I0692650

SPACE HAWK

SPACE HAWK

The Greatest of Interplanetary Adventurers

BY ANTHONY GILMORE

COPYRIGHT 1931, 1932, BY CLAYTON MAGAZINES, INC.

COPYRIGHT 1952, BY GREENBERG : PUBLISHER, A COPORA-
TION.

PUBLISHED IN NEW YORK BY GREENBERG : PUBLISHER AND
SIMULTANEOUSLY IN TORONTO, CANADA, BY AMBASSADOR
BOOKS, LTD.

ALL RIGHTS RESERVED UNDER INTERNATIONAL AND PAN
AMERICAN COPYRIGHT CONVENTIONS.

Library of Congress Catalog Card Number: 52-6108

Foreword

Hawk Carse came to the frontiers of space when Saturn was the outpost planet, which was years before the swift Patrol ships brought Earth's law and order to those vast regions.

From a casual glance at his slender figure it was impossible to imagine that he was to rise to be the greatest adventurer in space, that his name was to carry such deadly connotations among certain people in later years. But on closer inspection, a number of little things became evident, such as the steadiness of his light gray eyes, the easy movements of his strong-fingered hands, the wiry strength of his perfect athlete's body. Summing these things up, and adding the man's brilliant resourcefulness and his complete ignorance of fear, one can perhaps understand why even the brilliant egomaniac Dr. Ku Sui, his blood enemy, devoid of every kindly human trait, could not face Carse unmoved in his moments of cold fury.

His name, we know, enters most histories of the period 2100-2120 A.D., for he has at last been recognized as the one who probably did most—unofficially, and not with the authority of any planetary government—to shape the raw frontiers of space, to push them outward, and to lay the foundations of the present tremendous commerce between Earth and the many planets of greater orbit. Little of his fascinating character may be gleaned from the dry words of the histories, however; so it is Hawk Carse the adventurer, he of the spitting ray-gun and the phenomenal draw, of the reckless space-ship maneuverings, of the queer bangs of flaxen hair that from a certain year hid his forehead, of the score of blood feuds and the one great feud that jarred nations in its final terrible settling—it is this Hawk Carse we are concerned with here.

A number of his adventures, never recorded, are still among the favorite yarns spun by lonely outlanders in the scattered trading posts of the planets, and among them is that of his great duel with Dr. Ku Sui in the matter often called "The Affair of the Brains." It shows typically the resourcefulness, the nerveless daring, the prompt repayment of an injury to a friend or a blood debt of his own, that were outstanding qualities of this almost legendary figure.

The affair began early one crisp morning on Iapetus, eighth satellite of Saturn, and ended with the birth of a colossal meteorite in the atmosphere of Earth.

Carse pioneered Iapetus, and considered a fair share of its product his by right of prior exploration. One or two ships had landed there before he came to the frontiers, and reported the satellite habitable, possessed of an atmosphere only a little thinner than Earth's, along with a gravity very slightly greater than Earth's, despite its twelve-hundred-mile diameter; but they had gone no further. They had noticed certain odd animals in the jungles, but they had not investigated them. It was Carse who captured one and saw the commercial possibilities of the pointed seven-inch horn that grew on its head, and who named the creature phanti, after the now extinct Venusian bird-mammal.

There were great herds of phantis on Iapetus, and they constituted its highest form of life. Carse cut off a few of their opalescent horns and sent them as samples to Earth; and, upon their being valued highly, he established a ranch on Iapetus, and thus unknowingly set the scene for the first action in the spectacular duel to be recorded here.

There is no doubt that Carse expected trouble over the ranch. To protect the valuable twice-yearly harvest of horn from Ku Sui's several bands of pirates and other semipiratical traders who roamed space, he built a formidable ranch house with generators for powerful offensive rays and a strong defensive ray-web, and manned it with six competent men. Moreover, he came personally twice a year to transport the cargo of horn, and let it be known throughout the frontiers that the sign of the Hawk was on that portion of Iapetus, and that all who trespassed would have to answer to him. This should have been enough. But there was always the sinister Eurasian Dr. Ku Sui plotting against him, and reckless others to whom the ranch might look like easy pickings. From these, a raid had long been anticipated.

SPACE HAWK

I

The Swoop of the Hawk

Now, Hawk Carse was worried. He was standing in the control cabin of his new cruiser, the space-ship *Star Devil,* clad as usual in a faded blue tunic, open at the neck, soft blue trousers and old-fashioned rubber-soled shoes. He showed his worry in characteristic manner by pulling occasionally at the bangs of flaxen hair that had been trained to cover his forehead nearly to the straw-colored eyebrows.

He was within an Earth-hour's time of Iapetus on the third of his semi-annual voyages for the harvest of horn. Iaeptus lay dead ahead of the bow observation ports of the control cabin where he was standing, an immense buff-tinted globe, dark-splotched by the seas and jungles. Away to the left, scintillating in the blackness of space, whirled Saturn, his rings clear-cut and brilliant, his hard light filling the control cabin. Carse was staring unseeingly at the magnificent spectacle when the big Negro standing nearby at the controls rumbled:

. "Well, I can't think there's anything wrong. Nobody'd *dare* touch that ranch! Not Hawk Carse's ranch!"

This was "Friday," the big black Earthman whom Carse had rescued years before from one of the Venusian slave-ships, and who now was a member of that strange trio of totally dissimilar comrades—Carse, Friday, and Master Scientist Eliot Leithgow, now absent and at work in his secret laboratory. Friday thought the Hawk just about the greatest

1

man in the Solar System, and many times he had given proof of his devotion.

Carse looked at him. "You're a good mechanic, Friday," he said, "but in some ways you're very innocent. Crane hasn't replied to us for seventy Earth minutes. He knows we're coming and he should be on duty. That cargo's valuable, and it's all ready and packed."

"Well, who'd dare touch it when we're so close?" Friday asked, and he promptly gave himself an answer: "Nobody. Unless maybe one of Ku Sui's gang."

"That's what I've been thinking. I haven't heard anything of Ku Sui for some time, and he's never more dangerous than when he keeps silent," said the Hawk thoughtfully. "But Crane might be sick. Or his radio might have broken down. Still. . . ."

The third man in the cabin, Harkness, the navigator, now sat up and abruptly put an end to Carse's reflections by calling out:

"Radio, sir!"

A red light showed on the switchboard. Friday watched the Hawk step to it in his quick, effortless way and pull down a lever, all in the same motion—and then the Negro's neck muscles tightened as he listened to the words that came, choking and barely intelligible, from the speaker:

"Carse—Hawk Carse—Crane speaking from the ranch. We're besieged—pirate ship—outnumbered—can't hold out much longer. We've got the cargo inside here, but our generators—they're fading—and I'm fading, too, I guess—and all the others are dead or wounded. Carse—hurry—hurry—hurry—hurry. . . ."

Five words went back into the microphone before the receiver went dead.

"I'm coming, Crane! Hold on!"

Friday had seen the Hawk in such moments before, and he knew his characteristic reaction; but Harkness had not served with him very long, and he was a little frightened at

2

sight of the Hawk's controlled rage at this news—his set face, the tight-pressed bloodless lips, and the gray eyes, cold now as space itself. He flinched when the man turned and in passing looked him in the eyes.

"I want speed," came the Hawk's low, deceptive voice. "I want that hour's running time sliced by a third. Burn through that atmosphere."

"Yes, sir!" answered Friday.

"And you"—to Harkness—"use every watt you're given. Tell the engineer what's happened."

"Yes, sir," answered the navigator—and he felt some relief at getting away. For Carse at such moments seemed less human than the Indrots at the far end of the space he roamed. Blood had been shed, and for each drop another had to be shed, to balance the scales.

At a mike that connected aft to the three other members of the crew, Carse whispered, "Action posts. Arm and be ready. Pirates are attacking the ranch"; then he stepped noiselessly to the miniscreen. Friday put his eyes on the dials before him and sensitively touched the control-lever, while aft, in the ship's other compartments, three men with beating hearts strapped on ray-gun belts and wondered who was doomed to be caught in the swoop of the Hawk.

Carse himself wondered that. To judge by the boldness of his attack, the raider was a newcomer to the frontiers of space —one who had never faced the Hawk, one to whom the tales that were told must have seemed incredible, and to whom the rich consignment of horn must have looked like a gift. Certainly such an open attack did not resemble Ku Sui's subtle methods, or those of his several henchmen, all pirates of space; these men would strike behind his back, and, even then, only when the Eurasian had prepared what seemed a fool-proof plan.

"Foolish to raid when I'm so close!" Carse murmured as he adjusted the miniscreen. "Stupid! Unless. . . ."

Friday, at the control-lever, mopped trickles of sweat from his brow, and with an intake of breath slightly shifted his bulk. The job of entering and traversing an atmosphere at high speed always was ticklish, and it was with some tension that he shortly reported, "Into atmosphere, sir," according to routine. He waited for the usual acknowledgment, and when it did not come repeated his observation. The silence continued. Finally, Carse turned from the screen, and this time even the Negro trembled at sight of the expression on his face.

For the ranch house in its clearing had dimly appeared on the screen just before Friday had spoken, and Carse had seen certain things.

Carse spoke frigidly, almost in a whisper.

"More speed, if it burns us up. I want much more speed."

Friday gulped. "Yes, sir," he said, and, moistening his lips, he turned to his controls. The icy gray eyes swung back to the sight that was revealed on the screen.

A glittering space-ship rested on the soil some three hundred yards from the ranch house; in the space between moved the blurred figures of six men, each dragging a box towards the craft. The boxes contained the half-year's harvest of phanti horns, and obviously just had been removed from the house. The resistance had been overcome; the pirate raid had succeeded. The trim, gray-painted ranch house must be lifeless. . . .

His lips compressed, the Hawk lowered his eyes from the screen. "I'll take it," he said curtly to Friday. "Turn on the defensive web, and check all ray batteries."

"Yes, sir!" The Negro's big yellow-palmed hands moved among the instruments to his right; then, from amidships, came a shrill whine which keened upward in pitch. A few sparks raced by the *Star Devil's* after ports, quickly to disappear after they left the almost invisible envelope of delicate bluish light that entirely wrapped her hull.

The ship was making dangerous speed. Outside, she

4

screamed as she streaked through the satellite's atmosphere, and the friction of her passage raised the temperature of her outer shell to the point of danger. The finger on the dial of the altimeter almost jumped from forty thousand to thirty-five.

"Ready for the bow ray."

"Aye, sir!" replied Harkness, and a moment later repeated crisply, "All ready for bow ray, sir!" His voice showed no sign of the fear within him—fear that the *Star Devil's* outer hull would reach the softening point—but his expression lost its discipline at what the Hawk did next.

"Steady," came a whisper to his ears; then he saw the control-lever being shoved smoothly well forward.

II

Pursuit

That was the Hawk's way, and it had given him the name which he had made famous. It was characteristic that he preferred to strike at an enemy ship in a breath-taking swoop, much as the hawk plummets down on its prey. Nerves were uncomfortable things to have on such occasions, and Harkness had them, and accordingly he felt his heart hammer and his throat grow tight. He tried to copy the unshakable calmness of the figure at the controls, but could not. Through the forward port the navigator with wide eyes watched the surface of Iapetus rushing toward them, watched it spread rapidly outward on all sides until with unassisted eyes he could see the pirate ship lying there, and the nearby figures of men tugging at the heavy boxes of horn.

His eyes were on those figures when the men broke apart. First, they hesitated, gesturing with excitement at the silver comet streaking from above, and then the group melted. Three of the men scrambled towards the rim of jungle foliage close at hand, while their fellows made for the open port of their ship. Harkness saw them tumble headlong through, and slam the door shut. Then a web of blue streaks appeared around the pirate ship, and softened until her hull was bathed in ghostly bluish light.

"Their defensive web's on, sir!" he reported—unnecessarily, but according to routine. Carse, though close, might not have heard, so intently was he watching. The finger of the altimeter reached for one thousand and slid past. Harkness's face now was pale, his teeth clenched; he expected to crash into the ground amid molten fragments of steel. But Friday was grinning, his teeth a slash of contrasting white.

"Stand by bow projector," sounded the Hawk's clipped voice. The Negro extended his hands and rumbled:

"Ready, sir."

"Fire."

"Fire!" Friday roared.

His rich laugh rang out as he whirled the wheels over. With a hissing as of a hundred snakes, the ray pierced outward.

Well aimed, it sped true. The distance was short, and it came from generators perhaps not equaled in space; no ordinary space-ship's web could resist its annihilating energy. The orange stream was a narrrow cone that enclosed the brigand ship and held it accurately. For just a tick of time there was a turmoil of color as offensive ray met defensive web; then the air cleared—and the pirate was unmarked!

She should have glowed and caved inward, melting! To Carse, one eye on the screen, it must have been a shock that she had not; but his face showed nothing.

With firm control he pulled the *Star Devil* out of her plunge and brought her a hundred feet up over the rim of the jungle. Friday gaped; Harkness, still numb from the danger of the dive, stared foolishly; and then the brigand bared her fangs in return.

A brilliant orange light flashed from her stern, only to carom harmlessly off the side of the *Star Devil*—and on the heels of that one bolt, the pirate craft trembled, lifted a little, then with mounting speed raised up into the atmosphere, abandoning the boxes of horn without further fight.

"Running for it! Scared stiff!" exclaimed Friday, joy

7

gleaming in his eyes. He looked at the slender figure at the ship controls. "Follow them now, sir, and wear them down?"

"Plenty of time for that," Carse said shortly. "Some of the men on the ranch may still be alive; we must care for them. I'm going to land. Tell the engineer to keep that ship under observation. I'll start after it later."

"Funny our rays didn't hurt it," Friday ruminated aloud. "That's no ordinary craft, Captain. There's more in this business than hits your eyes!"

"Now you're getting cynical, Friday," the Hawk said coldly.

A quarter-mile block of land had been fenced off as a corral for the ninety-head herd of bull phantis Carse kept on Iapetus. These creatures resembled the extinct ostrich of Earth more than any other animal, but there were no feathers in their brown-gray leathery skin. Their neck was shorter, and their powerful hind feet, on which they stood erect, were armed with short stabbing spurs. Their forelegs were really arms, which they used for plucking the delicate shoots and young leaves on which they lived. There was a dim flicker of intelligence inside their horned heads; they recognized men as their enemies, and hated them. They required careful handling. Their horns were dangerous, but with their sharp-spurred feet alone they could rip a human being into shreds in seconds.

The phantis were clustered now behind the wire fence of the corral—electrified to prevent them from breaking through. They bellowed angrily and shoved each other about as their wicked little blood-shot eyes caught sight of the *Star Devil*, dropping gently down.

At the miniscope of the descending craft was the ship's engineer. The fleeing pirate craft by now was leaving the satellite's atmosphere, but he maintained a large image of it on the screen above the view ports, and kept a steady eye on it. The ship touched ground. At once the inner door of the port-lock opened, the outer door swung down, and Carse walked through, followed by Friday and Harkness.

An ugly scene lay before them. The Hawk had only gone a few paces when he came to an outsprawled thing that had once been a man. Stooping, he gently turned the mess of charred flesh over and looked at what was left of the face. There were small, burnt holes in it, and the flesh surrounding them looked as though it had been suspended for some time over a slow fire.

Carse straightened.

"Ruthers," he said softly, as if speaking to himself. He walked on.

Another heap of flesh was pitched before the front wall of the ranch house. This man evidently had been running for the door when the rays had got him. His gun was lying a few feet away. Again Carse stooped and gently turned the body over.

"Why—why—" stammered Harkness suddenly, "that's Jack O'Fallon! Jack O'Fallon! Why, we went to navigation school together! We—"

"Yes," said the Hawk. "O'Fallon, overseer." He stepped into the house. Friday, wide-eyed and grim, pulled Harkness away from the distorted body.

Three more were found behind a splintered table in the main room. They were partially welded together. Again the Hawk's frigid whisper spoke their names.

"Martin . . . Olafson . . . and this—Antil. . . . Antil was the only Venusian I ever really liked. . . ."

The chairs and tables in the room were overturned, and most of them bore seared scars from ray-guns, which showed plainly that there had been a desperate last minute hand-to-hand struggle there, after the defensive web had been penetrated and the pirates rushed the building. The radio alcove was choked with seared, cracked wreckage. Crane, the operator, still was in his seat, but he sat slumped forward, and his head and chest were pitted with slanting

9

burnt holes. One reaching hand lay just short of a switch. The other was twisted and charred.

"And Crane, the last," said Hawk Carse, and for some moments he stood there, his face cold and unmoving save for a tiny twitching of the left eyelid. Complete silence rested over the three—a silence broken only by the occasional roar of an angry phanti bull in the enclosure nearby.

Carse took a deep breath and turned to Friday.

"You'll see to their burying," he ordered quietly. "Get the power ray from the ship and burn out two big pits on that knoll outside the corner of the corral."

Friday looked at him in puzzlement. "Two, sir?" he repeated. "Why two? Why not put them all in one?"

"You will put all *my* men in one. I'll need the other later. You," he went on, to Harkness, "get the cargo of horn aboard. We can't leave it out there, for three of the raiders fled to the jungle. I haven't time to go after them; they'd take away the horns and bury them. I'll be with you soon. I want to take off in ten minutes."

"Yes, sir," answered the navigator, and he and the Negro went out.

For a little while Carse stayed in the radio alcove, reflecting, stroking the bangs of flaxen hair over his brow. He visualized what had happened inside that house of death, piecing a number of things together and forming a whole. On the surface it seemed plain enough; yet there were one or two points. . . . His face showed a trace of doubt. He shook his head slightly; then he stooped and picked up the radio operator's body, with an ease that might have seemed surprising in such a slender man, and walked out of the house.

Outside one corner of the corral, upon a slight rise in the ground, Friday was melting out the second grave with the ship's portable ray-projector. Carse laid Crane's body by the first grave, then went to where Harkness, with the *Star Devil's* radio-man and cook, was loading the cargo of horns

10

aboard. He opened several of the boxes, glanced at the upper layers to inspect the quality, then closed them again. All the boxes soon were trundled through the open port of the craft, and aft to her cargo hold.

The engineer on watch at the screen felt a hand on his shoulder and looked around to find Carse standing by him. He pointed up at the screen. On it, the brigand ship, four inches in size, stood bearing straight out on an unwavering course. "I reckoned their speed to be about ten thousand an hour, a minute ago, sir," the engineer reported.

"How soon," Carse asked, "do you think we could overhaul them?"

The other grinned. "Depends on their speed capacity. But probably, if you're in a hurry, sir, about two hours and a half."

"I am in a hurry. I want all the speed you can muster."

"Yes, sir. Might be able to get it down to two."

The Hawk nodded. "Try. Return to your post."

Outside, through the port, he saw Friday smoothing over the grave, and he beckoned him in. At that moment Harkness reported the cargo fastened down, and Carse snapped out further orders.

"Harkness," he said shortly, "you and Friday stay with me in the control cabin. Sparks, you can get an hour's sleep, but leave the radio receiver open. Cook, an hour's rest if you want it—and I think you'd better want it. There's war ahead. Close port!"

With a hiss, one after the other, the outer and inner doors nestled snugly into place. The rows of gravity plates in the ship's belly angled ever so slightly. The ship quivered, and in a surge of silent power lifted straight up; then, answering to the touch of her controls, she began to angle through the atmosphere on the trail of the reckless craft that had left its bloody mark on Iapetus and provoked the vengeance of the Hawk.

11

III

Death Rides the "Star Devil"

Usually, when pursuing an enemy, Hawk Carse was impassive, icy, apparently emotionless. But now he seemed disturbed.

He moved about restlessly, now studying the course of his quarry in the miniscreen, now watching Friday ease the ship through the skin of atmosphere into outer space, now standing apart for a moment, reflecting.

There was something about the affair he didn't like. Something that was obscure, that could not be grasped; something that might, on the other hand, be pure imagination. And yet, why——

Why, for instance, had the raiders taken to their heels with just the barest semblance of fight? Why, with their powerful defensive rays, had they left without more of an attempt to retain the horn? Why were they so willing to flee, knowing as they surely must that he, the Hawk, would follow? It was widely known that his new ship was the fastest in space—thanks to Master Scientist Eliot Leithgow; they surely could expect him to overtake them.

Were they Ku Sui's men? It seemed so, from the great strength of their defensive web. No ship in space except those devised by Ku Sui possessed such power—none that he knew of. But—it wasn't the brilliant Eurasian's customary style. It was too simple for him.

Carse stroked his bangs. The factors were all mixed up. He didn't like it.

The atmosphere of Iapetus was left behind; in minutes the light blue wash of her sky changed to the hard blackness of lifeless space. The *Star Devil's* light tubes glowed futilely, for Saturn's rays, coming through the wide bow windows, still lit the control cabin with hard brilliance. Inside, light and color, life and action; outside, the eternal, sable void, sprinkled with its millions of sparkling motes, each a world. And ahead—shown now on the miniscreen only by the bright dots of its observation ports—was the brigand craft.

The *Star Devil* was smoothly building up the speed that would eventually bring her up to the enemy. Carse's Earth-watch told him that an hour and a half had passed. A vague anxiety oppressed him, but he shook it off with the thought that the time for accounting soon would arrive. Only forty minutes more; probably less. His fears surely were foolish. He was getting too suspicious. . . .

Then came the voice.

It echoed loudly through the control cabin from the speaker above the radio switchboard. It was rough and mocking. It said:

"Hawk Carse? Hawk Carse? You hear me?" Many times it repeated this. "You hear me, Hawk Carse? Yes? I've a joke I want you to hear—a very funny joke. You'll enjoy it!" Then followed the staccato sounds of a coarse laugh of great amusement.

At the first words, Carse froze. His left hand by old habit moved toward his ray-gun as he wheeled to face the loudspeaker. Friday, at the controls, stared at him; Harkness' face was puzzled as he looked at the speaker, then turned and watched his captain.

"But where," Harkness asked, "—where does the voice come from? From the ship ahead?"

As if thinking aloud, Carse whispered:

"From that ship ahead. I half expected . . . I know that voice well. Very well. It's the voice of . . . of . . . I can't quite place it. . . . In a minute. . . . The voice of—"

The chuckling had ceased. Again the rough voice spoke.

"Yes—a very funny joke! I can't share it all with you, Carse, not all, because you'd spoil it. But do you remember, some years ago, five men—and another who lay on the ground at their feet? Do you remember how the man on the ground said: 'Each one of you shall die for what you've done to me'? Remember? That man didn't wear bangs over his forehead then. Remember? Well, I'm one of the five the mighty Space Hawk swore he would kill!"

Again the voice broke into a coarse chuckle.

But the chuckle ended suddenly. It changed into words with a tone entirely different, a tone cruel and taunting.

"Bah! The avenging Hawk! The mighty Hawk! Well, in minutes, you'll be dead. You'll be dead! The mighty Space Sparrow will be dead!"

A long moment went by. Carse remembered, and his gray eyes grew colder.

"Judd the Kite," he whispered.

Friday's lips formed the same words.

Even Harkness, new to the frontiers of space, knew the name and echoed it haltingly.

"Judd the Kite!"

Of the henchmen Dr. Ku Sui had gathered about him and banded against the agents of Earth, and against Carse, and against all peaceful traders and merchant ships, Judd in his coarse way was perhaps the most cruel.

It was for good reasons he was called the Kite—behind his back. Physically, he was big and gross, with thick unstable lips and stubby, hairy fingers. More than once he and his motley gang of hi-jackers had painted a crimson splash

14

across the far reaches of the frontiers—daubed it to the tortured groans of the crews of honest trading ships. More than once he had plunged on an isolated trading post and left its factor wallowing in his life blood. There was yet more. . .

There are things that cannot be set down in print, that the carefully edited history books hardly hint at, and into this class fell many of the Kite's deeds. He was a master of the Venusian tortures. He and his band during the unspeakable debauches which always followed a successful raid would amuse themselves by practising certain of these tortures on the captives of the day; and his victims, both men and women, would see and feel indescribable things, and death would be kept most carefully away until the last ounce of life and pain had been squeezed out for his entertainment. . . .

"Judd the Kite," Carse repeated in a hardly audible whisper. "Judd the Kite . . . one of the five. . . ." His left hand was smoothing his long bangs. "I have been looking for him."

"Will you reply to him, sir?" asked Harkness.

"What use? His trap—Ku Sui's trap, of course—has already been set." His brain raced. "What could it be?" he whispered slowly. . . .

Friday was scratching his wavy hair, his smooth face puzzled, when Carse, with a return of the decisiveness that always came to him in action, looked up at the miniscreen. The pirate ship was still on a straight course, and rapidly being overhauled. Another thirty minutes and they would be within striking distance. He said tersely:

"Set up the defensive web. Zigzag the ship in two dimensions as sharply as you dare, altering the period of the swing each time. Harkness, you and I are going to make an inspection tour. General alarm if Judd's course changes, Friday."

"Yes, sir." The Negro gave his undivided attention to his

instruments as the Hawk and Harkness went aft into the next compartment, the engine-room.

It looked quite normal. The great dynamos were humming smoothly; the air-renewing machine was functioning steadily; the indicators of the gauges all slept or quivered in their usual places. Nothing uneven in the slight vibration of the ship; nothing that might possibly forbode trouble. Up on his perch, the engineer looked down curiously and asked:

"Anything wrong, sir?"

"Not yet," Carse answered shortly. "You're sure everything is regular here?"

"Yes, sir."

"Good. But check every vital spot again, at once—and quickly. Then keep alert."

They passed on into the following compartment, the mess-room and sleeping quarters for the crew. Solid, rhythmical snores were issuing from the cook's open mouth as he lay sprawled out on his bunk; the smell of coffee was in the air; the cabin was quiet and comfortable with an atmosphere of rest. The radio-man, reading in his bunk, looked over, and seeing it was Carse, sat up.

"Notice anything wrong?" he was asked.

"Wrong? What— Why no, sir."

"Stay here and keep your eyes open for signs of trouble. I'm expecting some. I don't know what it will be. General alarm if the slightest thing happens." And Carse went noiselessly into the last division of the ship.

This was the cargo hold. The boxes of phanti horns were lashed neatly in precise rows; the dim tube overhead showed nothing that gave the smallest cause for alarm. The Hawk examined walls, deck and ceiling in a search for signs of strain or buckling, but again found nothing.

Then he let himself down into the ship's belly, in the three-foot space between the deck and inner hull. He found

16

the rows of delicately adjusted gravity plates in good order. Harkness joined him.

Their flashes scanned every foot of the narrow compartment as they made the under-deck passage from stern to bow and up through the forward trap-door into the control cabin. They found nothing abnormal. The water and fuel tanks, set in the space between the deck and inner hull below the living quarters, also showed nothing; likewise the store-room.

Nothing. Nothing at all. The ship seemed in excellent condition. Everything was working as it should. Carse went forward again with Harkness, then turned and faced him with puzzled eyes.

"I can't understand it," he said. "Why that threat, when everything seems all right? How can Judd reach me to kill me, as he said? And in minutes?"

The navigator shook his head. "I don't get it, sir."

"It must be something new, something Ku Sui has devised," the Hawk said thoughtfully. "Well, we'll soon find out. You report to the engine-room and keep on watch there. Any sound or sign, give the general alarm."

"Yes, sir," he said, and left.

"He's talking foolish, that Judd," said Friday, seeing that the search had been fruitless. "He thinks maybe he can penetrate our ray-web! Huh!"

His captain said nothing. He was standing motionless in the center of the cabin, waiting. Waiting for he knew not what.

Then it came.

A preparatory sputter from the speaker spun Friday around. The Hawk looked up quickly. Again sounded the rough sneering voice of Judd the Kite.

"We're ready now, Carse: there was a little delay. I'll give you, say, five seconds. Five Earth seconds. One for each of the five men you did *not* kill. Shall I count them off? All right. You have till the fifth.

17

"One."

Friday's big eyes rolled nervously. He wiped a drop of sweat from his brow and cursed.

"Two."

Friday glanced at the Hawk, and tried himself to assume the steely calm of the great adventurer. But his fists would clench and unclench as he stared up at the miniscreen. No change! The pirate craft was running straight ahead as ever, apparently fleeing.

"Three."

The Negro's breath came more quickly; the tendons of his neck stood out. "What's he going to do? What's he going to do?" he asked himself.

"Four."

"Change course—a-starboard!" Carse snapped. The control-lever moved a little, all Friday dared, at their speed; the position dials swung; the fixed point of a super-brilliant star that had long been visible through the bow windows slid to the left and was gone. Till the fifth, Judd had said.

"Five!"

The two men in the control cabin of the *Star Devil* looked at each other. The bigger one moistened his lips. But there was nothing. No sound, no change. No alarm bell. No offensive ray spearing across the reaches of space; no slightest change in the pirate's course. The bigger man suddenly laughed loud in relief.

"All foolishness!" he exclaimed. "That Judd, he's crazy! Tried to scare us! Just tried to scare us!"

"What's that?" whispered Hawk Carse.

There had been a faint rustle.

It continued, at first hardly discernible; but it grew. It grew rapidly into a low, steady, prickling murmur, blended soon with muffled voices raised in frantic cries. There was one piercing, ragged shriek, then more and more the indefinite peculiar sound of something rustling, creeping, always growing.

18

Then came the shattering jangle of the alarm bell.

"Spacesuits!" Carse yelled. The alarm was the signal to run and get them on; it was a safeguard against a possible breach in the ship's hulls. Against that emergency Carse had drilled the ship often, so all over the ship, now, the men would be climbing into spacesuits hanging ready.

The control-lever automatically locked as Friday leaped with his captain to the nearby locker. The cries from aft had ceased. The clanging of the alarm bell began to dwindle, as if muffled into inaction. The two were scarcely sealed in their suits when there came the sound of running feet, and a man ran into the control cabin, his face white, his breath coming in gasps, his eyes lit with terror. It was Harkness.

He slammed the door tight shut behind him, jumped to the locker, and started to get into a spacesuit; and as his fingers fumbled clumsily at the fastenings he cried out in short bursts:

"Fungus! It's filling the ship! It got all the others! It grew on them—it grew! They're all dead already! There—look, look!"

He jabbed his whole arm toward the bottom of the door he had just entered. Carse and Friday turned, and saw the van of the enemy that had swarmed through the ship.

A thin, bright yellow line lay along the under crack of the door. Quickly, the line appeared on all four sides of the door. It was a yellow stuff; it grew; it reached out. Energy flowed through it; fingers of yellow dust lifted out from the cracks where the door fitted, hung wavering for a moment, melted together, then fell to the floor, there to continue the advance. It increased marvelously, in minor spurts of speed. It was delicate in texture, moldlike. The more there became, the faster it grew; in seconds, shreds of it had branched out from the main mass and affixed themselves to the walls and ceiling of the cabin, there to accelerate the horrible filling process.

All this happened more quickly than it can be related. In

19

half a minute most of the cabin was coated by the yellow stuff; grotesquely formed clumps and feathers began to hang from the ceiling; fernlike fingers kept spurting everywhere. Friday shrank back before the advance, his captain following more slowly. It was impossible to evade the stuff, the Hawk saw; but there seemed no immediate danger of its penetrating through the tough fabric and space-tight joints of the suits—assuming that none had entered before the suits were sealed. A surge of the stuff caught the shoe of his suit—crept up the leg—enveloped the body; but it could not get through. How could such stuff be fought? he was wondering.

"Cap'n Carse! Look here!" sounded Friday's voice in Carse's helmet radio.

He turned, brushed a film of feathery yellow particles from his face-plate, and found Friday pointing at Harkness.

The young officer lay under a blanket of yellow against the bottom of a wall. While the others were retreating, checking the fastenings of their suits, he had fallen silently.

Carse jumped to his side, stooped, brushed the fungus off the man's face-plate and his own, and peered through, Friday looking over his shoulder. The yellow enemy was inside the navigator's suit. All over his face it had laid its deadly fingers. Sprouts of yellow trailed from the nostrils, a clump covered the mouth, other clumps filled the ears and were rapidly threading in a deepening layer over the entire head, even as the two looked on.

"That's how the others died," the Hawk said slowly. "Harkness must have carried a bit of the stuff with him from aft. It was on him when he got into his suit. At least I hope it was that way. If it can get into a sealed suit. . . ." He left the thought unfinished.

"You think, sir," Friday began haltingly, "—you think maybe it'll get into our suits too?"

"Maybe," said Carse coolly.

They waited.

20

IV

The Hawk Prepares a Surprise

Hawk Carse's icy poise in times of emotional stress never failed to amaze friends and enemies alike. Most of them said he had no nerves, and therefore was not human. This estimate, of course, was foolish: Carse was human, perhaps too human, as was amply indicated by the several objects of his life. It was probably an inward vanity that made him stand composed in the face of probable death; vanity and the example of leadership that once, for instance, led him actually to file his fingernails when trapped and hotly besieged, with the hiss of ray-guns in the hands of fighting men all around.

And so he stood now within his spacesuit—cool, his face graven, while the yellow tendrils carpeted the entire cabin, penetrated between the twin banks of instruments on each side and clouded the bow windows and miniscreen until outside vision was completely cut off. Friday, waiting as the Hawk was waiting to know whether or not their suits, too, harbored the fungus, could easily have been scared into a state of panic; but the sight of the steely figure near him eased his nerves as it always did, and brought a degree of reassurance.

Minutes went by. Presently the Hawk said softly into his helmet mike:

"We're safe, now, I think. You'd better go aft and see what state the men and ship are in." As Friday waded out

21

through the fungus the Hawk made his way to the mini-screen.

He brushed a thin film of yellow silt from his face-plate and a thicker layer from the screen. What he then saw in the screen made him start.

The *Star Devil* was tumbling over and over, like a spinning football!

For he was looking out on a sky that wheeled by in crazy fashion. Now the cloud-patched globe of Iapetus, which had just before lain behind, came swinging into view, sliding rapidly from the lower right corner of his field of view to the upper left, and so out of sight—to give place to the bright ringed sphere of Saturn, which traversed his view in the same manner and in turn passed away out of sight. Then Iapetus once more. He turned from the screen when through the external receiver of his suit he heard Friday come clumping back.

"Swept everything clean, sir," the Negro reported gloomily. "That fungus is thick; can't even see the men's bodies, it's so thick. It's that way all over."

"It's down in the gravity plates, too," Carse said shortly. "It's ruined their adjustment and we're turning over and over. I won't be able to watch Judd's ship till the plates are cleaned, so we've got to go down and see what we can do."

It was a weird scene that faced him in the engine room. All the complex machinery was draped with straggling ferns of yellow; up above, a solid clump two feet thick hung on the platform where the engineer usually sat—a living tomb. So fecund was the fungus that the path Friday had cleared in his passage aft was already filling, and Carse had to clear a new one.

In the next compartment the fungus was still thicker, for there it had found acceptable food. It had settled on everything organic; had devoured all but the bones and clothing of the two men it had caught there—the radio-operator and cook. Carse pushed through the feathery sea till he came

22

to the cargo hold, where, in the deck, was a trapdoor that gave passage to the below-deck space where the rows of gravity plates were located.

Friday raised the cover; then, preceded by the rays of their hand-flashes, they climbed down and wormed forward, as best they could in their hampering suits. They found the surface of the plates fouled, covered by powdery coatings of yellow, far more than enough to disturb their fields and microscopically adjusted angles. On hands and knees, the Hawk said:

"We could get some use out of these plates if we could keep the fungus brushed off. Let's try."

But the fecundity of the yellow growth balked them. Sweating from their awkward exertions inside the unventilated spacesuits, they again and again brushed the plates clean with cloths used for this polishing—only to see the powdery particles regather as quickly as they were cleared away. There wasn't more than an eighth of an inch of the fungus, but that eighth of an inch kept returning. There was no removing it.

"No use, Captain," gasped the Negro at last, pausing. "Nothing to do but wait and see what the Kite does. He'll certainly want this ship and the horn."

"He certainly will," Carse answered slowly. "He'll want this ship—but I can't understand how he'll board us. I'm going up and see what I can find out. You stay here and try cleaning the plates again. Maybe the stuff will lose its vigor."

He went through the trapdoor and forward to the control cabin. Again the miniscreen held a surprise.

The speed of the *Star Devil's* rotation had lessened.

A moment later the reason appeared. As her bow dipped downward to the right, there slid across the field of view, about a mile away, the lighted ports of Judd's ship; and on the nose of the ship lay a brilliant spot of purple—the point of origin of a ray which held on the *Star Devil's* bow. It was a magnetic ray, being applied once during each rota-

23

tion of the ship. Carse could feel his craft steady as it struck. Judd was using it to stop the turning of the *Star Devil*, probably so he and his men could board.

Again and again the beam flashed across the Hawk's field of view, raying the bow of his ship neatly once each time around. Quickly the turning of the *Star Devil* was reduced. When it had ceased almost completely, the ray was cut, and Carse, continuously brushing the screen and his own face-plate, saw the enemy craft move to one side and draw abreast. The outer door of the port-lock of the pirate ship opened, revealing six figures clad in spacesuits and connected by a rope. Promptly they stepped out, pushed, and came floating toward the *Star Devil*.

Carse moved swiftly. He had already decided that it was useless to try and surprise them as they boarded; there was a better and surer way.

Quickly, he removed the fungus-choked body of Harkness from its spacesuit, and threw the suit into a nearby locker. From another locker he selected a loop of yellow-encrusted rope. Holding this over one arm, he made his way aft to the trapdoor, descended, closed the cover carefully behind him, and crept forward to Friday, who was still futilely dusting the plates. He told what he had seen, but nothing else.

Friday noted the rope, and he twisted his whole body to get a sight of Carse's face through the face-plate.

"What do we do?" he asked. "Try and surprise them?"

"Can't do that; we'd still be helpless without a way to remove this fungus. They probably know how to remove it, and we've got to give them a chance."

Friday was puzzled. "Then what you going to do with that rope?"

"You'll soon see," snapped the Hawk.

They waited.

It was hot and stuffy in the low compartment, and pitch

24

dark, for Carse at once had flicked off his flash. Friday, unhappily, was possessed of an active curiosity; he wanted to know what Carse's plan was, but he dared not ask, for he knew from past experience that the Hawk was impatient of detailing his schemes in advance. So he sat in silence, and sweated, and stared anxiously into the darkness, thinking uneasy thoughts.

He remembered a tale once told him by a survivor of a trading ship Judd the Kite had destroyed. It wasn't a nice tale. The Kite, according to the story, was diabolically ingenious with a peeling knife, and could improvise with it for hours. Friday pursued that tack of thought, and then suddenly began to sweat more than before. He recalled that Judd possessed a special dislike for colored men of all kinds.

"Oh, Lord!" he murmured, unconsciously—to have a cold voice say in his earphones:

"Quiet! They're entering!"

The Negro threw the switch on his helmet that enabled him to hear sounds outside his suit. His body tensed. From above, unmistakably, he heard the hiss of the opening of the inner door of the port lock. Moments later he heard it again. Twice! The lock could hold three men. That probably meant that all six men had boarded. In the darkness, Friday turned toward Carse, for whatever reassurance that could give him.

Without warning Carse flicked on his flash. The beam fell on the parallel planes of the yellow-covered gravity plates. At sight of them, the anxious Negro straightened. The moldlike fungus which had baffled them was slowly melting away!

"Gas," he heard spoken in his receiver. "As I expected, Judd's cleaning it out with some sort of gas. But the plates won't be reliable until they're polished." Unthinking, Friday raised his hand near his helmet fastenings. "Keep your face-plate shut!" came a crisp order. "The gas might be as fatal as the fungus."

Silence ensued, to be broken at last by the clump of feet of someone proceeding aft on the deck above.

Carse switched off the light. His voice was but faintly audible.

"He's coming down to polish the plates. He'll have a flash. Hide behind the truss-work at your side, and when he gets here grab him by the neck. I'll be with you right away. I want no noise."

Friday saw a great light. Of course! That explained the rope. The plan was so simple it had escaped him. Already he felt better. It was only mental worries, never physical hazards, that unsettled him. He squeezed around the truss-work and shrank into as small a space as possible—which wasn't very small, in his suit.

The clump of feet had died; now came the sound of the the trapdoor being raised. A white beam pronged down, felt around in the darkness and flicked off. Boots clanged on the short ladder. The light appeared again, down at their level, and came forward slowly, with many darts to the sides.

From the sounds the approaching man made, he was on hands and knees, moving cautiously. Suddenly, in a certain light, the two who awaited him saw a swarthy, black-stubbled face in profile. He wore no spacesuit! That meant that the pirates also had cleared the ship of the gas—or that the gas was harmless. It meant that the two hiding men could get out of their own suits.

But not then. The approaching pirate was close; they heard his breathing; heard him mutter an oath when he bumped an elbow. The Negro moved his muscular arms and held himself ready. At last the pirate was within reach.

It was over in seconds. Rounding the truss, Friday caught the man's neck in the crook of his arm. There was nothing but one startled croak, the thump of two bodies on the hull, the crack of a falling flash, and a slight squirming, which was quickly stopped by a belting punch.

26

At once Carse was there in the darkness, looping his rope around the pirate's arms and legs—a difficult job while wearing a spacesuit in such cramped quarters. He gagged the man with a polishing cloth, and then hauled him to a girder farther forward, and bound him sitting to it. By the time he had finished, Friday was out of his spacesuit.

Carse slipped out of his own spacesuit. After several minutes they heard voices raised in argument in the control cabin. Once more came the sound of feet overhead; another beam cut down through the trapdoor hole, another man came creeping through the compartment. He was obviously uneasy. He called:

"Jake! Hey, Jake! Are you there? Where the hell are you?"

Mumbling oaths, he advanced, the beam from his flash weaving before him.

"What are you doing, Jake? Jake!"

Friday was ready for him, unhampered now by the restricting suit. But something—perhaps light reflected by the round whites of his eyes—made the pirate suspicious, for he suddenly stopped and cried out:

"Who are you? Jake, is that you? Answer! I'll ray you—"

That was all he said. Friday was too far away to reach him; but the Hawk, closer, approached him from behind, then sprang and locked one arm around the man's neck in a strangle hold; and two minutes later the second man was bound and gagged.

Carse loosened his ray-gun in its holster.

"Now we attack," he whispered. "Four to two are fair odds, I think. You go aft and wait by the trapdoor; wait till you hear me call. Don't let yourself be seen—wait. When I call, come at once."

"Yes, sir. You going forward below the deck?"

Carse nodded.

"Then up through that—"

"Don't ask so many questions!" the Hawk ordered curtly.

They separated.

27

V

The Hawk and the Kite

In the deck of the control cabin, between a bank of instruments and the starboard wall, was a second trapdoor connecting with the below-deck compartment.

Only two men besides Carse knew of its location. The adventurer for reasons of his own had had it installed with a cover so well disguised that it could hardly be detected.

Crouched beneath it, now, by its three-rung ladder, Hawk Carse waited.

He could hear quite clearly the angry voice of Judd the Kite, haranguing his men.

"Rinker, you go down and see what's wrong. Just because Jake and Sako don't come back right away, you guys act as if the ship's haunted! Haunted! By Betelguese! A sweet bunch of white-livered cowards I've got for a crew—"

"Aw, lay off!" growled a deep, sullen voice. "I ain't scared, but this looks like a short-circuit to me. Something's wrong down there! We only found four skeletons, and four ain't the full crew for a ship like this. There oughta be a couple more somewhere. Carse's got nine lives, blast him! How do we know he was one of the four?"

Another man spoke up. "I say we all go down together."

"Stow it!" thundered Judd. "They didn't get away in their spacesuits, did they? Why, they hadn't a chance—none of 'em. They were killed, every one! Four's plenty to work the ship. Carse is dead, see, dead! This was one trick he didn't know—one time he couldn't worm out. He was clever, all

28

right, but he couldn't stack up against me. I swore I'd get him and I did. He's dead!"

"*Judd,*" said a low, clear voice.

The Kite whirled around. He stared. His hands went limp, so that the hand-flash he was holding dropped to the deck. In a weak voice, entirely different, he said:

"Carse! Hawk Carse!"

"Yes," was the whispered answer. "Hawk Carse. And not dead."

It was a scene that might have puzzled a newcomer to that orbit, one who had never heard of Hawk Carse. Certainly at that moment there seemed nothing dangerous about the slender figure that stood by the now open manhole, both arms hanging easily at his sides; the advantage, on the contrary, appeared to be all with the men whom he confronted. All these men were bigger than he, and each was armed with a ray-gun.

But, though there were four guns to one, they made no attempt to draw. For this was the Hawk they faced, the fastest, most accurate shot in all those millions of leagues of space, and in his two cold eyes they read a menace that locked both their arms and their wills.

Judd slipped his tongue through his lips and wetted them.

"Where did you come from?" he asked, after a moment.

"Friday!" called Carse.

"Yes, sir!" boomed the big black's muffled voice.

They waited. Judd's three men turned their heads when the Hawk's famous satellite stepped into the control cabin, a ray-gun in his hand, his face all white, flashing teeth, so wide was his grin.

"Well, well!" Friday chuckled. "Isn't this a pleasure! I certainly am pleased to meet visitors like this! Just drop in?"

But the Kite's head did not turn; he seemed not to hear Friday's words; his eyes held on Carse.

"Ku Sui is in back of this?" the Hawk asked him.

29

Judd's tongue slipped out and again licked his lips. Obviously, his part was to spar for time; to postpone as long as possible the settlement just ahead, until some lucky chance might come to his aid.

"That's right," he began eagerly, "it was Ku Sui. I had to do this, Carse; I hadn't any choice. I didn't want to. He's got something on me: I had to go through with it."

The Hawk's eyes were glacial; the ghost of a smile hovered around the corners of his lips.

"Go on," he said. "What was that fungus?"

"I don't know. Ku Sui developed it. He just gave me a phanti horn with a cartridge containing the spores hidden in it, and made me raid your ranch and plant it with the ones you were ready to ship. There was a mechanism in the cartridge that allowed us to release the spores by radio from our ship."

"I see. Very clever," Carse said. "Quite up to Ku Sui's standard. Those three men running for the jungle when I came down were to insure my taking the horn aboard, of course. The raid was for the prime purpose of getting me. And my man Crane, the radio operator, was dead when I received that call for aid. It was faked, to bring me there right on schedule."

Judd stared at him. "How the hell did you know that?"

"Where is Ku Sui?" asked the adventurer coldly.

Again the other licked his lips. His fingers clenched, unclenched, clenched again. "I don't know!" he protested at last. Carse moved his left hand slightly. At this the Kite's eyes widened.

"Talk!" came the frigid command.

"Carse, I swear it! No one knows where he is. When he wants to see me he comes right out of empty space. I don't know whether it's done by invisibility or the fifth dimension, but he appears at places and times that would be impossible unless he was close to his ship—but his ship's not there!"

30

"Where is his base?"

"I don't know! And if he knew what I've told you already—"

"How do you arrange your meetings, then?"

"By radio. They're always in a different place. Listen, Carse, I'm going to tell you something. I don't have to tell you; it's a favor, because I don't want any more trouble with you. The next meeting is in seven Earth days. I don't remember the figures: they're in the log of my ship. But I'll give them to you, then you deal with Ku Sui and leave me out of it."

"I'll deal with him, but I'll deal with you first," said the Hawk coolly. "Right now. We have a few accounts to be settled."

During the few minutes the Hawk had questioned Judd, the pirate crew had stood silent, fascinated at this contact with the almost legendary Space Hawk. But with his last words the spell was broken, and they began shifting uneasily.

They suspected what was coming. The adventurer went on inexorably:

"Six of my men were killed on Iapetus, treacherously, without a chance. Four more were slaughtered by the fungus. That's ten. You attempted to murder Friday and me. Back up beside your men, Judd."

Judd knew very well what that order portended, but he could not move. He saw that his "favor" was to get him nothing. His eyes remained riveted on the shabby holster that hung on Carse's left side; he was hopelessly paralyzed by fear. But there was no mercy.

"Back, Judd," repeated the Hawk.

The icy voice unlocked him, and he took one short backward step after another, until he was standing with his three men against the side wall. Friday moved closer to Carse, eyes never shifting from the faces of the four men, his gun still covering them from the hip.

31

"You goin' to shoot us down in cold blood?" one of the men asked hoarsely.

Carse looked at the speaker, in his eyes a trace of contempt.

"No," he said. "I leave that for rats like you. I'm going to give you a chance; more than a chance. Friday, do you want to come in on this?"

Without the slightest hesitation the Negro answered: "Yes, sir!"

"I thought you would. Come closer, then sheathe your gun."

Friday did so. He stood in position near his captain; the four pirates were some fifteen feet away. The two groups faced each other squarely.

"Good," whispered Carse.

They stood there, four men to two, deadly enemies; yet not one hand moved toward a ray-gun. Again, the ignorant outsider would have marveled why Judd and his men, the numbers on their side, did not draw and fire. But each man of the four knew what the least sign of a draw would entail and all preferred to wait, to receive the advantage of the cold vanity in Carse which demanded, in gun-play, that the odds of numbers be against him. Of course, each one was hoping that that vanity might this time lead the Hawk too far.

So they waited, and Judd was the most afraid.

"A little earlier," the Hawk's quiet voice went on, "there was some counting. To the number of five. Remember, Judd? Count to five again."

"You mean to count to five and then shoot?"

"Yes. On the fifth count, we draw and fire."

Judd seemed to get control of himself. His eyes narrowed, shifted. Hawk Carse smiled icily.

"Is that clear?" he asked.

Judd licked his lips. He said:

"All right."

32

Openly, for all to hear, Carse said:

"Friday, you take the one on the right,"—a brawny, black-browed man as big as Friday himself.

"Yes, sir," answered the Negro; then, keeping his eyes on this one man, he stood ready.

"Start counting," said the Hawk.

Judd crouched a little, and drew a deep breath; but before his lips could form the first word there was a quick movement in the pirate next to him—and at the same time Carse's left hand seemed to vanish in a spitting streak of orange light. Judd gaped at Carse's lowering weapon and turned his head.

The man at his side was standing with a puzzled look on his face, in one hand an unlifted, unfired gun. He was dead. Over his left eye was a neatly seared round hole.

But his knees were beginning to bend. His gun clanged to the deck. Quickly now his body bent, pitched forward, and lay sprawling, face downward. There was a burnt odor in the air. . . .

Carse returned his gun to the holster and again stood with arms hanging freely at his sides.

"I'm still waiting, Judd," he whispered.

With an oath, one of Judd's two remaining men said:

"He's a devil! Fast as light!"

Then an unexpected thing happened. All in a split second Judd's eyes looked past the Hawk, as if taking in something, then turned back.

This was old stuff, but the Hawk could not afford to take chances. Instantly he snapped:

"Look behind, Friday!"

The Negro turned his head. He was too late. There was a man standing behind him—Jake. A short steel bar was flashing in a short arc to Carse's head. Then it flashed to his own. For both, the cabin went dark, and together, white man and black crumpled to the deck.

VI

Back to Iapetus

An indefinite time later Carse awoke, pain beating in his head. He sighed, and tried to turn over. He found he could not move. Then his eyes opened.

He found himself lying on the deck of his control cabin, near the after wall, bound tightly hand and foot with rope. Over him, looking down, was Judd the Kite, hands on his hips, a gloating smile on his coarse lips, and in his eyes a look of sneering triumph. He drew back his foot and kicked the netted Hawk in the ribs.

"You get taken mighty easy, Carse," Judd said. "You're nothing but a damned fool with a big rep you don't deserve. You're careless. You ought to know by now not to leave bound men in reach of high-power cable. It can cut as good as an electric knife. Does your head hurt where you were hit?" Deliberately, still smiling, he kicked Carse in the head.

Carse glanced around blinking, trying to understand the situation. Friday, he saw, was in the control cabin too, lying stretched out and bound as he was, but evidently still unconscious. There was a bloody welt on his head. One of Judd's men was at the ship's controls, and another, at his side, was turned toward him and grinning. The two remaining pirates apparently were aft. The body of the dead one had been removed.

Through the port bow window, far out, Carse could see

34

a ship; that would be the other space-ship, the Kite's, on the same course. Large, dead ahead, loomed the sphere of Iapetus. Judd was returning, then, to the ranch, probably to pick up his three men, and perhaps to leave a small crew to take charge of the herd of phantis.

"This is gonna be the end of the Space Sparrow!" Judd said, sneering the name and laughing coarsely. "A lot of people will be glad to hear it. There'll be a big reward for me, too, from Ku Sui. Head still bad?" Again he kicked his prisoner in the head.

Carse's lips compressed until they were colorless, but he said nothing. Looking squarely into Judd's eyes, he asked: "What are you going to do with us?"

"Well," grinned the pirate, "I don't know exactly, but it's gonna be interesting. I'd like to do a few little experiments with a peeling knife. I know some very neat ones. Then finish off by burning you full of holes. Little holes, done with a mild needle-ray. But I guess Ku Sui'll want to do that himself. You're worth a hell of a lot of money alive."

"I go to Ku Sui, then?"

"That's right. I'll hand you over when I have my rendezvous with him, seven Earth days from now. Clever man, Ku Sui! Brain doctor, you know. He'll be tickled to get you alive."

"And Friday?"

Judd laughed. "Oh, he's not worth anything. I'll throw him in for good measure, maybe. Maybe not. How's the head?" Once more the foot swung.

Carse's gray eyes were frigid. His left eyelid began twitching.

"Judd," he whispered, so softly that his voice was almost inaudible, "I am going to kill you. I shall kill you very soon."

The Kite spat.

"Bah!" he exclaimed. "Just your old stuff, Carse. It's all over with you now. You'll be wishing it was me killed *you* when Ku Sui begins to touch you up!" He guffawed, again kicked the man at his feet, and turned away.

Hawk Carse watched him go to the forward end of the cabin. After a little while, he sighed. He could be patient. He was still alive, and he would stay alive, he felt. A chance would come; he did not know how or when; it might not come until he had been delivered to Ku Sui; but it would come. And then—

Then there would be a reckoning!

The Hawk closed his eyes.

Night had settled over the ranch by the time the *Star Devil* and Judd's accompanying ship were in the atmosphere of Iapetus. It was one of the rare, black nights when neither sunlight nor Saturn-light reached its night side— when even the other satellites, dispersed toward the day side, gave little light. Down through this rare blackness lowered the two ships.

Below, on the surface of the satellite, glowed a point that was a camp-fire. At a height of some fifteen thousand feet, by Judd's orders, a powerful beam of light speared out from the *Star Devil* and fingered the ground. It found the ranch house and then passed on to enclose the figures of three men standing by the fire. Through the miniscope the pirate chief saw them wave their arms in greeting.

Not long after, the two ships lay grounded side by side a hundred yards or more from the corral, and Judd was saying to his mate, in the control cabin:

"We'll have a little celebration tonight. Break out a few cases of alkite and send three of the boys to the store-room of the ranch after meat for a barbecue."

"What you want me to do with them two?" the other asked, indicating Carse and Friday.

"Keep 'em here. I'll detail a couple of men to guard them. I'm taking no chances; they gotta be in sight every minute. Carse is too damned dangerous." He looked back

36

at the captives. The Hawk's eyes were shut, and Friday still appeared unconscious from the brutal blow on his head. "Asleep. Well, they'd better sleep while they have eyelids to close!" Judd laughed, and his mate laughed too, in appreciation of the wit.

But neither the Hawk or Friday was asleep. Nor was the Negro unconscious. Carse had ascertained this some time before by cautious signals.

A little stir had come within him when he heard Judd say there would be a celebration, for a celebration, to these men, meant a debauch and relaxed discipline, and relaxed discipline meant—a chance. First, however, there were their bonds. The ropes were strong, and expertly tied, but the Hawk had not been particularly concerned about them.

He had dismissed them as a problem after a few minutes of consideration, and his mind now ran farther ahead, planning coldly the payment of this new debt of blood.

All in all, Judd was to blame for what happened that night on Iapetus. He was an old hand in those orbits and a capable one, and he should have known that extraordinary measures plus, had to be adopted when Hawk Carse became his prisoner. In the light of cold self-interest he should have killed Friday immediately, then steered straight for his rendezvous with Ku Sui, keeping his eye on Carse all the time. He would have had to loaf on his way, for it needed but five days to get there, and he had seven; and he would also have had to pick up his three marooned men later; but that was what he should have done.

As it was, he ordered a celebration. He felt like having one, and felt that he and his men had earned one. He had captured the man who, more than anyone else, had stood in his way, and in Ku Sui's way—the man who was dedicated to the quashing of their outlaw schemes, the man who had given more trouble to them than all the forces of law and order of Earth and the Patrol ships. More, he had cap-

37

tured him alive, and that meant a much fatter reward from Ku Sui. He possessed the valuable cargo of phanti horn, and he had taken a brand new ship, the fastest in space, alone worth millions. Judd naturally felt expansive at all this; and, having two nights and a day to spare, he ordered a celebration.

Such decisions—trivial when seen from the eminence of a hundred years—more than once have diverted the tide of history.

There were thirteen men left of Judd's crew, including the three posted on Iapetus. These three and the six who manned the pirate's own craft now came running to the *Star Devil* and piled into her control cabin, shouting in high spirits, swearing, throwing clumsy jests at the two silent figures on the deck; and Judd joined them. There was much loot to be split, and the Hawk was snared at last! Their chief stilled them long enough to shout:

"Well, I guess we deserve a little jamboree. I'm breaking out some alkite and meat. Make a big fire outside and dig some barbecue pits. Go ahead—get out of here! You, Sharkey, and you, Keyger, wait."

These last two men, more dependable than most of their fellows, he detailed as guards over Carse and Friday. He silenced their protests by promising them a larger slice of the loot, and then went to join the others.

The two guards loosened the ray-guns in their belts and looked over the captives. Angry at missing the carousal, the man called Sharkey kicked Friday, and then, somewhat gingerly, Carse. Friday never moved, but Carse opened his eyes and looked at him with an expression that caused him to back a little.

After that small diversion the two guards pulled out chairs and settled themselves by the open port-lock, where they could command a view of the celebration and at the same time keep an eye on the prisoners.

VII

Jamboree

Two hours later the eyes of the two guards were taking in a fanstastic scene, one comparable to those that occurred in the days when buccaneers roamed the Spanish Main, back in the Dark Ages of Earth.

A little over a hundred yards away, straight before them, was the corral of phantis; far behind it encroached the inky fringe of the jungle; to their right, closer to the corral than to the space-ships, was the ranch house, lonely now and silent. These places were the background for a barbarous scene in front of the corral fence.

A monster fire had been built, and it was sending splashes of crackling flames up through the black coolness of the night. Around the fire, dark shapes were clustered, bottles were raised and drained, and a frieze of shadows staggered and jumped and danced. The carousal was in full swing. A ragged chorus of lewd song seeped back into the surrounding jungle. Case after case of alkite already had been smashed open, and the poison still went gurgling down a dozen leathery gullets. The carcasses of three animals sizzled on the barbecue, now and then to be violated and the hot, dripping meat torn at with tooth and claw. Thicker and thicker grew the stew of songs and yells and oaths, till the black night became a thing distorted and mad.

Other heavier sounds accompanied the bedlam of human

noise: deep snortings and roarings and the scraping of scores of spur-shod feet. Behind their wired electric fence was clustered the herd of phantis, staring with their evil, red-shot little eyes at the flames of the fire and the shapes of the hated men. The big bulls bellowed, bucking their heads angrily, churning the soft soil with their strong, dagger-spurred feet; the welter of noise and the sight of so many excited men had wrought them up dangerously.

Judd the Kite, in one hand a bottle and in the other a huge joint of meat at which he was tearing with his teeth, suddenly paused with mouth full and squinted through the leaping flames. He gulped down the meat, then turned to the shapes staggering around him.

"Hey—let's get out the black!" he yelled. "A little enter-tainment, fellows! Bring him out; but don't touch Carse; he's Ku Sui's. Douse him with water if he's unconscious!"

The drunken crew yelled with delight at his words, and most of them reeled off toward the *Star Devil*. Judd, his coarse lips upcurved in a smile, drew his ray-gun and set the lever for the low-power, continuous ray-stream. It must be explained here that these guns, unlike our present ones, could shoot at two extremes: they could spit about twenty high-power discharges, each a small fraction of a second in duration and easily sufficient to burn a hole straight through a man's head; or they could deliver a long-lasting low-power stream, just strong enough to sear and crisp a human skin. For the entertainment Judd had in mind he needed the low power.

The men sent to the *Star Devil* shoved past the guards on watch and went over to the prisoners. They found them ly-ing very close together near the after wall.

"Gonna have some fun with the black. Judd's say-so," they explained to the guards. "Still unconscious?"

Certainly Friday looked unconscious, his eyes closed, his everted lips slightly parted, showing the powerful white teeth.

40

"I'll warm him a little," one of the pirates said, adjusting his gun. "That'll bring him to."

They got an unpleasant shock when the low-power stream hit the Negro's leg. With a bellow that rang through the ship, Friday resisted.

It was like seeing a dead man come to life, and it startled them. Then, bound as he was, Friday made things unhealthy for his escort; he shunted his legs up and down, he squirmed mightily, and once his teeth snapped into an arm, bringing a howl of pain and several minutes of cursing. The unexpected resistance infuriated the alkite-maddened men. One of them—the one who had been bitten—soon sneaked in and slapped the butt of a ray-gun on Friday's head, and he rolled over, stunned. After that the Negro was picked up and borne without resistance to the fire.

"The black devil was faking all the time!" one of the two guards exclaimed to the other. "He wasn't unconscious at all. Why was that?"

"Dunno," snarled the other, rubbing a bruised leg. "Must of suspected what he's gonna get. I wish we was over there."

"Well, we can watch from here," said his companion, and they returned to their seats by the port-lock.

They both sat down, their backs half turned to the figure still lying on the deck, by the side of each one a bottle of alkite to give consolation.

Carse had made no protest, had hardly moved, when Friday struggled in fierce resistance. He might have done something, but it would have been useless. Long before, he had seen the Negro's opening eyes and signaled him to feign unconsciousness, thus deflecting attention and making him appear more harmless. He had also broached a plan for escape to Friday. He had not, however, reckoned on Judd's having some "entertainment"; now, he saw, he would have to act with greatest speed, to save Friday from as much pain as possible.

41

The control cabin was dark with shadows and near-shadows. One lighted pilot tube seemed to make the room only more dim. In this indefinite quarter-light the Hawk set about stalking his prey.

Eyes steady on the two guards, who were completely absorbed by the happenings outside and some drops of consolation within, he drew his hands from beneath him. They were not bound. The rope which had encircled them had been gnawed through by the strong white teeth of the Negro.

Cautiously, without a whisper of sound, he reached towards the bonds on his legs. His fingers worked rapidly. Quickly the knots yielded and the rope was unwound. The legs were free. For a moment the Hawk stretched his cramped muscles, limbering them for use.

A voice spoke at the port-lock. He froze. One of the guards said:

"Look at him! This is goin' to be good! You can't beat that Judd!"

They were completely absorbed in the scene outside, and quite unconscious of the low blot preparing to move with fixed purpose behind them.

Unobserved, the Hawk got to hands and knees, and moved forward like a shadow. The two guards who were his quarry were sitting side by side, hunched a little forward in their interest at what was transpiring at the fire. Their heads were close together.

Carse crept near. He paused to judge the distance. In a sudden, snakelike movement, he sprang.

His arms clamped around the heads of the two guards and jerked them sharply together. There was a loud crack. Dazed, the men toppled off their seats and fell to the deck.

"Quiet!" Carse whispered. They gaped at him for a moment, then pushed to their feet.

They found that the ray-gun which had just been in the belt of one of them, now was leveled steadily at them, held

42

in the hand of that small, slender man who, more than any other man in the Solar System, they most feared. Their manner showed their fear.

"It's him!" one said.

"Yes," whispered the Hawk curtly. He took a few steps backward, eyes not moving. "What is your name?" he asked the shorter man, whose gun he now held.

"Keyger," was the frightened answer.

"Go to that locker," Carse ordered, indicating with a nod the place where the spacesuits were stowed. "Hurry!"

Hastily the man complied. Anything else might have meant quick and lonely and useless death. Shouts and laughter and drunken shrieks were coming from outside. No one would hear any cry of theirs.

When he had stepped into the locker, Carse closed and sealed the door.

"What you goin' to do with me?" croaked the remaining guard. He towered inches over the figure facing him, but his lips were trembling and his eyes were filled with fear.

"You kicked me when I was bound," the Hawk whispered. He sheathed his ray-gun, then spoke again. "Go for your gun."

The pirate trembled all over. His mouth fell open, and his eyes stuck on Carse's shabby holster. He seemed half hypnotized.

"Draw."

The man's brow beaded with sudden-starting sweat. His fingers twitched. A moment before, he had been secure; now death stared him in the face.

"Damn you, Carse!" he burst out suddenly, going for his gun.

Carse deliberately let him get it out. Not until then did his left hand move. But even then, there was only one streak of orange in the cabin, and that streak was from his gun. The pirate quivered, his face still contorted with his last desperate emotion; then he sagged to the deck. His body

43

twitched a little, and rolled over in a spasm. Almost square between the eyes was a crisp, smooth-burned hole.

Hawk Carse did not glance at the body, but sheathed his ray-gun, picked up the other from the deck where it had fallen and stuck it in his belt, then glided to the port-lock.

At what he saw, his face hardened.

A cluster of torches were lighting the near side of the phanti corral. The men who held them made a half-circle about something there, and from them came yells and uncontrollable laughter. Through gaps in the ring, Carse could see the torso of Friday, black in the torchlight, unbound, standing with his back almost touching the wire fence of the corral. The actions of Friday gave the clue to what was happening.

He was enveloped in a broad ray of orange light. He was hopping grotesquely from one foot to the other in an agony of pain, his lips drawn taut over his gleaming teeth, his face contorted, the whites of his eyes making large bright patches as the eyeballs rolled. The orange glow about him streamed from a ray-gun held by Judd the Kite. He was being slowly crisped alive! seared, hopping in a furnace of heat! and the men who ringed him were yelling at him between their laughter. Carse strained to hear. In a jumble, he caught these fragments:

"Jump over!"—"Go on, climb!"—"Climb! The juice's off!"—"Into the corral!"—"Climb over, you black buzzard!"—"Howee!"—"Look at him!"

About a foot behind Friday was the wire fence, and just behind the fence was the herd of phantis, snouts converged towards him, red-shot eyes glaring—jostling, bellowing, tearing at the ground with their powerful legs in ferocious excitement. Brutal death awaited Friday on the far side of the fence; slow, most painful death by burning on the near side; yet he still hoped, he still had faith in the Hawk, for he did not put a quick end to his torture, as he might have,

44

by trying to plunge through the devilish circle, or clambering over the fence.

Carse's mind moved with the speed of light. He could not rush the group: too many of them! Nor could he dive at them in the *Star Devil,* or ray them from above: that would mean Friday's death too. It would have to be something else. In a moment he had it. Quickly he examined the variations and checked the scheme back. It promised to be the decisive move, engendering the final meeting, and there must be no slip.

First, the Hawk slipped shadowlike to the entrance port of the pirates' space-ship, lying in the darkness nearby. He had to know if anyone was aboard.

Gruffly he called inside:

"Judd! Hey, Judd! You there?"

There was no answer. Again he called; then, satisfied that it was empty, he doubled back with noiseless speed, skirted the *Star Devil* and arrived at the rear wall of the ranch house.

A short leap and his hands closed on the copper drain. The muscles of his arms flexed in a quick pull-and-press-up which brought him over the edge. He rolled to his knees, then, stooping, hurried to the side which faced on the clearing and the corral.

He drew one ray-gun from his belt.

For seconds he reckoned the distance and the angle. He brought the weapon up, resting it on his right forearm. His deadly left hand began to squeeze.

A pencil-thin streak of orange light speared the air.

VIII

Stampede

Judd the Kite was enjoying himself hugely. His sense of humor was tickled. It was very funny, the contortions of the Negro in the ray-stream!

"Climb over!" he suggested, amid roars of laughter from the circle of men. "Climb over, why don't you? We've turned off the juice. There's no juice in the fence! We wouldn't want you to get a shock—would we, boys! Why don't you climb over?"

Friday hardly heard him. His lips were sucked tight in wordless agony; his cheek muscles stood out like welts; his huge body, bathed in the steady orange stream, bore patches of unnatural color. He hopped mechanically, changing from one aching leg to the other, his eyes closed, his whole body expressing one dumb agony. He did not know when it would end, but he still had faith.

Overhead danced the flames of six torches, seeming to leap to the gusts of laughter and yells and oaths that came ceaselessly from the group. Half seen behind the nine-foot fence, the waiting phantis jostled and bellowed. Only eight thin strands of wire separated beasts and men, and it was the current in the wires, not their strength, which kept the phantis from crashing through.

Judd smiled more widely. "Maybe you want a stronger beam!" he yelled. "I'll give you one minute to climb over.

46

After that you'll really burn. Now—will you climb? See—I'm moving the lever over!"

He stopped speaking. He had heard a new sound—a *spit*, and a *spang*. He looked about, but did not see what had happened. His men had noticed nothing; they were still laughing and yelling in drunken merriment. The Kite smiled again.

"Feel it now?" he yelled. "Are you going over?"

Again the *spit* and *spang*. Again Judd looked around. Others were doing the same, and the group quieted somewhat. Then someone saw what was happening, and cried out:

"Look! The fence!"

Judd's lips slackened and lost their smile. For a second the clamor ceased, so that there remained only the snortings and bellowings of the maddened beasts beyond the fence.

Then came another *spit* and *spang*—this time accompanied by a streak of orange light that came from somewhere behind. All saw it. And all saw or heard the parting of the third strand of wire—third from the bottom—as it whipped apart with a little singing swish.

"Someone's cutting the wires!" came a scared whisper. Yet still the pirates stood there, fuddled, staring at the fence or looking stupidly around.

Another *spit-spang*, another streak of light, and the fourth strand broke. The lower half of a whole section of fence was gone. Behind the opening the red-eyed phantis inched forward, still afraid of a shock, but powerfully attracted by their hatred of the two-legged creatures just beyond. Closer they came, and closer.

Someone cried: "They're coming out!"

At that, the fuddled pirates found their senses, and with one ragged yell of panic they turned and ran. Some made for their space-ship, others for the ranch house, still others, confused, ran toward the edge of the jungle. The phantis

47

followed in a thundering tide, all their fierce energies released, trampling in their drive the torches fallen to the ground, so that in a moment all light was gone, save that from the dwindling camp-fire. Quickly they closed on the heels of the fleeing pirates; then one, then another of the men went down under their trampling feet and shredding spurs, while others, a little ahead, less drunk or more lucky, profited by this and got a few steps ahead. Every one of those who started for the jungle was quickly enveloped by the leading edge of the tide and went down; most of those who started for the space-ship lasted a moment longer, then they too disappeared. The rest, those making for the ranch house, had more chance.

From his vantage point on the roof of the ranch house, the Hawk had confirmed his quick decision that this was the only way.

Rapidly, as was his custom, he had reckoned out the problem, considering every angle. He had to shoot the fence, not the men. For he couldn't hope to get more than three or four of the men; the first one falling over dead would quickly cause the others to scatter in the darkness, leaving the odds against him still too great.

As for Friday, he had to take his chance. There was, this way, a good chance, if he kept his wits. For, to the left, as close to the corral as the ranch house, were the grave-pits he himself had dug some hours before—one still empty, waiting to be filled. It offered an effective shelter—if he kept his wits. He, Carse, could do much to protect him from the stampeding beasts while he ran.

Some of the pirates would be trampled in the rush of the phantis. A few would probably reach the house. That was what he wanted.

And that was what he got. After his fifth shot the Hawk lowered his weapon and watched the scene he had produced.

He saw the herd sweep under the fence that for so long

had kept them back. Bellowing their hatred, they charged. Before them fled the thin fringe of men, Friday on one flank. Man after man went down with a grunt, with a cry; half-grown horns tore them; they were ripped, trampled, and left dying in a matter of seconds.

Now, Carse was shooting again, with the precision of a machine. There was Friday to be guarded. He was already separated from the other men—cut off and edging to one side—to the side toward the grave-pit! Dodging, wildly twisting and turning, he barely escaped a group of three phantis that singled him out and went thundering after him. The leading phanti made perhaps five leaps, then it suddenly tumbled headlong and lay flopping on the ground, a little wisp of smoke curling from its shoulder. In quick succession the other two went down. But there were many, and even as Friday melted into the shadows, another group detached themselves and thundered after him. The deadly ray-gun on the roof wrought swift slaughter amongst them, but some got into the darkness beyond vision of the phenomenal gray eyes.

The Hawk lowered his weapon, his face hard and set. Would they catch Friday? Tumble down on him, even if he reached the pit? Well, there was no helping it.

But the reckoning now was at hand. Carse tossed his used-up gun on the milling animals below, then drew the second gun from his belt and put it in the shabby holster. Like a shadow, noiseless and swift, he moved towards the far end of the roof.

IX

The Hawk Strikes

His face red, his breath coming in horse gasps, Judd the Kite
stumbled through the door of the ranch house on the heels of
four of his men. He turned and flung his weight against the
door, then locked and double-locked it. A second later fists
pounded on its outer side, and a voice cried in terror:

"Let me in! Let me in! Oh, God, let me in! Judd!"

There was the drum of running feet, and one hoarse,
despairing shriek from the man who had found the door
locked against him.

But the Kite was not even listening. A measure of courage returning with the protection furnished by the building, he snapped:

"Get those other doors locked quick! And lights. Then
search the house."

The light tubes glowed, filling the room with soft radiance. Judd surveyed his position.

He saw that it could have been far worse. But his men
needed courage.

The rapid change from orgy to deadly peril had sobered
them completely. But they were still frightened; nor was it
fear of the beasts. They came treading silently back from
their inspection and reported the house empty: but their
eyes kept shifting, and their hands still held their ray-guns.
Each one knew who had fired the shots that collapsed the
fence. They had taken two captives; Friday had been under
their eyes; there was only one other—the Hawk.

Hawk Carse! They had killed his ranchmen. They had killed his crew. They had tortured Friday. They were fugitives from the cold gray eyes, were targets now for the fatal left hand. The Hawk was loose!

Judd saw their fear, and he was fearful himself; but there seemed no immediate danger, so he summoned a blustering courage and said to the others:

"Yes, it was that damned Carse! He must of got loose some way. But pull yourselves together; we're safe here. He's somewhere outside."

He reasoned it out for them.

"He couldn't have done that shooting from the *Star Devil* —it's too far away. And he's not in it now or he'd be using it to try and find that black of his—if the black's still alive. No, he's not in the ship, and he's not in this house. He's somewhere outside, and he can't reach us while the phantis have the place surrounded. We can shoot them down from the attic; they'll soon beat it; and we'll get to the ships before Carse knows what it's all about. We'll leave him marooned. Then we'll get him later."

His words brought a return of confidence. It was so, the others agreed: the Hawk could not reach them as long as the phantis were there; and when they drove them away, the ships were near at hand and empty. All they had to do was get to one of the ships before Carse. He certainly was not in one of the ships or he would be hunting for Friday— and burning the house. No doubt he was up a tree somewhere. Perhaps he was gored and dead.

One of the men snickered, and Judd smiled. He took confidence from their confidence in him.

"We'd better get away as quick as we can," he said. "Get to the attic. We've got to shoot our way out of here. Some of those brutes are already horning at the door."

There were two rooms in the attic. The larger one, used as a store-room for staples, had four small windows, two in front and one in each side wall. The other, at the rear of the first, was a small one used to store tools and spare technical apparatus. It had two windows, set high up, and it connected with the larger room by a door set in the middle of the dividing wall.

Judd placed his men at the windows of the large room, taking one for himself.

Around the house still milled dozens of phantis, snorting and bellowing in futile rage at the men they knew were within. Two of the bulls fell foul of each other and fought in fury, only to turn suddenly for no apparent reason and hurl their bodies against a ground floor door. A lance of orange light from Judd's attic window sent one staggering, a pencilled hole burnt through its flank. Another lance brought the second down.

The huge fire the pirates had laid was already dying, and the night lay heavy over the clearing. Glinting slightly in the faint starlight were the two silent space-ships.

Then Judd the Kite, as he aimed and shot again, was struck by a disturbing idea. From where had Carse fired at the corral fence? What was the logical vantage point for him?

A shiver ran down his spine. He saw suddenly with terrible clearness where that vantage point was—and it had not been searched. The roof!

He turned swiftly, his lips opening to give orders.

But there, standing in the doorway to the other room, stood the figure of the man he so much feared, and in his left hand was a steady-leveled ray-gun that pointed as straight as his cold eyes right at Judd.

"Hawk—Carse!"

"Judd," said the quiet voice.

The Kite went white. As one, his men turned. One of them gasped at what he saw, another cursed, the other two simply stared with fear-flooded eyes. One thing only filled every mind—the never-failing vengeance of the Hawk.

"Carse!" repeated Judd stupidly.

"Yes," whispered the trader. "I've come to settle up. There are some lives—a few blows and kicks—and a matter of some torture to be paid for. The accounts must be squared, Judd."

Slowly he raised his right hand to his bangs of flaxen hair. He stroked them, gently. Judd's eyes, dry, hot, held fascinated on the hand.

"It's not by choice that I wear my hair like this," came the whisper. "That's another debt I have to settle—the largest of all. *Sheathe your guns!*"

The voice had hardened a little. The men obeyed at once. As their guns went into their holsters, Carse followed suit with his own. He stood, then, with both hands hanging at his sides. And he said, in the whisper that carried more weight than the yell of another:

"Once before we were interrupted. This time we won't be. This time we will see certainly for whom the number five brings death. Count, Judd."

With an effort, the Kite regained some control over himself. The odds were five to one. Five guns to one gun. Carse was a wondrous shot, but such odds were surely too great. Perhaps—perhaps there might be a chance. He said in a strained voice to his men:

"Shoot when I reach five. On five."

Then he swallowed and counted:

"One!"

Aside from a tiny flickering of his left eyelid, the Hawk stood motionless, apparently without feeling. Judd, he knew, was just fairly fast; as for the others—

"Two!"

—they were unknown quantities, except for one, the man called Jake. He probably had a lightning draw; his eyes were narrowed, his hands steady, and the body crouched, a sure sign of—

"Three!"

—a gunman who knew his business, who was fast. His

53

hip holsters were not really worn on the hips, but in front, close together; that meant—

"Four!"

—that he would probably draw both guns. So Judd must wait; the other three, being unknowns, disposed of in the order in which they were standing; but Jake must be—

"Five!"

—first!

One second there was nothing; the next, half a dozen spitting pencils of orange light had speared across the attic! And then two guns clanged to the floor, unfired, and the man called Jake staggered forward, crumpled and fell, a surprised look on his face and a little round hole just over one eye. Two others, similarly stricken, toppled forwards; the fourth, his heart burned through, lay back on the wall and sank slowly to the floor. Judd the Kite teetered a little, but he was still on his feet.

His lips were twisted; his hands seemed locked. His eyes met the two cold gray ones—and then his coarse face contorted, and he croaked:

"Damn you, Carse! Damn—"

They were his last words. His body spun around, fell, then flattened out on the floor, arms and legs flung wide. A tiny black hole was visible through his shirt. He had been last, and had been struck less accurately.

The Hawk was untouched. He stood there for several minutes, surveying what lay before him. He looked at each body in turn, his face devoid of expression. Silence hung over the attic, for the noises of the phantis had diminished as they straggled off to the jungle that was their home. The single living man of the six who had lived a minute before holstered his still warm ray-gun; and then the sound of a step on the stairs leading from the rooms below made him look up.

A man stood in the doorway of the attic.

He was big and black and brawny; and though his arms

and bare torso were scorched and streaked with blood, there was a tired grin on his face—a grin that widened as he understood what had happened in the room.

Neither said anything for a moment. Then the Hawk smiled, and there was all friendliness and affection in his face.

"You made the pit, Friday?" he asked, softly.

Friday nodded and gave a tired chuckle. "Yes. But only just!"

"Still feeling chipper," Carse said, "—in spite of your burns. Well, good for you. I guess you've had enough of Ku Sui for a while."

"You don't mean to imply I'm scared of him?" Friday said indignantly.

Carse, smiling slightly, said:

"I see. Well, then, if you're not too done in, drag these carrion out to your pit. Then we'll get some food, and then we'll sleep. And then. . . ."

There was something in the air, something big. Friday listened eagerly. "Yes?" he reminded his captain.

"Judd," said Carse softly, "was to have had a rendezvous with Dr. Ku Sui in seven Earth days. I am told the place of the rendezvous is entered in the log of his ship. I've got Keyger, the last of Judd's crew, locked up on the *Star Devil*. . . ."

The adventurer paused a moment, then he said:

"I myself am going to keep that rendezvous with Ku Sui. I want to see him very badly."

Friday looked at the slender man, at his gray eyes, at his calm face, at the bangs of flaxen hair which obscured his forehead. He understood.

"But you're not going alone?" Friday said. "Won't you take me?"

Carse looked at him and smiled slightly. He said:

"It will be dangerous."

Friday knew he would be taken.

55

X

Off to the Rendezvous

They ate. Carse annointed Friday's burnt body. Then they slept. Late the next Iapetus morning they awoke—Carse thoroughly refreshed, Friday much less so, but not complaining a word about the pain of his burns.

There was work to be done. At the Hawk's order Keyger, the prisoner, was released and fed; then, aided sullenly by this man, all three cleaned up the ravaged ranch, threw earth over the bodies of the dead, repaired the fence and generally brought order out of confusion. When they had finished, Carse ordered Friday and the captive pirate to hide his ship, the *Star Devil*, in the nearby jungle.

That morning, before Friday awoke, Carse had gone to the control room of the *Scorpion,* the pirate craft, and examined the log. Now, while they were gone, he returned to the ship and restudied an entry of great interest to him. The entry ran:

"E.D. (Earth Date) 16 January, E.T. (Earth Time) 2:40 P.M. Meeting ordered by K.S., for purposes of delivering the skeleton and clothing of Carse to him, at N.S. (New System) X-33.7; Y-241.3; Z-92.8 on E.D. 24 January, E.T. 10:20 P.M. Note: The ship is to stand by at complete stop, the radio open to Ku Sui's private wave (D37, P1293, R3) for further instructions."

He mulled it over, slowly stroking his bangs. It was a wonderful chance. Judd's ship would keep that rendezvous, but it would sheathe the talons of the Hawk. This time a trap would be laid for Ku Sui.

The plan was simple enough on the face of it, but the Eurasian was a master of cunning as well as a master of science, and high peril attended any matching of wits with him. Carse closed the log when a scuffle of feet brought his gaze to the port-lock entrance.

Friday, stripped to shorts, stood there. Shaking drops of perspiration from his face, he reported:

"Done it, sir—got the *Star Devil* in the jungle just where you wanted, and Keyger's locked up again. Now what? Are you still figuring on keeping that date with Dr. Ku in this ship?"

Carse nodded.

"Then where'll we pick up a crew? Porno? It's the nearest port."

"I'm not taking any crew, Friday."

Friday was surprised.

"No crew at all? Against Ku Sui?"

"I've lost enough men in the last two days," Carse said shortly. "And this meeting with Dr. Ku is a highly personal affair. You and I and Keyger can run the ship: we've got to." One of the man's rare smiles relaxed his face. "Of course," he murmured, "I'm risking your life. Perhaps I'd better leave you somewhere?"

"Say!" cried the Negro indignantly.

The Hawk's smile widened a little at this spontaneous exclamation of loyalty.

"Very well, then," he said. "Prepare the ship for casting off."

But as Friday went aft on a final thorough inspection of all mechanisms, he muttered over and over, "Two of us—against Ku Sui! Only two of us!" and he was still disturbed when, after Carse had had a few crisp words with the cap-

57

tive Keyger, telling him that he would be free but watched, and that it would be wise if he confined himself to his duties, he received the order, "Break ground."

Gently the pirate ship *Scorpion* stirred. Then, in response to the delicate incline of her control-stick, she lifted sweetly from the crust of Iapetus and at ever-increasing speed lifted through the satellite's atmosphere toward the limitless dark leagues beyond. The Hawk was on the trail!

Carse took the first watch himself. Except for occasional glances at the banks of instruments, the screens and celestial charts, he spent his time in thought, turning over in his mind the several variations of the situation his dangerous rendezvous might take.

First, how would Ku Sui contact the *Scorpion*? Any of three ways, he reasoned: come aboard from his own craft, accompanied by some of his men; stay behind and send some men over to receive the remains of the Hawk—for either of which variations he was prepared; or a third, more dangerous, direct that the remains of Carse be brought over to his ship, without showing himself or any of his crew.

Whatever variation their contacting took, there was another consideration revealed by Carse's celestial charts, and that was the proximity of the rendezvous to Jupiter's Satellite III, less than one hundred thousand miles. Satellite III harbored Port o' Porno, main refuge and home of the scavengers, the hi-jackers, and out-and-out pirates of space, so many of whom were under Ku Sui's thumb. Several pirate ships were sure to be in the vicinity, and one easily might blunder upon them, destroying whatever balance there might be in Carse's favor.

There was peril on every side. The Hawk considered that it would be wise to make provisions against the odds proving too great. So, his gray eyes reflective, he strode to the *Scorpion's* radio panel and a moment later was saying over and over:

"XX-1 calling XX-2. XX-1 calling XX-2. XX-1 calling XX-2. . . ."

A full two minutes went by, and there was still no answer from the speaker. He kept repeating: "XX-1 calling XX-2. XX-1 calling XX-2. XX-1 calling—"

He broke off as gentle words in English came from the speaker:

"XX-2 answering XX-1. Do you hear me?"

Carse's face softened.

"Yes," he said. "Set for tightest beam." He adjusted the knobs before him.

"All right," the gentle voice answered. "Tight. How are you, old man?"

The Hawk's face softened further. "As usual," he said, in a voice almost as gentle as the other's. "How are you, Eliot?"

"Just fine, Carse," came in the clear, cultured voice of Master Scientist Eliot Leithgow, probably the greatest scientific mind in the System, Ku Sui perhaps being the only exception. He was speaking now from his secret laboratory on Jupiter's Satellite III, opposite Porno—this surpassing genius who, with Friday, was one of Carse's two trusted comrades-in-arms. "I've been expecting you," he went on. "Has something happened?"

"I'm involved with Ku Sui again," the Hawk told him swiftly. "Please excuse me; I have to be brief. I can't take unnecessary chances of his hearing this."

He related the events of the last two days: Judd's attack on the Iapetus ranch, the subsequent fight and its outcome, and finally his present position and his intention of keeping the rendezvous. "The odds are pretty heavily against me, M.S.," he went on. "It would be stupid not to admit that I may not come out of this affair alive—and that's why I'm calling. My affairs, of course, are in your hands. You know where my store-rooms and papers are. Sell my trading posts and ranches; Hartz of Newark-on-Venus is the best agent.

But I'd advise you to keep for yourself that information on the Pool of Uranium. Look into it sometime. I'm in Judd's ship, the *Scorpion;* our *Star Devil's* on Iapetus, hidden in the jungle near the ranch. That's all, I think."

"Carse, I should be with you!"

"No, M.S.—couldn't risk it. You're too valuable. But don't worry, you know my luck. I'll very likely be down to see you after this meeting, and perhaps with a visitor who will enable you once again to return to an honorable position on Earth. Where will you be?"

"Let's make it Porno, at the house you know. I'm going in for some supplies. I'll get there five Earth days from now, and wait for you."

"Fine," the Hawk said shortly. "Good-by, M.S."

He paused, his hand on the switch. There came a parting wish from the loudspeaker:

"Good luck, old fellow. Get him! *Get him!*"

The Master Scientist's voice trembled at the end. Through Ku Sui he had lost honor, position, home—all good things a man on Earth may have; through Ku Sui he, the gentlest of men, was regarded by Earthmen as a murderer, and there was a price on his head. Hawk Carse did not miss the trembling in his voice. As he switched off, the adventurer's eyes went bleak.

XI

The Coming of Ku Sui

Straight through the vast reaches that stretched between one mighty planet and another the *Scorpion* arrowed, Carse and Friday standing watch and watch, Keyger always on duty with the latter. Behind, Saturn's rings dwindled, and ahead a dusky speck grew against the vault of space until the red belts and one great great crimson spot that marked it as Jupiter stood out plainly. By degrees, then, the ship's course was altered as Carse checked his calculations and made minor corrections in speed and direction. So they neared the rendezvous. And a puzzled furrow grew on Friday's brow.

What was bothering his captain? Instead of becoming more cool and impassive as the distance shortened, he showed signs of anxiety. This might be natural in most men, but it was unusual in the Hawk. Often the Negro found him abstractedly smoothing his bangs of hair, pacing the length of the control cabin, glancing thoughtfully at the miniscreen. What special thing was wrong? Friday wondered again and again—and then, in a flash, he knew.

"Why—how are we going to *see* Dr. Ku?" he burst out. "Didn't Judd say something about invisibility?"

The Hawk nodded. "That's just it. You remember Judd said that Ku Sui 'comes right out of empty space.' That might mean invisibility or the fifth dimension—and the

61

stars help us if he's solved the problem of dimensional traveling! I don't know . . . it's something I can't well prepare against." He fell to musing again.

A day and a half later found the usually-cheerful Friday in a state of continuous worry. The laugh wrinkles of his face were re-formed into lines of anxiety which gave his face a most lugubrious expression. From time to time he grasped the butt of his ray-gun with a grip that would have pulped an orange; and occasionally his rolling brown eyes sought the gray ones of the Hawk, only to return as by a magnet to the miniscreen, whose six adjoining squares mirrored the entire sweep of space around them.

Jupiter now filled one side of the forward observation window. It was a vast, red-belted disk, an eye-thrilling spectacle which dominated all that part of the sky. Against it were poised two small pale globes, the larger of which was Satellite III. Several hours before, Carse had scrutinized it with miniscreen magnification, and had made out above its surface a silver dot which was a space-ship. It was bound inward toward Port o' Porno, and might well have been one of Ku Sui's. But the *Scorpion,* slowing down for her rendezvous, had attracted no attention and had passed undisturbed.

Now she hung motionless—that is, motionless with respect to the sun. Only the whisper of the air-renewing machinery disturbed the tension in her control cabin where the three men stood waiting, glancing back and forth from the miniscreen to the Earth clock and the calendar attachment. The date the clock showed was 24 January, the time, 10:21 P.M. Dr. Ku Sui was one minute late.

Keyger, the captive, was sullen and restless, and made furtive glances at the Hawk, who stood detached, arms hanging at his sides, his gray eyes half closed, giving little hint in his quiet attitude of the strain all were feeling. But his attitude of being relaxed and off guard was deceptive— as Keyger found out. Suddenly his left hand seemed to dis-

62

appear; there was a streak of spitting orange light; and Keyger was gaping foolishly at the arm he had stealthily raised to one of the radio switches. It bore a smoking scar.

Hawk Carse sheathed his gun. "I would advise you to try no more tricks," he said coldly. "Cutting in our microphone is too simple a way to give warning to Dr. Ku Sui. Move away from there. And don't forget your lines when Dr. Ku calls. You will never act a part before a more critical audience."

Keyger mumbled something and tenderly touched his arm. A pitying smile came to Friday's face. "You damn fool!" he said.

It became 10:22 P.M. Still, in the screen, no other ship. Nothing but the giant planet, the smaller satellites poised against it, and the deep star-spangled curtain of black space all around.

They had carefully followed the instructions in the log. They were at the exact place noted there: checked and double-checked. The radio receiver was tuned to the wavelength given in the log. But of Ku Sui, nothing.

And yet, in a way, he was with them. His enigmatic personality and rarely seen figure were very present in their minds, and with them were overtones of all the diabolical cunning and suave ironic cruelty that men always associated with him. "He comes right out of empty space. . . ." Friday licked his lips. He was not built for mental strain: his lips kept drying and his tongue was like leather.

A little sputtering sound tingled the nerves of the three waiting men, and as one their eyes turned to the radio speaker. A contact question was being asked in the usual way:

"Are you there, Judd? Are you there, Judd? Are you there, Judd?"

The voice was not that of Ku Sui. It was a dead voice, toneless, emotionless, mechanical.

"Are you there, Judd?" it went on, over and over.

63

"The mike switch, Friday," the Hawk said, and then he was at Keyger's side, his ray-gun transfixing the man with its threatening angle. "Play your part well," was the whisper from his lips.

The switch went over with a click. Keyger faced the mike.

"This is Keyger," he said.

"Keyger?" the dead voice asked. "I want Judd. Where is Judd?"

"Judd is dead. The trap failed, and there was a fight on Iapetus. Judd was killed by Carse; so were most of the others. Only two of us are left, but we have Carse and the Negro prisoners, alive. What are your instructions?"

A half minute went by, and the three men hardly breathed.

"How do we know you are Keyger?" the voice said at last. "Give the recognition."

"The insignia of Dr. Ku Sui."

"What is the insignia of Dr. Ku Sui?"

"It is—" Keyger hesitated, reluctant. Carse's ray-gun prodded him in the stomach. "It is an asteroid," the man went on hastily, "in the center of a circle of the nine planets."

The unseen speaker was quiet. Evidently he was conferring with someone else, probably Ku Sui.

"All right," his toneless voice came back at last. "You will remain motionless in your present position, keeping your radio receiver open for further instructions. We are approaching and will be with you in thirty minutes."

Carse motioned to Friday to switch on the mike. Keyger stepped back a little and stood still. He was soaked with perspiration.

"Now we must wait again," the Hawk murmured, crossing his arms and scanning the screen.

They had heard from Ku Sui, but that had not answered the old tormenting question of how he would come. The screen showed nothing, and it should have shown the Eurasian's decelerating ship at many times thirty minutes away. They looked again upon the same vista of Jupiter and his satellites, framed in eternal blackness; there was no characteristic silvery dot of an approaching ship to give Carse the enemy's position and enable him to shape his plan of reception definitely.

Twenty minutes went by. The Hawk showed the strain he was under in his characteristic way—by pulling at the bangs of flaxen hair that came down over his forehead nearly to the eyebrows. He had expected a mystery in Ku Sui's approach, and here it was. There was nothing to do but wait; he had made in advance what few preparations he could.

Friday broke the tense silence in the control cabin. "He's *got* to be *somewhere!*" he exploded. "It isn't natural for the screen not to show anything! Isn't there something we can do?"

The Hawk was unusually patient with the nervousness of his Satellite. "I'm afraid not," he said. "It's invisibility he's using, or else the fifth dimension, as Judd said. But there may be a chance. He'll send more instructions by radio and perhaps, after that, his ship will appear—"

A new voice, bland and unctuous, spoke in the control cabin from behind the three men.

"Not necessarily, my honored friend Carse," it said. *"You will observe there is no need for a ship to appear."*

Ku Sui had come. He was *there.*

XII

The Wave of a Handkerchief

He stood smiling in the door-frame leading aft to the rear entrance port. There was all grace in his posture, in the easy angle at which one arm rested against the side bulkhead, in the casual way in which he held the ray-gun that bored straight at Carse. Height and strength he had, and a perfectly proportioned figure. Beauty, too, of face, with soft, sensitive mouth, ascetic cheeks, and skin of clearest saffron. His hair was fine and black, and swept straightly back from the high narrow forehead where lived his tremendous intelligence.

It was his eyes that gave him away, his eyes of rare green that from a distance looked black. Slanting, hooded, unreadable beneath the lowered silky lashes, there was the soul of a tiger in their sinister depths. It was his eyes that his victims remembered. . . .

"So you have arrived, Dr. Ku," whispered the Hawk, and for a second he too smiled faintly, though his eyes were as bleak as a polar ice-cap. Their glances met and held—the cold, hard, honest rapier; the subtle perfumed poison. The other men in the cabin were forgotten; the feeling was between these two. Strikingly contrasted they were as they stood facing each other: Carse, in loose blue work trousers, faded blue blouse, open at the neck, old-fashioned rubber-soled shoes on his feet and a battered skipper's cap askew

66

on his flaxen hair; Ku Sui, suavely impeccable in high-collared green silk blouse, full-length trousers of the same material, and red slippers, to match the wide red sash which revealed the slender lines of his waist. A perfume hung about the man, the indescribable odor of tsin-tsin flowers from the humid jungles of Venus.

"You see, I meet you halfway, my friend," the Eurasian said with delicate mock courtesy. "A surpassing pleasure I have anticipated for a long time. *No, No!* I see that already I shall have to ask you a small favor. A thousand pardons: it's my deplorable ability to read your mind that requires it. Your so justly famed speed of draw might possibly overcome this advantage"—he raised his ray-gun slightly— "and, though I know you would not kill me—save in an emergency, since you wish to take me a living prisoner—I would find it most distressing to have to carry a flaw on my body for the rest of my life. So, may I request you to withdraw your ray-gun with two fingertips and put it on the floor? Observe—your fingertips. Will you be so kind? You too, black one."

The Hawk looked at him for a minute, then silently he obeyed. He knew that the Eurasian would have no compunctions about shooting him down in cold blood, if necessary; but, on the other hand, even as the man had said, he could not kill Ku Sui, but had to capture him alive, in order to take him to Earth to confess to the crimes now blamed on Eliot Leithgow. "Do as he says, Friday," he instructed the still staring Negro; and reluctantly Friday obeyed.

"Thank you," the Eurasian said. He paused. "I suppose you are wondering how I arrived here, and why you did not see me come. Well, I shall certainly tell you, in return for your favor. But first—ah, friend Carse—your gesture! A reminder, I assume."

Slowly the Hawk was stroking the bangs of hair which had been trained to obscure his forehead. There was no emotion on his set face as he answered, no sign of feeling

67

unless it were a slight trembling of the left eyelid—significant enough to those who could read it.

"Yes," he whispered, "a reminder. I do not like to wear my hair like this, Ku Sui, and I want you to know that I've not forgotten. I'm now in your power, but there'll be a time—"

"But you wouldn't threaten your host!" the other said with mock surprise. "And surely you wouldn't threaten me, of all men. Must I point out how useless it has always been for you to match yourself, merely a skillful gunman, against me, against a brain?"

"Usually," the cold whisper came back, "the brain has failed in the traps it has laid for the gunman."

"Only because of the mistakes of its agents. Unfortunately for you, the brain is dealing with you directly this time, my friend. It's quite a different matter. But this small talk —although you honor—"

"Yes—this small talk is sickening," said the Hawk. "Of course you intend to kill me."

Dr. Ku gestured deprecatingly. "You insist on introducing these unpleasant topics! But to relieve your mind, I've not yet decided how I can entertain you most suitably. I have come primarily to ask you one trifling thing."

"And that is?"

"The whereabouts of Master Scientist Eliot Leithgow."

Hawk Carse smiled. "Your conceit lends you an extraordinary optimism, Dr. Ku."

"Not unfounded, I am sure. I desire very much to meet our old friend Leithgow again; his is the only other brain in this Solar System at all comparable to mine. And did I tell you that I always get what I desire? Well, will you give me this information? Of course, there are ways. . . ."

For a moment he waited.

The Hawk only looked at him.

"Always in character," the Eurasian said regretfully. "Very well." He turned his head and looked at Friday and

Keyger, standing nearby. "You are Keyger?" he asked the latter. "It is unfortunate that you had to deceive me a little while ago. We shall have to see what to do about it. For the present, move farther back, out of the way. So. You, black one, take a place next to my friend Carse; we must be going."

Ku Sui surveyed them with his inscrutable eyes. Gracefully, he drew close.

Carse missed not a move. He watched the Eurasian draw a square of lustrous black silk from one of the long sleeves of his blouse.

"This bears my personal insignia, you see," he murmured. "You will remember it." He waved it languidly just under their eyes.

Friday stared at it; Carse too, wonderingly. He saw embroidered in yellow on the black a familiar insignia composed of an asteroid in the circle of nine planets. And then alarm hit his brain. There was a strange odor in his nostrils and it came from the square of silk.

"Characteristic, Dr. Ku," he said. "Quite characteristic."

The Eurasian smiled. An expression of stupid amazement came over Friday's face. The design of asteroid and planets wavered into a blur as the Hawk fought unconsciousness; a hard sound came from his lips; he lurched uncertainly. The Negro crumpled to the deck. Carse's desire to sleep grew overpowering. Once more, as from a distance, he glimpsed Ku Sui's smile. He tried to back to the wall; made it; then a heavy thump suggested to his dimming mind that he too had fallen to the deck. He was unconscious at once.

XIII

Soil!

Carse awoke with a slight feeling of nausea and the smell
of the drug still in his nostrils. He found he was lying on the
floor of a large square cell whose walls and ceiling were of
some pastel green metal and which was bare of any kind of
furnishing. In one wall was a heavy, tightly-closed door, also of metal, and studded by the knob of a lock. Barred slits,
high in the opposite side walls, gave ventilation; a single
tube set in the ceiling provided illumination.

He was not bound. He got up and regarded the outflung
figure of Friday, lying to one side. Something in his look
seemed to reach the big Negro, for, as he watched, the
man's eyelids flickered, and a sigh escaped his full lips. He
looked up at Carse; then recognition, followed by gladness,
flooded his eyes. The Hawk smiled faintly also. There were
close bonds between these two.

"Lord, I'm thankful to be with you," said Friday with
relief. His eyes rolled as he took in the cabinlike cell. "Nice
homey little place," he remarked. "Where do you suppose
we are?"

"I think we're at last at that place we have searched for
so long—Ku Sui's headquarters—and I think his headquarters may be a space-ship, a huge one."

(Those who have read the history of that raw period a
hundred years ago will remember that the Eurasian's actual

70

base of operations was for a long time the greatest of the mysteries that enveloped him. Half a dozen times the Hawk and his comrade-in-arms, Eliot Leithgow, had hunted for it with all their separate skills of adventurer and scientist, and, although they had twice found the man himself, always they had failed to find his actual retreat. According to common opinion it was a place of frightening potential, where unthinkable experiments were performed.)

"I guess that means we're finished, then," Friday said lugubriously.

Carse had walked to the lone door and found, as he of course expected, that it was locked. At Friday's words he turned and responded crisply:

"It's not like you to talk that way, Friday. We're far from finished. We have succeeded in the first step—if, as I suspect, this cell is part of Dr. Ku's real headquarters. Surely before he decides to eliminate us we will be able to learn something of the nature of his space-ship. Perhaps it has a weakness, and can be attacked."

Conversation always cheered the naturally social Friday; he seldom had the opportunity for it with his usually reserved Captain. He objected.

"But what good'll that do us, if we take what we've learned to where it won't help anybody, least of all us, ourselves? And what chance have we got against Ku Sui now, when we're prisoners? Why, he's a magician; it isn't natural, what he does. Lands in our ship plop right out of empty space! Puts us out with a wave of his handkerchief!" With final misery in his voice he added: "We're sunk. This time we're surely sunk."

Carse smiled at his emotional friend. "All you need is a good fight, Friday. It's anticipation that disintegrates your morale; you shouldn't think so much. Why—there was an anesthetic on that handkerchief! Simple enough; I might have expected it. As for his getting into our ship, he entered from behind, through the after port-lock, while we were

71

looking at the screen in the control room. I don't understand yet why we could not see his craft. I still can't quite
believe he could make it invisible. Paint, perhaps, or camouflage? It doesn't seem likely. He might have a way of preventing the registering of his ship on our screen. Oh, he's
clever and dangerous, but somewhere there'll be a weakness. Somewhere. There always is." His tone changed and
he snapped: "Now be quiet. I want to think."

He thought, but arrived at nothing productive. Ku Sui's
easy assumption that the information as to Eliot Leithgow's
whereabouts would be forthcoming from his lips, puzzled
him, and brought some anxiety. Torture probably would
not be able to force his tongue to betray his friend, but
there were perhaps other means. Of these he had a vague
apprehension. Dr. Ku was preeminently a specialist in the
human brain—and he had implied his determination to
have that information. Suppose he should use something it
was impossible to fight against?

He alone, Hawk Carse, had assumed this responsibility.
He had asked Leithgow where he would be, and he remembered the place agreed upon for the meeting. He dared not
lose the battle of wits he felt was coming. . . .

His eyes turned to the door. It opened. Ku Sui stood
there, and behind him, in the corridor, were three other figures, their yellow faces strangely dumb and lifeless above
glistening gray smocks which extended a little below their
belted waists. Each bore embroidered on his chest the planetary insignia of Ku Sui in yellow, and each was armed with
two ray-guns.

"I must ask forgiveness, my friend, for these retainers
who accompany me," the Eurasian began suavely. "Please
don't let them disturb you; they are more robots than men,
obeying only my words. A little adjustment of the brain,
you understand. I have brought them only for your protection, for you would find it would result most unpleasantly
if you were to make a break for freedom."

"Of course, *you're* not the one who wants protection!" sneered Friday. "Or else you'd of brought a whole army!"

But the Negro recoiled a little when the Oriental's green tiger eyes caught him full. It was with a physical shock—such was the power of the man—that he received the soft-spoken reply:

"Yours is a most entertaining wit, black one; I am overcome with the honor and pleasure of having you for my guest. But perhaps—may I suggest it?—it would be well for you to save your humor for a more suitable occasion. I would like to make the last few hours of your visit as pleasant as possible."

He turned to Hawk Carse. "I have thought that an inspection of this, my home in space, would intrigue you more than anything else my poor hospitality affords. May I do you the honor, my friend?"

"I should like to see it," the Hawk replied coolly. "But Friday comes too."

The Eurasian bowed. "After you," he said, and waited until Friday and the Hawk passed through the door. Close after them came the three living automatons.

The passageway was square, plain and bare, and spaced at intervals by other closed doors. "Storerooms in this wing," the Eurasian explained as they progressed. He stopped in front of one of the doors and pressed a button. The door slid noiselessly open, revealing not another room, but a short metal spider ladder. Up this they climbed, one of the guards going first in the half-light; then a trapdoor above opened and they were flooded with ruddy light. They stepped out.

What they saw took them completely off guard. Friday gaped, and Carse so far lost his habitual poise as to stare in wonder.

Below was soil! Above, a great, glassy dome!

Not a space-ship, this realm of Ku Sui! Soil—with a whole settlement built upon it! Genuine brown soil, and on

73

it several buildings of a familiar green metal. And over-head, cupping the entire outlay, a colossal hemisphere of glasslike material, ribbed with silvery supporting beams and struts! And on its other side the glorious vista of space!

Ahead, at an angle of sixty degrees, hung the red-belted disk of Jupiter, with the pale globes of Satellites II and III wheeling close—*and all of them appeared the same size as when the two had last seen them from the* Scorpion!

Dr. Ku smiled blandly at the puzzlement that showed on the faces of his prisoners.

"Have you noticed," he asked, "that you are still in the neighborhood of the point in space where we had our ren-dezvous? But this is *not* another of Jupiter's satellites. Ah, no. This is my own world—my own personally-controlled little world!"

"Snakes of the Santo!" Friday gasped, the whites of his eyes showing all around. "Then we must be on an asteroid!"

They were. On the far side of the dome the outline of the asteroid was hard and sharp in the Jupiter-light against the backdrop of black space. It was a long, craggy, uneven body, seemingly about a mile in length, pinched in the mid-dle and thus shaped roughly like a peanut shell. One end had been leveled off to accommodate the dome with its cradled buildings; soil had been laid down; outside the dome all was untouched. The landscape outside was a gar-gantuan jumble of sharp rocks which had crystallized into a maze of hollows, crevices, facets and jagged out-thrusts. Without an atmosphere, with but the feeblest of gravities and without any form of life—save for that within the dome built upon its surface—it was a typical small asteroid, of which race only the largest are globe-shaped.

"Once," the Eurasian went on softly as they took all this in, "this world of mine circled with its thousands of fellows between Mars and Jupiter. I picked it from the rest because it contains great quantities of a certain fissionable mineral; and I had this air-containing dome constructed on it, and

74

these buildings inside the dome. Then, with batteries of gravity plates inserted precisely in the center of gravity, and with the enormous power of the atom, I nullified the gravital pull of the sun and other planets, wrenched the asteroid from its age-old orbit and swung it free into space. An achievement that would command the respect even of Eliot Leithgow, I think. So now you see, Carse; now you know. *This* is my secret base, *this* my hidden laboratory. I take it always with me, and I travel where I will."

The Hawk had a special interest in the scene of Ku Sui's great achievement. He was observing many things: the buildings, their nature, the exits from the dome, and how they could best be reached.

They were standing on the roof of the central building, the largest—a low metal structure with four wings which crossed at right angles to make the figure of a great plus sign. The hub was probably Dr. Ku's chief laboratory, Carse thought. On each side stood other buildings, low, long, like barracks, with figures of coolies moving in and out. Workshops, living quarters, power-rooms, he supposed; power-rooms certainly, for there was a soft hum in the air.

There was a great port-lock at ground level in the side of the dome nearest the tip of the asteroid, a lock big enough to admit the largest space-ship; and on one side was a smaller man-sized lock. To reach them—

"And over there," Dr. Ku's voice broke in—"quite near the lock—you see your borrowed ship, the *Scorpion*. But please don't let it tempt you to cut short your visit with me, my friend. It would avail you nothing, even if you reached her, for it requires a secret combination to open the port-locks, and my servants' brains have been so altered that they are physically incapable of divulging it. Of course I have offensive rays and other devices hidden about—just in case. All rather hopeless, isn't it? But surely interesting.

"Let us go; I have more to show. Below, in my main laboratory, in the center of this building, there's something far more interesting, and it concerns you, Carse, and me, and also Master Scientist Eliot Leithgow." He let the words sink in. "Will you follow me?"

And so they went below again, down the spider ladder into the corridor. There was nothing else to do; the guards, ever watchful, pressed closed behind. But a tattoo of alarm was beating in Hawk Carse's brain. Eliot Leithgow again —the hint of something ominous to be aimed at him, Carse, for the extraction of information he alone possessed: the whereabouts of his elderly friend the Master Scientist.

XIV

The Color-Storm

The corridor ended at a heavy metal door. As the party approached, it swung inward in two halves, and a figure clad in a white surgeon's smock emerged. He was a white man, tall, with a fine head but eyes strangely dull and lifeless, like those of the coolie-guards. His gaze rested on Ku Sui, and the Eurasian asked him:

"Is it ready?"

"Yes, lord," he replied—tonelessly.

"Through here, then, my friends." The door opened and closed behind them as they stepped inside. "This is my main laboratory. And there, friend Carse, is the object which is to concern us."

With one glance the adventurer took in the laboratory. It was an immense room, a circle in shape, with doors opening into the four wings of the building. Along the walls of the periphery were many complicated machines and much apparatus whose purpose he could not even guess at. In one place there was a table strewn with tangled shapes of wire, rows of odd-bulging tubes and other apparatus; and conspicuous near one door was an ordinary operating table, with a light dome overhead. At that place a tall wire screen placed a dozen feet out from the wall hid something from view. Carse noted all these things; then his gaze went back to the object in the middle of the floor which Ku Sui had indicated.

77

It was a hemisphere about five feet high, resting curve upward. Its substance was a network of extremely fine wire, woven in a shell. The wires seemed as thin as the threads spun by a spider. They wove upward and around, shimmering beautifully, and completely enclosing the interior; but they made so thin a wall that inside, in the center, a sort of chair could be discerned. Extending from the chair in front, and so placed that it would be directly in front of the eyes of anyone sitting in it, was a rectangular device. The wires of the web were supported by an internal frame of glasslike strips. Where they came together at the top there was a metal ring. In the ring was a hook attached to a rope reeved through pulleys in the ceiling; this, it seemed, was means for raising the web, to permit entrance. Standing ready were four men in surgeons' smocks—white men with intelligent faces and dull, lifeless eyes—one of them the man who had come to meet them.

"What is its purpose?" asked the Hawk—but he felt he already knew the answer.

"That," came the suave reply, "you will discover for yourself. I think you will have some novel sensations. Nothing harmful, though, however much they may tire you. Now!" He gave a sign, and one of the assistants touched a switch. The wire web rose, leaving the central seat behind. "We are ready. May I ask you to enter?"

Hawk Carse faced his old foe, his bleak gray eyes directed squarely at Ku Sui.

"If I don't?"

The Eurasian gestured apologetically to his guards.

"I see," Carse whispered. There was nothing to be done. Three coolies, each with ray-guns at the ready; four white assistants—robot men. He looked at the Negro. "Don't move, Friday," he warned; "they'll only shoot you down. I can resist this thing."

He turned back to the Eurasian. "Ku Sui," he said, clipping the words, "you have said that this would not permanently harm me. I know you for the most deadly, vicious egomaniac in the Solar System, but I do not know you for a liar. . . . I will enter."

The slight smile on the Oriental's face did not alter. Carse stepped to the seat, sat down, and was strapped in place.

The web of shimmering wires descended, cupping him completely. Ku Sui stepped to an adjoining switchboard and studied the indicators, finally placing one hand into a recess and drawing from it a little cone trailing a wire—something like a microphone. Dead silence hung over the laboratory. The white-clad figures stood like statues, dumb and apparently without feeling. The watching Negro trembled, his mouth slightly open, his brow already bedewed with perspiration. Through the web, Carse looked like a ghost.

Dr. Ku Sui pulled down a switch, and there sounded a low murmur. Immediately the wire web came to life. The shimmer disappeared, and in its stead was color, moving color, every color in the spectrum. In rhythmic waves tinted brilliances dissolved back and forth through each other, making the group of men seem like resplendent figures out of another universe.

Ku Sui pressed a button, and the side of the device in front of the Hawk's eyes started to glow. Colors began to float over its face, colors constantly weaving and clouding in an infinity of combinations and designs. Eyes staring wide, as if unable to close them to the brilliant kaleidoscopic procession, the adventurer looked on.

Inside the web of color Carse began to quiver, but still he sat unresisting in the chair and watched the color-maelstrom. His eyes began to throb with pain; but for some reason he could not close them. He was fully conscious, and was going to defend his secret if he had to die. He was sure, now, that the device was being used—or was going to be used—to extract from his mind the knowledge of Eliot

79

Leithgow's whereabouts; therefore he attempted to seal his mind. He fastened it on one thing—on Iapetus, satellite of Saturn, and his ranch there—and barred every other thought. Over and over he repeated to himself: "Iapetus. Iapetus. My ranch on Iapetus. Iapetus. The corral. The phantis." Hundreds of times. . . .

The blinding waves of color rioted in front of him, about him, submerged him, fatigued him. He came to have a mighty impulse to sleep, but he resisted it.

Days seemed to pass. . . . Years. . . . An eternity. This. . . . Continued without change. . . . To the end of time. . . .

Dimly he knew that the color-storm was affecting him. He sensed danger when a great drowsiness stole over him; but he fought it off, his brain beating out again, hundreds of times: "Iapetus. Iapetus. I have a ranch there. The phantis have a horn. It is very valuable. I'll have to collect another herd. Iapetus. Iapetus."

Then came excruciating pain!

It was an electric shock. His nerves seemed to tear; for a second his mind was thoroughly disorganized before it again could focus on Iapetus. Recovery . . . dullness . . . a kind of peace—and again the shock speared him. It was followed by a question in words which seemed to come from far off:

"Where is Eliot Leithgow?"

Somehow the question meant a great deal, and should not be answered. . . .

Again the stab of agony. Again the voice:

"Where is Eliot Leithgow?"

Again the shock, and again the voice. Alternating, over and over. He could brace himself against the shock, but the voice could not be avoided. Perhaps it was not really a voice, but only something in his head; but, whatever it was, it was everywhere about him—over, around, and under him; he began to *see* it. Desperately he forced his brain to

80

keep his thoughts connected with Iapetus. He no longer could remember why he must, but he knew there was a reason.

"Iapetus—Iapetus—I have a ranch there—Iapetus—Iapetus—*Where is Eliot Leithgow?*—Iapetus—Iapetus—I have a ranch there—*Where is Eliot Leithgow?*—I have a ranch there—a ranch there—Iapetus, a ranch—*Where is Eliot Leithgow?*—Where is Eliot Leithgow?—Where is Eliot Leithgow?*" . . .

After one hour and ten minutes the Hawk crumpled.

He was delirious. The combined effect of the pain, the physical and nervous exhaustion of the shocks and colored light, the endless, persistent question, his own attempted concentration on his Iapetus ranch—these were too much for any human body to stand against, even his. He lost his grip on his mind, lost the fine control that had never been lost before, the control about which he was so vain. The Hawk Carse that now was only a lump of flesh gave the information he had so valiantly tried to keep locked in the cells of his brain.

His voice gasped out:

"Port o' Porno, Satellite III! Port o' Porno, Satellite III!"

Dr. Ku Sui stepped forward.

"The house number?"

"574—574—574—"

"Ah!" breathed the Eurasian. "And Port o' Porno! So near!"

Ku Sui pressed another of the buttons and threw back the switch. The web of colors faded; the laboratory became, it seemed, midnight dark. Slowly, as all their eyes readjusted, vision improved. The machine in its center was again but a great shroud of shimmering wire.

Slumped in the seat within it was the familiar slender figure, flaxen head bowed, eyes closed, unconscious.

Lying on the floor was another unconscious figure. Friday had fainted.

81

XV

Port o' Porno

The pirate port of Porno is of course dead now, replaced by the clean lawfulness of Port Midway, but a hundred years ago, in the days before the Patrol ships came, she roared her bawdy song through the farthest reaches of the Solar System. For crack merchant ships and dingy trading tramps alike, she was haven; drink and drugs, women and diversions unspeakable lured to her ship-berths the cream and scum, the adventurers and riffraff of a dozen worlds. Spacemen and pirates paid off at her, staying as long as their wages lasted in the Street of Sailors; not a few remained permanently, their bodies flung to the beasts of the savage jungle that rimmed the port. There, only the cunning and strong could survive for any length of time. Ray-guns were the surest law. The most modern achievements of science stood side by side with murderous lawlessness as old as man himself.

The hell town had grown with the strides of a giant, rising rapidly from a muddy street of *tio* shacks to a small cosmetropolis. She was essentially a place of contrasts. Two of the big Earth companies had modern space-ship hangers there, well-lighted and well-equipped; but under their very noses was a festering welter of dark, rutted byways extending all the way from the comparative orderliness of the narrow Street of the Merchants to the drunken bedlam of the

Street of the Sailors. It perhaps can be understood why these men who needed a whole Solar System for elbow room, disdained setting to order the measly few acres of dirt they stopped at, but it is a mystery why they endured such narrow streets and cluttered houses. Whatever the reason, nervously exhausted, free at last after their long cramped cruises, impatient for physical release—they became just animals.

The riotous tangle that was this famous space port rested in the heart of Satellite III's primeval jungle.

Tall electric-wired fences girdled Port o' Porno to keep the jungle creatures back. It was equivalent to a death sentence to pass unarmed outside them; the monstrous shapes that lived and fought in the nearby swamps saw to that. Nightmare shapes they were, for the most part, some reptilian and comparable only to the giants that roamed Earth in Jurassic ages. Eating, fighting, breeding in the humid gloom of the vegetation-shrouded swamps, their bellows and roars sometimes at night thundered clear across the port, a reminder of Nature yet untamed. Occasionally, in the berserk ecstasy of the mating season, the reptilian ones hurled their house-high bodies at the guarding fences; and then there was panic in the town, and many lives were ripped out before a barrage of rays drove the monsters back.

They were not the only inhabitants native to Satellite III. Deep underground, seldom seen by men, lived a race of clawed man-mole creatures, half human in intelligence, blind from their unlit habitat, but larger than a man and stronger; and fiercer, too, when cornered. Their numbers no one knew, but their bored tunnels constituted a lower layer of life over much of the satellite.

Probably more vicious than these native "Three's" were the visiting bipeds, man himself, who thronged the *kantrans*—which politely may be defined as dives for the purveying of all entertainments. In them were a score of snares for the buccaneer with money in his pocket and dope in his

83

blood. The open doors on the Street of the Sailors all were loudspeakers of drunken oaths and laughter, pierced now and then by a roar or scream as someone in the sweating press of bodies inside knew rage or fear.

One interplanetarily notorious kantran made a feature of swinging its attractions aloft in gilded cages, where all of them, young and old, pale and painted, giant and dwarf, Square and Round, ogled and arrested the passers-by, inviting a sampling of their wares.

Of all kinds and conditions of men were these passers-by. Earthmen sailors, white, Negro, Chinese and Eurasian, most of them in the drab blue of space-ship crews, but each with a ray-gun strapped to his waist; short, thin-faced Venusians, shifty-eyed, cunning, with the planet's universal weapon, the skewer-blade, sheathed at their sides; tall, thin Martians with large chests, wearing the air-rarifying mask that was necessary for them in Satellite III's Earth-like atmosphere; and all the lesser breeds, including the Square and Round ones—who will not be referred to again, for they are still not generally accorded belief. Business men and sightseers, except the most bold, were apt to stay in their houses after their first visit to the Street of Sailors. Each face on the streets or in the kantrans that lined them bore the mark of drink, or the contemptuous, insolent expression bred by Porno's favorite drug, *isuan*.

Around Porno was the constant threat of savage life; below it were half-human savagery and mystery; in it, in the very shadow of their mighty engines of space, were the most vicious animals of all—degraded men.

This was the Port o' Porno of a hundred years ago.

This was the Port o' Porno where Master Scientist Eliot Leithgow for very good reasons had told Hawk Carse he would meet him. 574. The house of his friend.

Night descended suddenly on the outlaw space-port that day the elderly exile waited in vain for his comrade Hawk Carse to show up.

84

There were four hours when the light received by Satellite III from the sun and near-lying Jupiter would be gone, and in its place a cloying darkness, heavy with the odors of town and exotic products and the damp, lush vegetation of the impinging jungle. The night would be given over to carousing; for these four hours the Street of the Sailors came lustily to life. It was a time to keep in hiding.

In the middle of that night, when the pleasures of Porno were in full stride, there emerged from one of the dark, crooked byways that angled off the Street of the Sailors, a squad of five men whose disciplined pace and regular formation were in marked contrast to the confusion around them. They were slant-eyed men, with smooth saffron faces; they were strongly built, and they were armed, each one, with both a ray-gun and a black, pointed, two-foot tube. When they crossed the Street of the Sailors, the carousing crowd fell silent and hastened to get out of their path. It was not their numbers, formation, or weapons that caused this; rather, it was the insignia embroidered on the breasts of the gleaming gray smocks they wore—an asteroid in a circle of the nine planets.

The squad pressed along rapidly. A still-comely woman, new to Porno, plucked at the leader's sleeve; but his pace did not slacken, and she fell back, puzzled and afraid because of a feeling of something lifeless, dumb, machinelike in the man. Ahead, an isuan-maddened Earthman fell foul of a Venusian; a circle cleared in the mob, a ray-gun spat and missed, and the Venusian closed, the gleam of a skewer-blade playing around him. This was combat; this was interesting; but none of the squad's five men gave the fight a glance, or even turned his head when, as they passed, the butchered Earthman coughed out his life in the muck at their feet.

So they crossed, and soon they were gone down another black-throated byway.

They padded noiselessly along in the darkness, to turn

85

again presently, pausing finally before a low, steel-walled house, typical of the strongholds of the prudent merchants of the port. No lights were visible. All within seemed asleep.

There was silence and darkness along the narrow street. Occasionally a desultory breeze brought sounds of a burst of revelry, and once the ports of an outbound space-ship flashed overhead for an instant; but the street was wholly theirs. The five men stood close together, parleying in toneless whispers.

After a little they separated. On cat's feet four of them stole around the sides of the house. The fifth, drawing the black, pointed tube from his sash, crept up to the front entrance-port and held the tip to it. Blue light flowed from it amid a shower of white sparks, revealing an impassive Oriental face and the front of a crouching body. The port melted inward, and the man disappeared into the blackness of the interior.

Presently, inside, there was a stir of movement, a whisper, a rustle. A challenge, shouts volleying forth, a scream, another. And the peculiar rattling sound that sometimes comes from a dying man's throat. Then again silence.

Five shadows melted from the front entrance-port. They were carrying something black and still and heavy among them.

The errand was done. . . .

XVI

The Coming of Leithgow

Hawk Carse awoke to the touch of a hand on his brow. He came slowly to full consciousness. His pain was great.

His whole body was sore; every joint, every muscle in it ached; his brain was a pumping turmoil. When at length he opened his eyes he found Friday's face bent close down, anxiety written large over it.

"You all right, sir? How do you feel now?"

A harsh sound came from the Hawk's throat. He pressed a hand to his temple and tried to collect his senses. Sitting up helped. He glanced around. They were back in the same cell, and they were alone. Shortly, he asked:

"Did I tell him?"

"Where M.S. is?"

"Yes."

"I guess you did." Friday answered mournfully. "I didn't hear you, but Ku Sui said you did. But you couldn't help it!"

Carse forgot his pain as his brain extracted from these words their overwhelming consequence. He murmured:

"I couldn't help it. I really don't think it was possible. But I could have refused to get into the machine. I thought I could resist it. I took that risk, and failed." He stopped. Suddenly his body twitched with uncontrolled emotion, and in decency the Negro turned his back on the man's anguish. A broken whisper reached him: "I have betrayed Leithgow!"

87

For a little neither man moved or said anything. Carse's emotion was something new to Friday. He guessed what must be going on in Carse's mind, and was afraid to intrude. But the Hawk soon showed that he was himself again.

He got up and stretched, to limber his muscles. "How long have we been here?" he asked.

"Don't know, sir; I was unconscious myself when they brought me here."

"Unconscious?" asked the Hawk, surprised. "You fought, and they knocked you out?"

The big Negro looked sheepish and scratched his head.

"Well, no," he explained. "I wanted to butt in, but you said not to."

"Then how did you get unconscious?"

Friday fidgeted, acutely embarrassed. "Don't know, sir. I just can't figure it, unless I fainted."

"Oh." The Hawk smiled. "Fainted. Well, so did I, I guess. I suppose," he went on seriously, "you haven't noticed whether the asteroid has moved."

"I haven't felt any movement, sir."

"The door is locked?"

"Oh, yes. Tight."

"Very well. Now please be silent. I want to think."

He leaned against the wall of the cell. His right hand rose to the bangs of flaxen hair and with a slow regular movement began to smooth them.

He had expected to subject himself to great risk in keeping the rendezvous with Dr. Ku Sui, but it had never occurred to him that his action would endanger Eliot Leithgow also. It was torture to know he had put the gentle old scientist into the Eurasian's web.

He thought: if he could not somehow break out of that web, Leithgow would be better off dead. He himself probably would wish it. For he had no doubt whatever that Ku Sui's reason for wanting the Master Scientist was an ugly one.

Break out of the web. How? Where was the weak strand in Ku Sui's carefully laid plot? The Hawk visualized what he had noted of the asteroid's arrangements. The large port-lock flanked by the little one; secret opening combinations —not much hope in that avenue. Judd's ship, resting above; could he reach it and raise it and douse the buildings with its rays? Dr. Ku had spoken of defense rays; but being land based they would be far more powerful than the *Scorpion's.* Then, somewhere there was the mighty atomic fission plant which provided the power to control the movement of the asteroid in space. Two men, working swiftly, might wreak great damage in little time, and in the resulting confusion, anything might happen. If!

Into the depths of his concentration came the sound of someone at the door; then the indescribable odor of tsin-tsin flowers, followed by the familiar, suave voice of his arch-enemy.

"I see you are deep in thought, my friend. I trust it indicates your complete recovery."

Dr. Ku Sui stood smiling in the doorway, the same body-guard of three armed men behind him. His sardonic words brought no reply. He went on:

"I hope so. Thanks to your kindness, I have been able to arrange a meeting with an old dear friend; he already honors my establishment with his presence. I have come to ask you to join us."

The Hawk's grey eyes turned frigid.

"God help you, Ku Sui," he said.

The Eurasian turned the words aside. "God always helps those who help themselves," he said. "But come with me, if you'll be so kind. We are expected in the laboratory."

This exchange passed quickly. Friday was a very un-happy man as they again were escorted down the corridor outside. Ku Sui's general attitude did not fool him. He knew that the man's suave mockery and flowery courtesy were camouflage for a very real fear of the quick wits and brilliant, pointed action of his famous captain, the Hawk —but what could even the Hawk do, trapped, along with Leithgow, like this?

Carse walked steadily enough, but he was tortured with remorse. For he had betrayed into the hands of the Eurasian his loved and loyal friend. Betrayed him! Despicably egotistical he had been in submitting to the chair, in not making one last wild break for freedom at that time. He had thought he could beat Ku Sui at his own game. Ku Sui, of all men!

Hands on the other side opened the metal laboratory door. They passed through and the close-fitting halves were closed behind them. Ku Sui went to the main switchboard and Carse glanced rapidly around. Leithgow was not there. The wire web was gone, but otherwise the details of the room were unchanged, even to the four white-clad assistants whose eyes were so lifeless and faces so expressionless. Emphasized, now, somehow, was the tall screen that hid something on one side of the room, and an intuition told the Hawk that what lay behind the screen was concerned in some way with what was to come.

He waited quietly.

"Now," Dr. Ku said. "Believe me, this is a pleasure." He smiled at the Hawk and pressed one of the switchboard's array of buttons. A door opposite them swung open.

Escorted by a slant-eyed guard, a frail figure in a rubber apron entered.

Master Scientist Eliot Leithgow blinked as he looked about the laboratory. Helpless, pitifully alone he looked, his face so deeply lined, his small body stooped under the weight of his misfortunes. The blue veins showed under the transparent skin of his forehead; his light blue eyes, set deep under snow-white eyebrows, moved from side to side, dazed by the light and perhaps still confused by the events which had snatched him so suddenly and numbingly from his accustomed way. Such years and frailty might have

90

been suited to some seat of science in a university on Earth —not here amid the raw life of the frontiers of space.

Hawk Carse found words, but could not control his voice.

"This is the first time I've ever been sorry to see you, M.S.," he said, his voice breaking.

XVII

Dr. Ku Shows His Claws

The scientist brushed back his thinning white hair with a trembling hand. He knew that voice. He walked over and put his hands on his friend's shoulders.

"Carse!" he exclaimed. "Thank God, you're alive!"

"And you," said the Hawk simply.

Ku Sui interrupted.

"I am most glad to welcome you here, honored Master Scientist," he said in the flowery fashion that he affected in his irony. "For me it is a memorable occasion. Your presence graces my home, and, however unworthily, distinguishes me, rewarding as it does aspirations which I have held for a long time. I am humbly confident that great achievements will result from your visit—"

Quickly Eliot Leithgow turned and looked squarely at him. There was no bending of spirit in the frail old man. "Yes," he said, "my visit! Your sickening verbal genuflections evade the details—the house of my friend raided at night; he, himself, unarmed, rayed down in cold blood; his house gutted! You are consistent, Dr. Ku. A brilliant achievement, typical of your best!"

Five faint lines appeared across the Eurasian's high, narrow brow. "What?" he exclaimed. "Is this true? My servitors must be reprimanded; but meanwhile I beg you not to hold their impetuousness against me."

Carse could stand it no longer. This suave mockery and the pathetic figure of his friend; the mention of raid and murder—

"It's all my fault," he blurted out. "I told him where you were. I thought—"

"Oh, no!" Dr. Ku broke in, pleasantly protesting. "Captain Carse is gallant, but the responsibility's not his. I have a little device—most ingenious at extracting secrets which persons attempt to hold from me. The Captain couldn't help himself, you see—"

"It was not necessary to tell me that," said Leithgow.

"The end justifies the means," the Eurasian said—seriously, for once. "Master Scientist, I have for some time been working toward a certain end. This end is now in sight, for with you here, the final achievement can be attained. An achievement—" He paused, and something of the look of a fanatic came to his eyes. Never before had the three men standing there seen him so. "I will explain," he ended.

His expression changed; imperiously he gave an order to his assistants. "A chair for Master Leithgow, and one for Carse. Place them there." Then, "Be seated," he said with a return of his usual seeming courtesy. "I'm sure you must be tired."

Slowly Eliot Leithgow lowered himself into the metal seat. Friday, ignored, shifted his weight from one foot to the other. The Hawk did not sit down until from old habit he had sized up the whole layout of laboratory, assistants and chances. The two chairs faced toward the high screen. At each side two coolie-guards took positions, mechanically alert as always. The four white assistants made a group of strange statues to the right.

Ku Sui took a position before the screen. Never did the hard purpose of the man show through the velvet of his manner as it was beginning to do now.

"Yes," he repeated. "I will explain. I will tell you some-

93

thing of my purpose. When I have finished you will know why I have wanted you here so badly, Master Leithgow."

The Eurasian began to speak, and for the first time in the Affair of the Brains, he showed his claws.

"For a long time," he said, "we four gathered here have fought each other. All over the Solar System our conflict has ranged, from Venus to beyond Saturn. I suppose there never have been more bitter enemies; I know there has never been a greater issue. I said we four, but I should have said we *two*, Master Leithgow. Captain Carse has commanded a certain respect from me, the respect one must show for courage, fine physical coordination, and a remarkable capacity for self-preservation—but, after all, he is primarily only like the black here, Friday, and a much less splendid animal. It is a *brain* that receives my respect! A brain! Genius! I do not fear Carse; he is only an adventurer; but your brain, Master Leithgow, I respect.

"For brains will determine the future of the planets of this System. The man with the most profound and extensive scientific knowledge united to the greatest audacity—remember audacity!—can rule them every one!"

He paused and looked into the eyes of the Master Scientist. Pointedly he said:

"You, Master Leithgow, have the brains but not the audacity. I have the audacity *and* the brains—now that *you* are here."

He began—and as never before he hid nothing of his monstrous ambition, his extraordinary preparations. With mounting tension his captives listened to his well-modulated voice as it proceeded from point to point. He had fine feeling for the dramatic and knew well the value of climax and pause, but his use of them here was unconscious, for he spoke straight from his dark and feline heart.

"You shall soon know what I mean," he said. "You will see that right now, in this laboratory, the fate of the planets is being decided!"

94

Hawk Carse licked his dry lips.

"Big words!" he said.

"Easily proved, Captain Carse, as you'll see. What can restrain the man who can instantly command Earth's master-minds of science—the man who not only has a considerable brain of his own, but has the mightiest brains in existence to call on, all coordinated for perfect, instant use? Why, aided by such brains, he can become omnipotent! He can proceed with irresistible steps toward universal power! Only chance, unpredictable chance, always at work, always powerful, can defeat him; but my audacity allows me to disregard what I cannot anticipate."

"This is raving," said Leithgow. "It would be impossible to force the ablest men to aid you."

"Impossible was ever a foolish word, Master. But you said *men,* and I said *brains.* You know that the brain has been my special study. As much as ten years ago, I was universally recognized as the greatest expert in my specialty. But I tell you, my knowledge was as nothing then to what it is now. I have been very busy these last ten years. Look!"

With a graceful sweep of a hand he indicated the four coolie-guards and his four white-smocked assistants.

"These men of mine," he continued, "—do they appear normal, would you say? Or rather, mechanicalized; lacking in certain things, but thereby gaining enormously in the values which can make them perfect servitors? I have removed from their minds certain superficial qualities of thought. The four men in white were, a few years ago, highly skilled surgeons, three of them brain specialists noted for exceptional intellects and bold, pioneering thinking. I needed them and took them, diverting them from their natural state, in which they would have resisted me and refused my commands. Certain complicated adjustments on their brains—and now their brains are mine, all their separate skills at my command alone!"

95

Leithgow sat back suddenly, astonishment and horror on his face. His lips parted as if to speak, then closed tightly together again. At last, he uttered one word.

"Murderer!"

Dr. Ku smiled. He went on:

"The reshaping of these mentalities and of the mentalities of all my coolies were achievements, and valuable ones; but I wanted more. I wanted very much more. I wanted the great, important part of all Earth's scientific knowledge at my fingertips, under my control. I wanted the exceptional brains of Earth, the brains of rare genius, the brains that lived like lonely stars, far removed from the common herd. And more than that, I wanted them *always;* I wanted them *ageless.* For I had to seal my power!"

The Eurasian's words were coming more rapidly now, though the man's thoughts and tone were still under control. Carse, listening closely, felt that a climax was being reached; that something unthinkable, something of dread, soon would be revealed. The voice went on:

"The brains I wanted were not many—only six. You knew the bodies that held them, Master Leithgow—these brains, the cream of Earth's scientific ability. Professor Estapp, the handsome young American; Dr. Swanson, the Swede; Master Scientist Cram—the great English genius Cram, already legendary, the only other of that rank beside yourself! Professor Geinst, the hunchbacked, mysterious German; and Dr. Norman—Dr. Sir Charles Esme Norman, to give him his English title. I wanted these men, and I got them! All except you, the sixth!"

Again Dr. Ku Sui smiled in triumph. To Eliot Leithgow his smile was unspeakable.

"Yes," the elderly scientist cried out, "you got them, you murderer!"

"Oh, no, no, Master Leithgow, you are mistaken. I did not kill them. Why should I be so stupid as to do that? Kill the men I wanted so badly? No, no. Because these five scientists disappeared from Earth suddenly, without trace, without hint of the manner of their going, were they necessarily killed? Stupid Earthmen, to believe they were killed! Abducted, of course; but why assume they were killed? And why, of all people, decide that Master Scientist Eliot Leithgow had something to do with their disappearance? Of course I planted that evidence pointing to you, but if they had the sense of a turnip they would know that you were incapable of squashing a flea, let alone destroying five eminent brothers in science! You, jealous, guilty of five *crimes passionel! Pour la science!* Credulous Earthmen! Incredible Earthmen! And here you are, a hunted man with a price on your head!

"So for six years you have thought I murdered those five men? No, no. They were alive for three years—and very troublesome prisoners, too. It took me three years to solve the problem I had set myself.

"You will meet them in a minute—the better part of them. You'll see for yourself that they are very usefully alive. For I succeeded completely with them. *I have sealed my power!*"

He turned to the screen behind him, his silk clothing rustling in the strained silence which followed his words.

"Observe!" he said, and pushed the screen aside. An assistant threw a switch on a nearby panel.

"The ultimate concentration of scientific knowledge and genius! My gateway to all power!"

XVIII

The Brains Speak

A case lay revealed.

At first it seemed nothing more than a case like those with glass sides and tops found in museums, one perhaps four feet high, four feet wide and two feet deep. Under the glass upper part of the case was an enclosed section a little more than a foot in depth. The whole structure was supported at each corner by short, strong metal legs on rollers. And that was all.

But as the prisoners took in these details, a change came over the interior, no doubt the result of the increasing effect of a flow of electrical current from the throwing of the switch. The inside of the glass case gradually lightened, until it became apparent that it was full of a pinkish liquid that seemed to have the property of glowing with soft light. As this light increased, a row of five shadowy bulks began to take form in what looked like a forest of silk fibers.

In a few more seconds a miracle of complicated wiring came into visibility. The silk fibers were seen to be wires, threads of silver gossamer that interconnected the five emerging bulks in a maze of ordered complexity. Thousands interlaced the interior; other thousands were gathered in five close bunches that emerged from the floor of the case and then spread fanwise, to various groupings of liquid-immersed instruments.

In several seconds more Eliot Leithgow and Hawk Carse were staring at the five inhabitants of the now brightly

98

glowing liquid. Together, they rose and stepped to the cabinet, and gazed with fascination.

"Brains!" exclaimed Leithgow. "Human brains! But not alive—surely not alive!"

"But yes," contradicted the triumphant Eurasian. "Alive."

Five human brains lay immersed in the glowing case, each resting in a shallow metal pan. There were pulsings in narrow gray tubes which led into their under-sides— theatrical evidence that the brains there imprisoned were, as the Eurasian had said, alive—most strangely, unnaturally and horribly alive. Stark and naked they lay there, pulsing with life that should not have been.

"Alive!" exclaimed Ku Sui again. "And never to die while their needs are attended!"

One of his long artistic fingers tapped the glass before the central brain, which was set somewhat lower than the others. "This," he said, "is the Master Brain. It controls and coordinates the thoughts of the others, avoiding the useless, pursuing the relevant and retaining the valuable. It is by far the most important of the five, and is, of course the superior intellect. It is the keystone of my gateway to all power."

Eliot Leithgow's face was ashen, but, such was his fascination, he could not tear his eyes away from the revolting achievement of his brilliant enemy. The Eurasian with the cruelty of a cat picked that moment to add:

"This Master Brain is all that was best of Master Scientist Cram."

The frail old man took this statement like a blow.

"Oh, dear heaven—not Raymond Cram! Not Cram, the physicist, brought to this! Why, I knew him when—"

Ku Sui smiled and interrupted. "But you speak of him as if he were dead! He's not! He's very much alive, as you shall see. Possibly even happy—who knows? There is no good— *Keep back, Carse!*"

His tiger's eyes had not missed the adventurer's slight crouch in preparation for a shove which might have toppled the case and ended the abominable servitude of its gruesome tenants. Carse had been caught just in time. He stepped back and burned his enemy with the frigid glare of his eyes. The Eurasian continued as if nothing had happened, addressing himself chiefly to Leithgow.

"The others, too, you once knew; you are even charged with their murder. Let me introduce you once more to your old colleagues and friends. There, at the right, is the Brain you once compared notes with in the person of Professor Estapp. Next to him is Dr. Swanson. To the left of Master Scientist Cram is Professor Geinst, and this last is Dr. Sir Charles Esme Norman. Now think what this group represents!

"Estapp, Chemistry and Bio-Chemistry; Swanson, Psychology; Geinst, Astronomy; Norman, Mathematics. And Cram, the Master Brain, of course Atomic Physics, although his encyclopedic knowledge encompassed every major subject, well fitting his Brain for the position it holds. All this, gathered here in one! The five outstanding intellects of Earth here gathered in one priceless instrument! Here are my advisors; here my trusty, never-tiring assistants. I can have their help toward the solution of any problem; obtain from their individual and combined intelligences even those rare intuitions which I have found almost always precede brilliant discoveries.

"For they not only retain all they ever knew of science, but they can *develop,* even as brains in bodies can develop. Their knowledge does not become outmoded, for they are kept informed of the latest currents of scientific thought. From old knowledge and new they build their structures of logic, once my command sets them on. Wills of their own they have none.

"I have not succeeded in all my secondary alterations, however. For one thing, I have been unable to deprive them

100

altogether of the memory of what they formerly were; but it is a subdued memory, to them something like a dream, familiar yet puzzling. Because of this, it is possible they hate me—yet they lack the ego and will which would enable them to refuse to answer my questions and do my work.

"Frankly, without them this whole structure"—his hands swept out widely—"my whole asteroidal kingdom would have been impossible. Most of my problems in constructing it were solved here. And in the future other problems, far greater, will be solved here!"

Hawk Carse by now understood very well Dr. Ku Sui's purpose in bringing M. S. Leithgow to his laboratory, and was already searching for a way to thwart it. Death for Leithgow was by all means preferable to the life that the Eurasian intended—death self-inflicted or by Carse, and death that mutilated the brain.

If Leithgow suspected what was in store, his face gave no sign of it. He said:

"Dr. Ku, of all the things you have ever done, this is the most heartless, the most vile. I should have thought there was a limit in you somewhere, but this—this thing—this horrible existence you have condemned five men to—"

He could not continue. The Eurasian only smiled, and replied, with his perpetual seeming-courtesy:

"Your reaction is natural, Master Scientist; I expected no other. But when great ends are to be gained, he who would gain them must strip himself of those atavistic things we call the tender emotions. The pathway to power is not for those who wince at the need for death. I hope, for special reasons, that you'll make an effort to understand this before we come to the phase which will follow my demonstration. . . .

"Now, allow me to show you my Coordinated Brains in useful operation. Will you be seated again? You, too, Captain Carse."

They slowly obeyed.

"Thank you," the Eurasian said, and went to the panel flanking the case. There, he turned and remarked: "Before we begin, I must ask you to remember that the opinions of my Brains always may be accepted as the probable truth, and that always, absolutely, they are honest and without prejudice." He threw a small knife switch and again turned. Nothing seemed to happen.

"I have of course contrived an artificial way of communicating with my helpers. This inset grille here contains both microphone and speaker—ear and mouth.

"The receiver picks up my words and transmits them to every Brain. If I have asked a question, it is individually considered and the respective answers sent to the Master Brain; they are there coordinated and the result spoken to me by means of the speaker. When the opinions of the individual Brains do not agree, the answer is in the form of a poll, often with brief mention of points pro and con. Sometimes their meditations take considerable time; but simple questions always bring a prompt and unanimous answer. Shall we try them now?"

The man's spectators did not answer. Dr. Ku paused dramatically, a slight smile on his lips; then he turned his head and spoke into the grille.

"Do you hear me?" he asked.

For a moment the silence in the laboratory was total. Then, from the grille, came a thin, metallic inhuman voice.

"I do," were its words.

"Strange," mused the Eurasian, half aloud, "that their collective answer is always given as 'I.' What obscure telescoping of egotisms can be the cause of that?"

He dropped that mood at once. "Tell me," he said, looking deliberately at Leithgow: "Would the brain of Master Scientist Eliot Leithgow be more valuable in the position of the Master Brain than Cram's?"

102

An eternity seemed to pass. Again came the inhuman voice:

"I have answered that question before. Yes."

Dr. Ku quickly broke the stunned silence that followed.

"Don't forget that several ray-guns are centered on you, Carse," he remarked casually. "Others, black, are on you. Earthmen would no doubt consider your emotions very creditable; I only suggest that you keep them under control."

But the Hawk had given no intimation that he might attempt anything. He sat quietly, his face a mask, only the freezing shock of his steady gray eyes betraying his emotion as they bore straight at those of the Eurasian. No man could meet such eyes for long, and Ku Sui looked away.

Friday still stood trembling in back of the chairs in which his two comrades were seated, his eyes large rolling white marbles. He was scared to death. Eliot Leithgow was a man crushed. His head was sunk down on his chest, and Dr. Ku's next words, though aimed at him, did not seem to penetrate his consciousness.

"You see, Master Leithgow, you are honored. My purposes require this substitution. Were your intellect of lesser stature, I would have no interest in you whatever."

Hawk Carse stood up.

The Eurasian stopped speaking. The ensuing silence lent a razor sharpness to the whisper that reached him from thin lips that barely moved:

"God help you, Ku Sui, if you do it."

Dr. Ku Sui smiled deprecatingly and shrugged.

"I have told you before that God helps those who help themselves. I have always had splendid results from helping myself."

For a moment he looked away as if considering something in his mind. Then his hooded eyes turned back, and he said:

"I think perhaps you'd like to observe the operations, my

103

friend, and I'm going to allow you to. Not here; I could never have you interrupting; the operations will be of infinite delicacy and require weeks. But I can make other arrangements; I can give you as good as ringside seats for each performance. A small miniscreen might be attached to one wall of your cell to enable you to see every detail of what transpires here." His tone suddenly stiffened. *"I wouldn't, Carse!"*

The Hawk relaxed from the brink on which he had wavered. A sudden mad rush at the case—what else remained? What else? For an instant he almost had lost his head—one of the few times in his life. Just for an instant he had lost his phenomenal patience under torture, had forgotten his own axiom that in every tight place there was a way out.

"That was reckless," said Ku Sui. "Perhaps you and the black one had better return to your cell."

The Hawk's left eyelid was twitching as he turned to go, and his balance was uncertain. Friday followed just behind. The ray-guns of the coolie-guards covered their every move.

As the adventurer came to the door he stopped and turned, and his eyes sought those of the frail, elderly scientist.

The doomed man met the gray eyes with a smile.

"It's all right, old comrade," he said. "Just remember to destroy this hellish device, if ever you possibly can. My love to Sandra; and to her, and to all my dear ones on Earth, anything but the truth. . . . Farewell."

Carse clenched his fists. He tried, but could not speak. The Eurasian said:

"All right, Carse, you may go."

The robot-guards nudged white man and black out, and the door swung solidly closed behind them. . . .

XIX

In the Miniscreen

Friday declared subsequently that a month went out of Hawk Carse's life for every minute he spent afterwards in the cell. For the insight into the real Carse afforded by that scrap of information, we must thank Sewell, the great historian of that generation, who personally traveled many millions of miles to get what meager facts the Hawk would divulge concerning his life and career, equally with Friday, who shared this particular adventure with him. Friday's emotional eyes no doubt colored his memory of the scenes he passed through, and it is likely that the facts lost nothing in the direct, dramatic way he would relate them. But certainly the Negro was as fearful of his Captain during that following period in the cell as he was of what he saw acted out on the screen.

We can picture him telling of the ordeal, his dark eyes wide and his deep voice trembling with the memories stamped in his brain; and picture too the men who, at one time or another, listened to him, fascinated, with a tickling down the length of their spines. It was unquestionably only Friday's talent as a narrator which later caused some of his listeners to swear that new lines were etched in Carse's face by the minutes he spent watching Eliot Leithgow strapped down on that operating table, close to the wonderful surgeon fingers of Dr. Ku Sui.

105

To what extent that period of torture pierced through the Hawk's iron emotional guard and set its permanent mark on him, it is impossible to say. There were deep things in Hawk Carse, however, and the deepest things among them were the ties binding him to his friends; and there was also his undoubted cold self-esteem; and considering these it is probable that he came close to the brink of a genuine emotional abyss, before which he had few shreds of mind- and body-discipline left. . . .

He reentered the cell like a ghost. He stood very still, his hands slowly clenching and unclenching behind his back; his pale face inclined low, so that the chin rested almost on his chest. So he stood for some minutes, Friday not daring to disturb him, until the lock of the single door that gave entrance clicked and the door opened again. At this he raised his head. Five men came in, all robot-coolies, three of whom had weapons which they scrupulously kept directed at the prisoners while the other two rigged up an apparatus near the top of one of the walls of the cell.

The device they attached was a two-foot video screen and associated components, connected to a length of black, rubberlike cable, which was passed through one of the ventilating slits high in the wall. Carse watched them remotely until they were finished and the two were once more alone. Then his head returned to its bowed position and Friday approached the apparatus and began to examine it with the curiosity of the born technician he was.

"Let it be, Friday," the Hawk ordered tonelessly.

A dozen minutes passed in silence.

The silence was outward: there was no quiet in the adventurer's head. He could not stop the sharp remorseless voice which kept sounding in his brain. In pitiless words it flailed him unceasingly. "You, whom they call the Hawk," it would say; "you, the infallible one—you, always so egotistically confident—*you* have brought this to pass! Not only have you allowed yourself and Friday to be trapped,

106

but you've been a traitor to Eliot Leithgow! He is out there now; and soon his naked, living brain will be condemned forever to a pitiful existence in a glass case! The brain that trusted you! And *you* have brought this to pass! *Yours* the blame, the never-failing Hawk! All *yours—yours—yours!*"

A voice reached him from far away. A deep voice which said, timidly:

"They're beginning, sir. Captain Carse, they're beginning. On the screen."

This was more torture. The real ordeal was approaching.

Friday spoke again, and this time his words seemed to roar into Carse's ears. He raised his head and looked.

The tubes behind the screen were lit and the screen itself had come to life. He was looking at the laboratory. But the place was changed.

What before had been a large circular room, with machines and unnamed scientific apparatus following its walls, was now a place of deep shadow pierced by a broad cone of white light which shafted down from a source overhead and threw into brilliant emphasis the center of the room.

The light enclosed an operating table. At the head of the table stood a squat metal cylinder out of which extended a flexible tube which ended in a cone—no doubt the anesthetizing apparatus. A stepped-back tier of white surfaces stood off to one side, upon its several levels an array of gleaming surgeon's instruments. In neat ranks they lay there; long thin knives with straight or curved cutting edges; handled wires, bent into hooks and eccentric shapes; scalpels of different sizes; forceps, clasps, retractors, odd metal claws, circular saw-blades and a variety of other instruments. Sterilizers lay convenient nearby, thin wraiths of steam drifting from them up into the source of the light.

Four men worked within the brilliant shaft of illumination—four white-clad figures, hands gloved and faces hidden behind surgeons' masks. Only their eyes were exposed, concentrated on their tasks of preparation. Steam rose in

107

increased mists as one figure lifted back the lid of a sterilizer and dropped in some gleaming instruments.

All this in complete silence. From the darkness outside the cone appeared another figure, tall and commanding, a shape in a smock of delicate green which contrasted vividly with the general whiteness of the scene. He was pulling on operating gloves. Unseen through the eyeholes of the mask he wore, his slanted eyes surveyed the preparations. Fateful, the tall figure looked, among the white-clad assistants.

He seemed to give an order; one white figure looked off into the surrounding darkness and raised one hand. A door showed in faint outline as it opened. Through the door two vertical shadows moved, wheeling something long and flat between them.

Two attendants came into the light, wheeled their conveyance alongside the operating table, then turned again into the darkness and were gone.

"Oh!" gasped Friday. "They've shaved his head!"

They lifted the frail form of Eliot Leithgow to the operating table. He was clad to the neck in loose white garments, and, as Friday said, his hair was shaved off close—stunning verification of what was now to happen. Pitifully alone and helpless he looked, yet his face was composed and he lay quiet, watching the soulless vandals at their preparations. His expression altered, however, when Dr. Ku appeared over him and prodded his naked head.

"I can't stand this!"

It was a whisper of agony in the silence of the cell where the two men stood watching, a cry from the Hawk's very core. Leithgow had trusted him! Trusted him! And now this!

Ku Sui's fingers were prodding Leithgow's head like that of any dumb animal, a subject for experimentation. Prodding that head. . . .

"I can't stand it!" the Hawk whispered again.

The mask on his face, that famous all-concealing mask,

108

had broken. Lines of agony creased it, sweat beaded it. Carse saw Ku Sui pick up something and adjust it to his grip while looking down at the man who lay, now strapped, on the table. He saw him nod to an assistant; saw the anesthetic cylinder wheeled up a little closer, and the dials on it set to moving. . . .

His hands came up and covered his eyes. But only for a moment. He had to look. *Had* to. *That* was the exquisite torture the Eurasian had counted on. But he could not look long. Again he covered his eyes. When next he took away his hands and looked up, the screen was blank!

Friday was kneeling before the knob on the door of the cell. Carse saw that the knob was of metal, centered in an inset rectangle of some dull plastic composition.

"This door has an electric lock," the Negro explained rapidly. "And things worked by electricity can often be short-circuited!"

Quickly and silently he had disconnected from the television projector the wire which led back through the ventilating slit in the wall, and now, with the end of one conductor, he was twisting out the screw which retained the knob. "Anyway, won't hurt to try," he said, picking out the screw and laying it on the floor. In another second he had laid the knob beside it, and was squinting into the hole where it had fitted.

"Be quick!" Carse whispered.

Friday did not answer. He was guessing at the structure of the mechanism within, and trying to summon up the knowledge he had of such things. After a moment he bent the end of the same conductor into a mild curve and felt his way down into the lock with it, carefully keeping the other end clear of all contacts.

Seconds went by as his fingers delicately worked—seconds that were torture to Hawk Carse. For the screen was blank, and there was no way of knowing how far the work in the laboratory had progressed. In his mind remained

109

each detail of the scene as he had viewed it last: the strapped-down figure, the approaching anesthetic cylinder, the knives lying in readiness. How was he to know if one of those instruments was not already tinged with scarlet?

"Oh, be quick!" he cried again.

"If I can short the circuit through the lock," grunted Friday, absorbed, bringing up the end of the other conductor, "there ought—to—be—trouble."

Suddenly, with a sputtering hiss, a shower of sparks shot out of the knob-hole. The current path had been completed. It remained to be seen whether the mechanism of the lock had been destroyed—or welded solid. Friday dropped the hot, melted wire he was holding and reached for the knob, but the other was ahead of him.

Carse stuck the shaft of the knob in the hole and turned its holding screw part way in. Gently, then, he tried the knob. It turned!

But precisely at that moment he was stopped by the voice of Ku Sui. From some source within the room it came—a strong note of irritation in its tone:

"Hawk Carse, you are beginning to annoy me—you and your so-clever black satellite."

Carse's eyes searched the ceiling. They found there in one place a small disklike object, almost unnoticeable.

"Yes," continued Ku Sui, "I can talk to you, hear you, and see you. I see you have succeeded in destroying the lock. So open the door and glance into the corridor—and escape, if you still want to. I rather wish you'd try, for I'm critically occupied and must not be disturbed again."

Carse turned the knob, opened the door a little, and looked through, Friday looking also, over his head. They looked right into the muzzles of eight ray-guns, held by four coolie-guards waiting there. Quickly, Carse closed the door.

"So that's it," Friday said, dejectedly. "He saw me work-

110

ing on the lock and sent those guards. Or else had them there all the time."

The Hawk considered what to do. Ku Sui's voice returned.

"Yes," it sounded metallically, "I've an assistant here who is watching every move you make. Don't, therefore, hope to surprise me by anything you do.

"Now I am going to resume work. Reconnect the screen; I've had the burned-out fuse replaced. If you won't, I'll have it done for you—and have you so bound that you'll be forced to look at it.

"Don't tamper with any of my audio and video apparatus again. If you do, that will be the end of my patience.

"But—if you'd like to leave your cell, you have my full permission."

The voice said no more. Carse ordered Friday harshly:

"Reconnect the screen."

The Negro hastened to obey. Carse looked anxiously upward, fiercely smoothing his bangs.

The laboratory flashed into clear view again. There was the shaft of white light, the operating table, the anesthesia apparatus, the banks of instruments, the sterilizers with their wisps of steam. There were the mute, efficient, white-clad assistant surgeons, their dull eyes hidden behind the eyeholes in their masks. And there was the green-tinted figure of Ku Sui, a trace of irritation in his face, and before him his victim, resigned and helpless old Eliot Leithgow.

The Eurasian gestured. An assistant found the pulse in Leithgow's wrist, and another bent over him in such fashion that the prisoners could not see what he was doing. Ku Sui too bent over, something in his hands. The prelude to Leithgow's most unnatural living death had begun. . . .

From that moment Hawk Carse became a different man, recovered from his weakness of a short time before. The old, cold characteristic Carse returned. He would act!—

even though he must die. "I've been cautious too long!" he exclaimed under his breath. "Friday!" he whispered.

"Yes, sir?"

"Four men outside—a sudden charge through that door when I nod. Willing?"

Without hesitation Friday whispered back:

"Yes!"

Their whispers had been low. Dr. Ku Sui seemed not to have been warned, for the screen showed him still bending over at his work.

"You open the door for me—I'll go through first," the Hawk whispered. Friday grasped the handle of the door. Carse nodded.

Friday pulled open the door and white man, then black, went charging out.

Immediately there sounded the imperious clanging of an alarm bell.

XX

Trapped in the Laboratory

In the chain of his plans, so carefully welded, Ku Sui had left one weak link. Probably he was not aware of it at the time, for it could only appear in the test, and he had not expected it to be tested. Carse of course acted recklessly; perhaps, in the light of cold reason, senselessly. How could Dr. Ku have thought he would dare make that break? But the adventurer did dare, and the weak link cracked.

The Eurasian had a paranoic's vanity, and with it an ever festering lust to exact the most terrible vengeance he could from the adventurer who had frustrated his schemes so often. His arrangement for subtly forcing Carse to watch the operation was part of his plan of vengeance, but only part. He wanted his old foe, broken by guilt at having been the cause of the living death of his old friend, to die slowly under that guilt—crushed, overwhelmed. He wanted to crumple utterly the flinty will of that other egotist, the mere "adventurer" who had opposed him so often and so successfully. And—no doubt—he wanted to control this process of mental and physical murder, and be there to mock at the agonies of his hated enemy. Ku Sui was capable of this. It would have been characteristic. What a weapon against Carse he would have, in Leithgow's brain *installed!* But there lay the weak link. Carse had to be kept alive.

If Ku Sui had instructed his robot-guards to kill, Carse

and Friday could not possibly have broken out of the corridor alive. Eight waiting ray-guns were too many; their lives would have been burned out in a few seconds. The few shots fired at them by the guards were directed only at their legs—and their legs were moving very rapidly. Ku Sui's orders, their speed, their mad, fighting start, made the result of that first hectic scramble in the corridor inevitable.

It was with an ear-shattering war-whoop that drowned out the alarm bell that Friday, a living thunderbolt of fighting Negro, flung his two hundred and twenty pounds of brawn after Carse, taking no more notice of the ray-guns than if they had been water-pistols. The guards, standing together, were scattered like ten-pins. Three were knocked flat, one of them dropping both guns.

At once Carse darted at the fourth coolie and closed his wiry hands around his throat; but hardly had he done so when Friday bashed the man to the floor with one vertical bounce of his fist. Again the Negro's war-whoop drowned out the alarm bell.

Carse picked up the two guns and stuck one out for Friday. The black took it, and in his excitement he gave the Hawk an order!

"Get to the Master!" Friday roared, an ebon god of war at that moment. "I'll be following!"

But that was precisely what Carse intended to do; he ran down the corridor toward the laboratory. Behind, pawing over four guards in various stages of unconsciousness, remained Friday, wrenching from them their weapons. When he could see no more he started after the Hawk.

He had run only a few steps when an orange spear of light streaked past his legs. Turning his head, still running, he saw two of the men sitting on the floor aiming guns in his direction. Guns he had missed! Even as he took this in, another spear streaked by. Friday fired three times and they fell—or lay—back.

Their triumph so far had been a matter of but a few sec-

114

onds. The alarm bell was still jangling, awaking the defenses of the asteroid to action. Here and there, in the doors spacing the corridor, appeared the heads of other coolies. These had not heard Ku Sui's order. If they had guns they would shoot to kill!

Three suddenly appeared in Carse's line of vision ahead; three ray-guns settled on him. His left hand flashed, his trigger finger squeezed three times, and the three coolies fell, almost as one. Just ahead was his goal, the door leading into the central laboratory. A streak speared past his legs. Flattening himself against a wall, Carse glanced back. All he could see was Friday.

"Coming!" Friday yelled.

He was bringing up the rear as fast as he could. He came sideways in a zigzag course, ducking and whirling and firing at any portions of enemy bodies that dared project into the line of the corridor. The Hawk covered the last few yards of his retreat, and then they were together at the door of the laboratory.

"The knob!" Carse ordered, spraying the corridor in general warning.

Friday tried it, but the door was locked. He thrust himself against it, but the door was of heavy metal and did not budge.

How to get through? On the other side of the door was Leithgow, and probably Ku Sui; on this side they were trapped in a blind end. They could never run back down that gauntlet and live, and anything like concerted action on the part of the yellows would do for them where they were.

An unexpected action came at once. Seventy feet back, a movable ray-projector was pushed out on its little rollers from one of the rooms. An arm reached out and turned it so that its muzzle bore straight down the corridor at them. Carse shot at the hand, but the target was too small and he missed. Instantly, hand and arm disappeared.

It looked hopeless! But Carse watched that doorway like the Hawk he was, waiting, gun dead on the spot where the hand must reappear to fire the projector. He had to get that hand—and any others that took its place. An almost impossible shot. He never could rush the projector. Not in time.

A few seconds passed. Again the hand flashed out; again Carse shot and missed; and at once there was a narrow orange cone along the corridor, a blinding light, and a deafening crackling rasp. Instantly the air was stifling.

Both Friday and the Hawk were untouched. The shot had been taken by the door—and the door now lay ajar!

At once Carse was moving. "Inside!" he yelled, then was through, the other right behind. His eyes swept the laboratory. It was a place of shadows, the sole light being a gleam from a tiny bulb-tipped surgical tool which glimmered weirdly from the bank of instruments waiting by the operating table. Carse saw no one.

"Hold the door!" he cried.

Friday jumped to obey. He found the inner bolt melted and the lock inoperative; but when he placed his forearms on the two halves, to close and brace them, he jerked back in pain. The door was hot! Instantly he began pushing both halves into place with his hips—and that was hot, too, even through his clothing.

At once a furious pounding shook the door. Stifled and in pain, Friday pushed against it.

"Something to wedge it!" he panted. "Quick!"

"Coming!" the Hawk cried. "Hold it!"

He was already dragging a small metal table to the door. Quickly, with Friday's help, he up-ended it under the knob, so that it made an angle with the floor. So placed, it held stoutly against the blows given the door from the other side. Momentarily relieved, the panting Negro sat down on the floor to rest; but then he rose almost at once to help with the placing of additional blocks.

116

That finished, the Hawk at once, pantherlike, ray-gun ready, stalked the room. There was no sign of the enemy. He approached the operating table.

With great relief he found Eliot Leithgow lying there, conscious and apparently untouched. The elderly scientist was strapped down tight, but he was smiling.

"I knew you'd come, Carse, if you could," he said simply.

There was no time for visiting. "Where's Ku Sui?" the adventurer asked.

"Gone," Leithgow answered. "I heard a door open and close—which one, I couldn't see. He went as soon as that bell began to ring. The assistants, too."

Over the shouts and batterings at the barricaded door came a new sound—from another direction. Like a streak the Hawk was at one of the three other doors, throwing its inside hand bolt; then as he shot over and secured the second, Friday ran and locked the remaining one.

The Negro let out a vast breath. "Umph!" he said. "I'll tell the stars that was close!"

Hawk Carse said nothing. Pausing several times, watchful for sign of a trick or a trap in the apparently deserted laboratory, he unbuckled the bands that held Leithgow to the operating table. Friday lifted him to the floor, where he stood and stretched weakly.

This was no soft moment for the adventurer. Crisply he said:

"I think we're trapped. There'll be men outside each of these four doors. The bolts may hold them for a little, but they'll get through. We must look for further weapons. If only there were better light! Friday," he ordered, "look for a switch. Ah!"

With a thud and a booming reverberation a systematic battering had begun on the metal door through which they had entered. It quivered visibly and rang from the powerful blows from the other side—blows evenly spaced, delivered in the middle. *Whrang.* . . . *Whrang.* . . . *Whrang.* . . .

117

Then a similar bombardment began on another door; then a third; and then the last. The doors jumped with each blow. Friday scowled, forgot he was looking for the switch, took a few short, indecisive steps, and then stood still again, looking questioningly at his Captain. The Hawk stood silent also, thinking, smoothing his flaxen bangs.

He had first assumed that they would use the projector on the door, and had been somewhat cheered by the reflection that they wouldn't dare, for fear of destroying the contents of the laboratory, especially the irreplacable Brains. But this was just as bad. Ku Sui was directing their efforts now. And that being the case, he could expect to see one door after another battered down—and then a concerted, four-point rush which would end everything. Carse didn't know what to do.

Eliot Leithgow said the extraordinary thing that pointed a way out. "May I suggest," he said mildly, "that we try to get Dr. Ku Sui's Brains to help us?"

"What do you mean?"

The old man smiled, somewhat sadly. "Those Brains— they once were in people who were friends of mine. It is possible they'll answer our questions. It won't hurt to try. We'll ask them how it might be possible to get out."

Hawk Carse cried: "Of course, Eliot! It's a chance!"

He went to the case and shoved back the screen.

"We know where this switch is," he said. "If only the current's not been turned off!"

"Probably not," the Master Scientist said, out of his own technical thought-train.

The Hawk was at the switch, but for a moment his hand hesitated. This thing he was about to do . . . this fearful human mechanism before him . . . weird . . . unnatural. . . .

He heard a faint click inside the laboratory, in a place where no one should be. Instinctively, he whirled and crouched—and an orange ray lanced over his head with a

118

vicious spit. Almost in the same motion his own ray-gun answered to the spot whence the shot had come—and then he was flat on the floor, eeling toward the wall opposite.

A high wide panel in the wall had slid aside, making the faint noise Carse had heard. For a few seconds it stayed open. The Hawk covered the last few feet in a rush, but he reached it too late. It clicked shut in his face, and there was no hold for his hands when he tried to force it back.

A voice showed that someone was on the other side. In familiar tones it said:

"Carse, I still will take you and Leithgow alive. It would be idle to ask you to surrender, but it's not necessary, for you're trapped and will be taken in five minutes. I intrude only to warn you away from my Coordinated Brains. I will destroy without compunction anyone who meddles with them."

Dr. Ku's voice dropped away; the last words seemed to have come from below. He might have been descending by a stairway or hidden elevator.

"Without compunction!" Leithgow echoed with a bitter smile.

Carse curtly ordered Friday to watch the panel, then he returned to Leithgow.

"Eliot," he said, "we've got to be quick."

With his words the delicate, overused filament in the tiny instrument bulb gave out, and the laboratory was plunged into total blackness.

XXI

Out Under the Dome

Within the blackness rang the metallic reverberations from the battering on the four doors all around. The nerve-shattering clangor made the laboratory a place of fear.

The Hawk at once exercised control. His curt voice cut through imperatively:

"Keep your heads. We'll have a light in a second. Light of a sort."

He threw the switch by the side of the chamber of the Brains.

Seconds passed, and where was darkness came a faint glow. The switch had operated; current, probably from the device's own batteries, was there! Quickly but steadily the liquid within the case took on its self-originating glow, until the midnight laboratory was faintly washed with the delicate rosy light. The wires emerged in their complexity as before, and then the Brains, naked and gruesome in their cradles.

Around the glowing case, half shrinking from it, were grouped the three besieged Earthlings, half in blackness, the light from the front making devilish patches on their faces. Acolytes at some sorcerer's rite they looked, with the long vague shadows that left them to dissolve formlessly among the apparatus in front of the far walls of the room.

Grotesque in the operating garments he wore, his shaven

head shining in the eerie light, Eliot Leithgow approached the microphone Dr. Ku had used to communicate with his pathetic subjects. He looked down at the Brains, at the wires which threaded the pans they lay in, at the narrow gray tubes that pulsed with blood—or whatever might be the fluid used in its stead. All electrical and mechanical was the apparatus—all of metal and other cunningly-fashioned man-made material—all but the Brains. . . .

To the old Master Scientist the clangor of the room dissolved away in a vision of five human figures, rising specter-like from the case in which they were entombed: straight, proud young figures, two of them; two others, old like himself, and the fifth a gnarled hunchback. Very different were they one from the other, but each face had its mark of genius; and each face to Eliot Leithgow was warm and smiling, for these five men were friends. . . .

So he saw them in vision, for just a few seconds. Then, rousing himself, he said:

"Another switch has to be thrown to talk with them, Carse." The Hawk indicated one inquiringly. Leithgow nodded. The switch was thrown.

The old man steadied himself and said into the speaking grille:

"I am Eliot Leithgow—Master Scientist Eliot Leithgow. Once you knew me. Professors Geinst, Estapp and Norman, Dr. Swanson and Master Scientist Cram—do you remember me? Do you remember how once we worked together; how, long ago on Earth, we were friends? Do you remember your old colleague, Leithgow?"

He stopped, deeply shaken. Again his mind had sped back through the years to the bodies of those five men as he had last seen them—and to two women he had met, wives, calm-faced as their husband-scientists. . . . God forbid those women should ever learn of this!

Carse watched his old comrade closely, fearful of the strain on him.

Then came a cold, thin, mechanical voice.

"Yes, Master Scientist Eliot Leithgow, I remember you well."

It was "I" who remembered. That surprising *I*! Unable, quite to control his voice, the scientist continued:

"Two friends and I are trapped here. Dr. Ku Sui wants my brain. He wants to add it to—to—" He stammered, halted; then burst out: "If it would help you in any way, I'd give it gladly! But it couldn't I know! It would only aid his power-mad schemes. So my friends and I must escape. And we can see no way!

"Can you hear that banging? It's very loud; men are outside each door, battering at them, and at any moment they will break through. How can we escape? Do you know of a way, out of your knowledge of conditions here? Will you tell me, old colleagues?"

He waited.

Fifty feet away from this scene, and missing most of it, was Friday. From his post at the panel he kept throwing fearful looks at the nearest door, which was shuddering and clanging and threatening at each blow to give way.

Carse waited tensely for the response—if there was to be one. His ears were throbbing in unison with the irregular crash of the four rams, but his brain hardly noted the noise at this moment, for his eyes were on the convoluted mounds of intelligent matter so fantastically featured by the internal radiance of the life-surrounding liquid. Impossible, it seemed, that thought could be taking place inside those gruesome things. . . .

There sounded a particularly loud crash.

"Please hurry!" Carse said in a low voice; and Leithgow repeated desperately:

"How can we escape? Please be quick!"

Then the miracle of dead and living matter functioned again. The cold voice said:

"It is my disposition to help you, Eliot Leithgow. On a

122

shelf under one of the tables in this room you will find a portable heat-ray. Melt a hole in the ceiling and go out through the roof."

"Then what can we do?"

"*In lockers behind the table there are spacesuits, hanging ready for emergencies. Don them and leave through one of the asteroid's port-locks.*"

"Ask if the ports are sealed," Carse interjected instantly. Leithgow asked the question.

"Yes," replied the unhuman voice. "*But twice four to the right will open any of them.*"

The Master Scientist wiped his brow. Trembling, still not in control of his voice, he said:

"But the asteroid's gravital pull would hold us close to it. Is there a way of breaking free?"

"*The spacesuits are self-propulsive, and have generators and gravity-plates which I helped Ku Sui develop. The switch and main controls are on the breast.*"

"Thank you! Oh, thank you! You give us a chance!" exclaimed old Leithgow.

He turned, and saw the Hawk already laying the heavy cone of a portable heat-ray on a nearby table, ready to hand. A moment later he was pulling three spacesuits from the locker. The increasing heat and a new smell of burned metal sent their eyes on a quick quest about the room—and they saw, in the door they had just entered, a glow which told them that the large projector in the corridor was at last being used to burn a way in.

With surprising strength in one so slender, Carse lifted the heavy heat-ray and pointed it upward at an angle. He pulled its lever. A blinding stream of orange radiance splashed against the ceiling above. It hissed and sputtered where it touched; molten drops splattered to the floor; then suddenly the flood of orange light disappeared. The Hawk lay down the heat-ray, stepped carefully forward among the smoking splatters on the floors, and looked up.

123

He looked up through an irregularly-melted round hole
—up at the great glass-like dome which arched over the
whole settlement—up, past it, into the vast face of Jupiter,
hanging oppressively near!

Friday, energized now, already had left his post and was
dragging a long low cabinet to position under the hole. He
heaved up the operating table to a place on top, locked its
small wheels, and added still another table to the pile.

"You first, Friday!" his Captain ordered as he finished.
"I'll pass the suits to you. Then pull Leithgow up."

The Negro swiftly climbed the rude pile and reached for
the edge of the hole. It was very hot. He cried out; but he
did not let go, and levering himself up, he got a leg through
and then his body. A second later he looked back in and
lowered his hands.

"No one up here yet!" he reported. "The suits!"

Carse passed the three bulky suits to him, also one of
two extra ray-guns he had found in the locker.

"Now, Eliot—up!"

With the Hawk's help, Leithgow clambered onto the cabinet. He was just mounting the operating table when, from
behind, came a thin, metallic voice:

*"Master Leithgow—Eliot Leithgow—will you do me a
favor?"*

For just an instant, Leithgow was startled, then he understood. It was the Coordinated Brains. They had forgotten to return the switches. This time the cold voice was
speaking of its own accord; and somehow—though it might
have been imagination entirely—there seemed to be a tinge
of wistfulness to the words from the speaker.

Instantly Leithgow got down and hurried over to the
case. Seconds were precious, but Carse and he were heavily
obligated to the Brains.

"I shall do anything I can," he said. "What is it you
want?"

The lower hinge of one side of the barricaded door gave,

124

burned out, and the door wrenched inward at a resumption of the battering. The other hinge still held, but it was bending with each blow. Outwardly calm, Hawk Carse listened to this strange conversation, but he watched closely the weakening door, a gun in each hand.

"This," said the toneless voice: *"Destroy me. Utterly. Leave no trace. I live in hell, and have no way to move. . . . There are old memories. . . . things that once were dear. . . . Earth . . . my homes . . . my lives there. . . . Eliot Leithgow, destroy me. But promise on your honor as a Master Scientist never to let a single word regarding my fate reach those on Earth who knew me, loved me. . . ."*

Leithgow looked at the Hawk. The adventurer himself answered.

"Yes!" he promised. "I'll do it. I'll use the heat-ray."

He ran to it, but he had hardly picked it up when the second hinge of the yielding door wrenched free with a screech—and the door fell, half twisting into the room.

As if by a signal the crashing at the other doors stopped. In an extraordinary silence a number of gray-smocked bodies pressed forward from the lighted corridor into the gloom.

Orange streaks laced the laboratory. The Hawk shouted, "Up, Eliot! Up! Up!" as with deadly effect, he poured his two ray-guns at the advancing men.

For a second, shaken by the terrific barrage, they fell back over the smoking door, leaving several sprawled bodies on or near it; but they came right back again.

Leithgow got safely to the top of the pile and was snatched out to temporary safety. Frantically Friday called down to his Captain; he seemed on the point of jumping down to fetch him. But Hawk Carse had made a promise.

He was behind the pile of furniture under the hole. One of his guns was spitting at the guards, while the other was stabbing at the case of Brains. Two intermittent orange

125

lances angled from him, one holding back the coolies, only three-score feet away, and the other—absolutely useless. All over the still-glowing case it spat its hits, but the glass-like substance resisted it, and remained unscathed.

Carse swore. He hurled one empty gun at the case, and sent a parting shot at the coolies, and then was up on the pile and leaping for Friday's hands.

They caught and gripped his hands, swung him once—twice—then hauled him out. But as the Hawk disappeared he shouted down toward the case:

"I'll be back!"

XXII

Answer to a Mystery

On the roof, Carse considered their situation. They were standing on the hub of the four-winged building. Far to the left were the dome's port-locks, large and small; not far from them lay the *Scorpion*. The entire area enclosed by the dome was a flat plain of brown soil.

Looming over the great transparent dome hung the great globe that was Jupiter, so near that it seemed it might crash into the asteroid. Its rays poured in a ruddy wash over the entire settlement, illuminating each detail. Comparatively close against the face of the mighty planet lay the whitish globe of Satellite III. It offered the nearest haven. They might arrive famished, but in the power-equipped space-suits which Friday was lugging they might be able to span the gap.

The Hawk pointed to the port-locks.

"There," he snapped. "We'll have two chances, the *Scorpion* and the port, but the port's safest; we could never get the whole ship under way and through the lock in time. To prevent pursuit, all we have to do is leave the lock open after us."

They hastened along the roof of the wing that ran that way, Friday bringing up the rear with the space-suits. As yet, there was no sign of activity outside; but it could be only a matter of seconds before men would begin to emerge from the hole in the ceiling. Just as the three arrived at the

127

end of the wing an orange lance passed between Carse and Friday, perilously close. Carse glanced back, to see one man already out of the hole and the head of another emerging. The one already out was on his knees, aiming a ray-gun at them. Even as Carse took this in, a second lance sizzled by.

Friday took the fifteen-foot drop without hesitation. Carse lowered Leithgow to him and then swung down himself. They panted forward again over the level brown soil.

Nearly a hundred yards of open space lay between them and the port-locks for which they were headed. Friday now led the way, weighted down under the heavy suits as he was; the scientist came next; then the Hawk, his sole remaining gun replying at intervals to an ever-thickening barrage from behind. They had covered perhaps half of the distance when the Negro's steps suddenly faltered.

"Look there!" he exclaimed. "They're cutting us off!"

Carse looked where he pointed, and saw a squad of half a dozen men emerging from a building well to their left. They were running at full speed for the lock, and, as Friday had said, it was obvious that they would get there first. He glanced quickly around. Many guards had jumped from the laboratory roof and were now hot in pursuit in their rear; moreover, three of them were angling sharply out on each side, to outflank them! In a minute they would be surrounded! Unable to reach either the port or the ship!

Then came another piece of ill-luck. The Hawk winced; staggered; clapped a hand to his shoulder. A lucky shot from an enemy gun had caught him.

"You're hit!" cried Leithgow.

"It's nothing," Carse said calmly.

The slender adventurer stood still, thinking. He was trapped. But he was never more dangerous than when he was trapped.

Leithgow timidly ventured a suggestion.

"Why can't we put on our spacesuits and rise up in the dome?"

Crisply the answer came back:

"We'd be perfect targets—unable to get out." Almost without pause he cried, "I have it!"

Tersely he gave the two men orders:

"We've a bare chance—if I'm lucky. Now listen, and obey me exactly. Put on your spacesuits. Shut them tight. Lie flat. You, Friday, use your ray-guns *and keep the following guards from coming close*. Wait here. Do nothing but keep them off. And keep your suits intact or you're dead!"

He grabbed one of the suits from Friday and turned toward the *Scorpion*. The three outflanking men had already cut him off from the ship. Friday cried:

"But you can't get to the ship through those guards! And if you did, you couldn't run it yourself—and pick us up!"

Carse turned with anger. "When will you learn to obey me implicitly?" he said harshly—and ran toward the ship.

Old Leithgow trusted his friend more. "Get your suit on, Friday," he said, and he got into his own. The Negro, abashed but still anxious, did so; then both were flat on the ground, back to back, sniping at the two groups of men who, in short rushes, kept coming ever nearer.

The Hawk's plan might have appeared half-brained to one who did not know the man, and what he was capable of accomplishing under pressure. The first step in this plan required the destruction of the three outflanking coolie-robots who had interposed themselves between him and the space-ship.

As often in the career of the great adventurer, he was lucky. Everyone knew his luck, but the unthinking have never seen that he *forced* it—forced it by doing the unexpected—attacking when he was attacked. He was doing that now. If the three guards knew who he was, their alarm at finding themselves, the attackers, attacked, would fully account for their making a move of poor strategy. Instead of scattering and defending the entrance-port of the space-ship from the outside, they made haste to get inside, to defend it from there. The interior of course would be the best place to defend the ship—if they were already inside—for they could either close the port and shut Carse out, or they could cut him down when he came through.

But to try to enter the port with Carse only fifty yards away—that was bad judgment. It was only necessary for Carse to hold bead on the port and fire when they crossed his sights.

This was the present "luck" of the adventurer. He might have sniped the guards anyway, but he had it easier. Prone, ray-gun supported and carefully sighted, he took what was left of the three lives that already had been so unnaturally altered by Ku Sui.

A moment later, the way cleared, he was inside the ship —and his space-suit lay on the ground outside.

Leithgow and Friday had their hands full. From two sides the attacking guards closed in. They did what they could to slow the advance, but the cramped interiors and stiff fingers of their cumbrous suits did not permit accurate shooting—not even by Friday, who was a crack shot. They could not hold out long—nor did they expect to.

They were much too occupied to notice what had become of Carse. They had not had time to learn the mechanisms of their suits, so within them all was silence; they heard neither their own shots nor the Hawk's, as he burned out the three men. Quick glances at the ship's open port revealed nothing. Probably the Hawk was dead, they thought; even if he were not, all soon would be. A matter of a minute, at most. Their suits were still intact, but even a grazing shot would open them. The shots kept coming closer. Their attackers had become a ring, completely encircling them.

Then, in those last few seconds, with death staring them in the face, Friday did a foolish, magnificent thing. It happened that Carse saw him do it, as he stood in the open port of the *Scorpion*—just before he jumped and with utmost speed got into the spacesuit he had left ready on the ground outside. Friday stood straight up, a hundred feet from the enemy, a bloated target in his bulky suit—and charged. He yelled; but it was silently, to the guards, that he rushed them—slowly, because of his hampering suit—his ray-gun spitting lances of orange contempt, while lances from them passed him narrowly by.

And then, while he still charged, the lances stopped coming, and he saw the faces of the guards turn upward. So surprised was the expression on their faces that he turned and looked too—and saw the *Scorpion,* her entrance ports still open, forty feet off the ground and rising with high acceleration.

Faster and faster she rose, all ray-guns silenced before her astounding ascent. Higher and higher—faster and faster —till she struck the great dome and crashed through.

Then came chaos.

A huge, jagged gash marked the ship's place of exit, and through this the air inside the dome poured with cyclonic force, snatching into its maelstrom everything unfastened and drawing it spinning into space. For seconds the torrent of air rushed out, a visible thing, brown from the soil which it sucked up; and while it continued every building on the asteroid quivered and creaked.

And where, a moment before, men had been—two white men and a black, and a score of robot-coolies—there now was nothing save the rock that had underlain the soil. The soil had been sucked off and flung forth like a concealing veil around the bodies that had departed. . . .

For an interval Hawk Carse knew nothing. It was as if he had ceased to live, and was floating through eternity. He never knew how much time passed before his numbed senses began to return and he became aware of roaring in his head.

He felt that he was floating—though in fact he was moving at great speed. Something kept intermittently flashing

131

before him—a wide, vertical stream of ruddy light; his dazed brain could not account for it. As his mind cleared, however, he saw that the orange stream came in regular bursts, pitch blackness filling the intervals; and then, suddenly, he saw that the stream was the vast lighted ball of Jupiter, streaking across his line of vision as he tumbled over and over, head over heels—free in space!

As he had planned.

He manipulated the controls he found on the breast of his suit, and found a way to slow the relative motion of Jupiter. As his orientation improved, he looked around through his face-plate. To one side he glimpsed two tumbling spacesuits, half of each one lost against the blackness of space, the other half vivid in the near-by planet's light. He saw other figures, too, spread out in a scattered fringe —figures of men in gray smocks—dead and bloated and white.

They were the guards, these last, and the other two were of course Leithgow and Friday. But had they survived the outrush of air? Carse tentatively moved a short lever on the breast of his spacesuit. A change in the pressure of the suit on his body indicated an acceleration away from the side of pressure. He experimented further, and found the switch for a radio transmitting and receiving set encased inside the helmet. He called:

"Leithgow! Leithgow! Can you hear me? Friday!"

The radio broadcast his words. The others, too, had experimented, and soon welcome answers sounded in his receiver—Eliot Leithgow's voice, tired, and the Negro's emphatic baritone. He instructed them in the operation of the suit controls.

"Maneuver together," Carse then ordered. "We must stay close."

Slowly, with many false movements, the three figures made toward each other, and presently they were reunited in a close group. Carse pointed an arm into the face of

132

Jupiter, to a place where hung poised an attendant planet, misty white, and dappled with dark splotches.

"Satellite III," he said, "—our goal. And we'll get there without danger now that Ku Sui, his laboratory, and his Coordinated Brains, are destroyed. . . . You are very quiet, Eliot. Are you hurt?"

"I am just very tired," the old scientist said. "Oh, but we'll sleep and feast and gam when we get back to my hidden lab on Three—won't we!"

"Chicken for me!" exclaimed Friday. "Even at twenty dollars a can!"

"Your shoulder, Carse—how is it?" asked the Master Scientist. "And how did you ever get out of that space-ship in time, after you had given it such an acceleration?"

Habitually curt, the adventurer replied:

"My shoulder—it's nothing. I have a dozen such burns. But my feet still hurt from the twenty-foot drop I took. I had to get out: the shock of the crash would have killed me.

"But I've been looking for the asteroid," he went on— and interrupted himself. "By the stars!" he exclaimed in amazement. "Look, Eliot! That explains it!"

He angled his spacesuit, so as to be able to look back and "upward." Friday and the Master Scientist followed his example, and they gaped in wonder.

For there was nothing above or around them—no dwindling fragment of rock—no sign of any asteroid; only darkness and the eternal stars.

"Yes," said Eliot Leithgow slowly, "that explains it all. . . ."

"It explains what?" asked Friday, staring. "And where is the asteroid?"

"It's up there," the Hawk replied. "Don't you see now, Friday, why no one's ever found it; why we could hunt forever, and never find it? Ku Sui made his whole asteroid invisible!"

133

XXIII

The Stump

Thirty thousand miles (it has been estimated) was the gap between Ku Sui's asteroid and Satellite III, the nearest haven. Thirty thousand initial miles in a space-ship is about the time of a peaceful cigarro. Thirty thousand initial miles in a cramped spacesuit grow into a nightmare journey, an eternity of suffering, and they will kill some people.

For, leave the security and companionship of a space-ship and get out in a hard, confining spacesuit, and space loses its face of friendliness, or harmlessness, and is seen for the impersonal killer it is. There is the terrible quiet and aloneness, the unthinkably remote distances, the sense time-lessness; there is the "weightless" feeling from pressure-changes in the blood-stream—changes which may be sickening and result in delirium. Nothing definite; no apparent gravity; no "bottom," no "top"; no contact; no apparent motion: it is no wonder that fear along with illness sometimes overwhelms the mind, so that the encompassing vault of glittering stars comes to stagger and swirl and the universe goes mad. Such a trip is enough to churn the resistance of the hardiest traveler; but for Hawk Carse, Friday and Eliot Leithgow there was more. On Ku Sui's asteroid they had gone through hours of mental and physical tension without break or relaxation, and they were starved for food and rest before they started. What would have been a strong

134

reaction in any case, hit them, on that journey, with extra force.

So Friday (our ultimate authority) remembered little of the transit. As time passed, his periods of consciousness decreased and the degree of his illness increased, yet it was only during these periods that he could on occasion see the other two figures, sometimes separated, sometimes close, always only partially lit by the light of nearby Jupiter. From time to time he was aware that one of the other two was requiring them to keep together—Carse, of course—Carse, who hardly slept, who by will power alone drove off unconsciousness and fought down nausea to keep at his task of shepherding them down to the satellite, of preventing their angling apart and becoming hopelessly separated. He became expert in the manipulation of a short metal rod on the breast of his suit, which gave movement in the direction it was pointed when its switch was thrown; and he became skilled in chasing the others and making, himself, small adjustments of their direction rods.

But though it seemed endless, the journey was not. Satellite III grew and grew. Its pale circle spread outward; dark blurs took definition; one took the color blue—the Great Briney. The globe eventually appeared concave, then, later, convex. The last stretch—through the atmosphere—was the most grueling.

Friday remembered it in dim snatches. Time after time he dropped into nightmarish sleep, each time to be awakened by Carse's shouting at him, bumping him—giving him no peace, so he would be attentive to the job of decelerating. The adventurer's efforts must have been tremendous, taxing all his enormous driving power, for he at that time should have been more exhausted than they. But he persisted, and he was a haggard-faced, feverish shell of himself when at last he held them in a drunken dangle a thousand feet from the surface of the satellite.

Primal savagery lay on all sides, and there seemed to be

135

no safe spot whereon to land. The swamp that was concealed by the tree tops, the trees themselves, with their crown of leaves, the interlaced vines and creeper-growths —all was a-stir with tropic animal life, varied and voracious, and exotic and untamed. From the tiny poisonous bansi insects layers deep on the nearest tree to the monster gantor that crouched in a clump of weeds slowly sawing his fangs, all the creatures of this world were hostile to man.

Carse scanned the scene through overwhelming weariness. They had to land; had to sleep under normal conditions, had to eat and drink, before they could go farther. But how could they do this? Where was the haven? He angled his direction rod, touched the accelerator and glided forward. Not far away he glimpsed a small peninsula of firm soil jutting into a pool of fairly clear water which contained nothing but an old uprooted stump. It seemed safe and uninhabited. He came back to the others, roused them, and led them down to the place he had discovered.

The two men landed with a thump and fell over. They were asleep almost immediately. Carse extracted a ray-gun from the belt of Leithgow's suit and prepared to stand watch. But that was too much. He overestimated his capacity. He had come through an interminable period of sleeplessness and delirium, and he could not hold out any longer. He slumped and went down, and his eyelids were glued in sleep when his body hit the ground.

But with an instinct that even sleep did not relax, his left hand kept clasped around the butt of the ray-gun in his belt. . . .

It was just before the setting of Jupiter that the three spacesuited figures landed and sprawled out unconscious on the little peninsula. Quickly the sweeping rim of the titanic planet plunged down over the horizon, and night fell over the land.

It was night of fierce darkness. In jungle and swamp

136

awoke the creatures of the surface. Swift shapes swooped down from trees, prey-hungry eyes gleaming green. From all sides came bellowings and stirrings from monster mud-encrusted bodies, awakening to the nocturnal quest for food. The darkness was jarred by the harsh cacophony of a hundred kinds of cries.

With lumbering caution, its knob head weaving on a long reptilian neck, its heavy armored tail dragging behind the flesh folds of its body, a giant night-thing emerged from a copse of jungle growth—a buru. Its sore eyes were watchful to all sides, but they ever returned to one edge of the spit. Its drinking water was there. With many pauses, it went out on it, and a flat-bottomed foot larger than an elephant's set down only inches from the head of one of the sleeping forms. But the buru cared nothing for these odd objects. Its undulating neck curved downward, its head dipped, and it sucked up water—until it caught sight of the uprooted stump projecting from the surface a little way out. The beast drank no more after that, but retreated as cautiously as it had come.

Two or three of its fellows followed at intervals, grotesque shapes of foul odor, plastered with slime and mud. Each drank from the same spot; each ignored the figures lying unconscious close by; but each one noted the outthrust roots of the stump, and watched them with care, and drank briefly, and promptly backed away.

From time to time there came smaller and more cautious animals which noted the stump, sniffed, hesitated, and finally retreated from the pool without drinking at all.

There was good reason for this caution. For, with the setting of Jupiter, the stump had been at least thirty feet out in the water; now it was not ten feet out, and only fifteen from the sleeping figure lying nearest on the spit. The suits that clad the three figures were sealed, the faceplates closed, so—after their trip through the void—there

137

was no man smell to attract the animals of the land; but those three figures occasionally had moved. That was lure enough for one monster.

When the first pink rays of returning Jupiter began to lace through the jungle's highest foliage, the twisted stump was settled right on the peninsula's rim, half out of the water. And when day burst its roots eeled forward in sudden sinuous attack.

In one second Hawk Carse was snatched from sleep into a fight for his life.

Something hard and enormously powerful wrapped his waist with a grip that threatened to cut him in two. He felt one leg go up and crumple back, almost breaking under the force of a sudden pressure. He was squeezed in, caged, compressed, by a score of tough, encircling tentacles, and his whole body was drawn toward a flexible, black-lipped mouth yawning in the center of the monster he had thought a stump. Moving with loathsome life, its sinewy root-tentacles sucking him whole into the maw, the thing shrunk back under the surface.

The water frothed around Carse. He was too dazed to do more than tense himself; he did not know what had gripped him as he lay unconscious and weak. But he remembered the ray-gun clasped in his hand.

The lips of the hideous mouth were pressing close. Both man and monster were now under the surface, but the man's suit was tight and he could still breathe. He strained his left arm against the branchy tentacles that looped it, worked the ray-gun in line with the center of the thing that held him, and at once, gasping and sick, squeezed the trigger.

An orange stream boiled a path through the water and bit into the gaping mouth. At once the faceted eyes on each side of the mouth bulged, the woodish body quivered. Then the root-tentacles of the monster slackened, and, half fainting, the Hawk wrenched free and staggered up onto

138

the spit, where he toppled over, streams of water running off his suit. From the ground he saw the thing writhe back along the surface of the pool. When well out from the shore it again subsided into a "harmless" uprooted old stump. . . .

XXIV

Alone on the Danger Trail

Carse lay resting and collecting himself for a quarter of an hour, while Leithgow and Friday slept on; then he got to his feet, opened their face-plates and bathed Leithgow's pale brow with water. The scientist awoke more readily than Friday, but the latter stirred and stretched and blinked and sat up at last, yawning.

The Hawk answered their questions about his wet suit with a brief explanation of the fight, then got down to business.

"There's water here, but we must have food," he said. "Friday, you go back and find fruit; some isuan weed, too, if you can find any growing near-by. A chew will stimulate us. Keep your ray-gun ready. I wouldn't be here if I'd not had mine."

They chewed some isuan and it was a big help. In its prepared form isuan is habit-forming, eventually destroying mind and body, but the leaves in its natural state give a strong and comparatively harmless stimulation. The leaves that the Negro brought back called up reserves that brought renewed vitality and strength to their bodies, so that they came, for the first time since they had started their flight through space, to a near-normal state. Meaty, yellow globules of a pearlike fruit, followed by prudent drafts of water, aided also. Friday's long-absent grin returned as he

140

bit into the juicy fruit, and he announced through a mouthful:

"Well, things're looking sunny again! We've got food and water inside us; we can reach Master Leithgow's laboratory in these suits; and to top it all we've finished Ku Sui. He's dead at last! Boy, it sure feels good to know that!"

Eliot Leithgow was lying back, breathing deeply of the fresh morning air, his lined face relaxed. "Yes," he murmured, "it is good to know that Dr. Ku is now just a nightmare of the past. He and his unthinkable Coordinated Brains." He glanced aside at the Hawk, sitting silent and still, and stroking, as always when in meditation, the bangs of flaxen hair which obscured his forehead. "Why so serious, Carse?" he asked.

The adventurer's gray eyes were cold and sober. No relaxation showed in him. At the question his hand paused in its slow smoothing movement.

"Why I overlooked it before," he said quietly, almost as if to himself, "I don't know. Probably because I was too tired, and too busy, and too sick, to think. But now I see."

Leithgow sat up straight. "What?" he asked.

"Eliot," said the Hawk clearly, "doesn't it seem strange to you that Ku Sui's asteroid continued to be invisible after we had smashed through its dome?"

"What do you mean?"

"We've assumed that our smashing the dome and opening it to space killed Ku Sui and everyone inside, and destroyed all the mechanisms, including the Coordinated Brains. But the means which gave the asteroid invisibility was not destroyed. The whole asteroid remained invisible."

The old scientist's face tensed. Carse paused for a moment.

"That means," he went on, "that Ku Sui provided the invisibility apparatus with special protection for just such an emergency. Do you think he would give it such protection and not his Brains? Wouldn't he first protect the

141

Brains, a much more valuable possession? Didn't he give the Brains a separate power supply?"

There was no evading the logic of this reasoning. The Master Scientist nodded. "Yes," he answered. "He certainly would."

"I couldn't damage the case they were in," Carse continued. "The whole device seemed—and was—self-contained. It means just one thing: special protection. Since the means for invisibility survived the outrush of air, we may be sure that the Brains did too. And more than that: we may assume that there was special protection for Ku Sui's most valuable possession of all—his own life."

Friday's mouth gaped open. The old scientist cried out: "Merciful heavens! Ku Sui—still alive?"

"Probably," said the Hawk.

He amplified his argument. "Look at these spacesuits we're wearing; they're Dr. Ku's. Couldn't he have protected himself with one too? He had plenty of warning. And then the construction of the asteroid's buildings—all metal, with tight, sealed doors! Oh blind! Why didn't I see it all before! Here, in my weakness, I thought we'd killed Ku Sui and destroyed the Coordinated Brains!"

Leithgow looked suddenly very old and tired. The calamity did not end there. There were other angles, and an immediate one of high danger. In a lifeless voice he said:

"Carse, our whole situation's changed by this. We intended to go straight to my laboratory, but we may not be able to. The laboratory may already be closed to us. And even if not, there'd be a big risk in going there."

"Closed to us by what?" the Hawk demanded sharply. "A risk from what?"

Old Leithgow pressed his hands over his face. "Let me think a moment," he said.

(It may be stated here that there were special reasons why Eliot Leithgow maintained his laboratory on the dangerous Satellite III. Other satellites would have offered

142

less hostile locations; but Three possessed stores of accessible minerals valuable to his work, it lay close to the orbits of his friend and protector, Hawk Carse, and it was far distant from Earth, where the authorities still were looking for him. He had negated the danger inescapably associated with the laboratory's location by ingenious camouflage, intricate defenses and hidden underground entrances—had, indeed, hidden it so well that not one of the scavengers and pirates who infested Port o' Porno, not even Ku Sui himself, suspected that his headquarters were on the satellite at all. Ships and men could pass over it with never an inkling that it lay below.)

The scientist sighed, and then he explained.

"You remember that Ku Sui's men kidnapped me from Kurgo's house in Porno. There were five of them; robot-coolies. They took us entirely by surprise, and killed Kurgo and bore me to Ku Sui's asteroid.

"Well, I had come to Kurgo's house in the first place to arrange for supplies for building an addition to my laboratory, and I had with me a sheaf of papers containing plans for this addition. The plans themselves are not important —they tell nothing—but there was a figure on one of the papers that might reveal everything! The figure 5,137. Can you guess what that stands for?"

The adventurer thought for a moment, then shook his head. Leithgow went on:

"Few would. *But among the few would be Ku Sui!*

"You'll remember that on building my laboratory we considered it extremely important to have it on the other side of the globe from Port o' Porno—diametrically opposite—so that the movements of our ships to and from it would be hidden from that pirate port. Diametrically opposite—remember? Well, the diameter of Satellite III is 3,270 Earth miles. This diameter multiplied by pi gives 10,273 miles as the circumference, and one half the circum-

143

ference is 5,137 miles—the exact surface distance of my laboratory from Port o' Porno!"

The Hawk sighed. "I see," he murmured. "I see."

"That figure meant nothing to you, nor would it to the average person; but to a mathematician and astronomer— to Dr. Ku Sui—it would be a challenge! He would be studying carefully the paper on which it is written down. One of Eliot Leithgow's papers. Plans for an addition to a laboratory; therefore, Eliot Leithgow's laboratory. And then the figure: half the circumference of Satellite III. Why, he would at once deduce that it gave its precise location!"

The Hawk rose. "If those papers fell into Dr. Ku's hands—"

"He would know exactly where the laboratory is," Leithgow finished. "He would search. Its camouflage would not hold him long. And that would be the end of it—and us too, if we were caught inside."

"Yes," snapped the Hawk. "You're sure that the papers were left in Kurgo's house?"

"I had them in the bottom drawer of the clothes-chest in the room I always use when I'm there. The coolies did not take them. At that time they wanted nothing but me."

Friday, rubbing his head, interjected: "But, even if Ku Sui's still alive, he wouldn't know about those papers. As far as *I* can see, they're safe."

"No!" Leithgow cried. "That's it! They're not! Follow it logically, point by point. Assuming that Dr. Ku's alive, he has one point of contact with us—Kurgo's house, in Porno, where I was kidnapped. He wants us badly. He will anticipate that one of us will go back to that house: to care for Kurgo's body, to get my belongings—for any of several reasons. So he will radio down—he probably won't go himself—for henchmen to station themselves at the house and wait for us to come—and meanwhile to ransack it thoroughly for anything pertaining to me. The papers would fall into their hands!"

"All right," said Carse levelly. "We must get those papers. They will either be still in the house or in the possession of Dr. Ku's men at Porno. But whichever it is—*we must get them before Ku Sui does.*" He paused.

"Well," he said, "that means me." He turned and looked down at the old man and smiled. "It would be foolish to risk the three of us. I'll go to Kurgo's house myself."

Leithgow and Friday got to their feet.

"If the papers are gone, then what?" asked Friday.

"I don't know. What I do will depend on what I discover there."

"But," said Leithgow, "there may be guards! There may be an ambush!"

"I have a powerful weapon, M. S. Ku Sui himself supplied it. This spacesuit."

The Hawk scanned the "western" sky and began giving brisk orders.

"Eliot, you've got to go to some place of safety until this is all over. You too, Friday, to take care of him. Let me see. . . . There's Cairnes, and Wilson. . . . Wilson's the one. He should be at his ranch now. You remember it: Ban Wilson's ranch on the Great Briney, fourteen miles from Porno. Both of you will go there and wait. I'll meet you there when I'm finished. And at that time I'll either have the papers or know that Ku Sui has the means to find the laboratory."

The old Master Scientist regarded anxiously this slender, coldly calculating man who was his closest friend. He was afraid. "Carse," he said, "you're going back alone into probable danger. The papers, the laboratory—they're important—but not so important as your life."

There was visible now in the Hawk's face the hard purpose that was one of his most characteristic attributes. "Did you ever know me to run from danger?" he asked softly. "Did you ever know me to run from Ku Sui? . . ."

He glanced again at Jupiter, hanging massive in the sky.

145

"About three hours of Jupiter light left," he observed. "Now, close face-plates. We must go up—far up—and get our bearings."

Altitude swept back the horizon as they arrowed up. From far in the heavens, perhaps twenty miles, Carse saw what he looked for—bright points in the subdued polychrome of the terrain, where Jupiter-light was reflected from the silver sides of the space-ships resting in the satellite's space port, Porno, a hundred or more miles away. Into the helmet's microphone he said:

"That's Porno, over to the 'north,' and there to one side is the Great Briney. It's not far: you won't have to hurry, Eliot. Head straight for the lake and follow the near shore-line toward Porno, and you'll come to Ban Wilson's ranch. Now we part."

The three bloated forms drew near. There were last touches of gloves on the suits, nods and smiles through the face-plates, and a few parting words:

"Good luck, old comrade!—in Leithgow's gentle tones; and the Negro's rich voice: "I don't know the range of these suit radios, sir, but if you need me, call. I'll keep listening!"

And then two men, white and black, were speeding off through the sky, and Hawk Carse faced the danger trail alone.

XXV

The Smell of a Venusian

Caution, rather than speed, had to mark the Hawk's journey. A number of ranches lay scattered in the smother of jungle between him and Porno—stations where the weed isuan was collected and refined into the deadly finished product. They were worked for the most part by Venusians allied with Ku Sui—the Eurasian practically controlled the drug trade—and therefore, if any alarm had been broadcast, many men would already be on the lookout for him.

So the Hawk dropped low, and chose a course through the screening walls of the jungle. It did not take him long to complete his mastery of the suit's controls, and soon he was gliding cleanly through the hollows created by the mammoth outthrusting treetops in a course obstructed and twisted, but one which kept returning him always towards Porno. Presently he found an easier and smoother highway, a sluggish yellow stream, quite broad, which ended, he was sure, in a swamp within a mile of his destination.

Flanked by the jungle growth which sprouted thickly from each bank, a gray, ghostly shape in the shadows lying over the water, he sped upright through the dying afternoon. He kept at least ten feet above the surface, well out of reach of such water beasts as from time to time reared up through the placid surface to scan him. Once a huge gantor, gulping a drink from the bank, snorted and went

trumpeting away at the grotesque sight of this odd creature
—flying without wings!—and once, too, on rising cautiously above the treetops to reconnoiter, Carse saw life far more
perilous to him: a small party of men, stooping over the
brink of a swamp, plucking the ripe isuan weed. At this he
lowered quickly and sped on; but he was sure that he had
been unobserved.

Jupiter lowered as the miles streamed past, breeding a
legion of shadows, welcome alike to the skimming spacesuited figure and to the creatures who blinked and stirred
below. The stream broadened, spread into wide areas of
swamp and was absorbed, and Carse knew he was close to
his destination.

He cut his speed and glanced around. Ahead, the dark
crown of a giant sakari tree climbed into the gloom. It
would be a good place, he thought. He rose slowly, carefully lifting into its topmost branches; and there among
the broad, cuplike leaves, he warily ensconced himself.
For man-sounds came into his opened helmet, and through
a fringe of leaves, across half a mile of swamp and marsh,
he could just make out the boundary of the clearing in
which lay the cosmetropolis of Porno, precariously safe behind its electrified fence.

A last slice of the blotched red rim of setting Jupiter still
lighted Porno, brushing the hell town with soft beauty. The
rows of tin shacks which housed its dives, the clustered,
nondescript hovels, the merchants' grim strongholds of
steel—all from his distance made a scene of peace, one far
alien to the brooding swamp and savage jungle in whose
breast it lay. At intervals the space-ships showed their sun-
set-tinted flanks, glittering high-lights in the final burst of
Jupiter-light. . . .

The planet's rim vanished abruptly, and Porno began to
awake. Beads of light appeared, some still, some winking,
most of them making one crooked line marking the Street
of Sailors, along which the notorious kantrans flourished—

148

now rousing to receive the nightly broods of interplane-tarians who sought forgetfulness there in revelry. Soon, Carse knew, the faint man-noises he heard would grow into a broad ribbon of sound, stitched by shrieks and roars as the isuan and alkite flowed free. And all around the lone watcher in the sakari tree the night-monsters were rousing, too—and slithering in jungle and swamp on the dark routine of their appointed lives.

The night flowed thicker around him.

From somewhere behind and below Carse heard a half-fluid suck as a giant body moved in the mud. A tree close to him began to flutter with the unseen life it harbored. A hungry gantor raised its long deep bellow to the night, and another answered, and another.

It grew quite dark. Only an irregular sprinkling of pin-points of light marked Porno. The sky beyond the town matched the sky to the rear. Jupiter's light now had fled even the higher levels. The time had come.

Cautiously, Carse brushed the branches aside, rose up-right and moved a switch on his breast to repulsion. In instant response he lifted, then sped upward, straight and fast; and at two thousand feet, still untouched by the sunken planet's rays, he brought himself to an approximate halt and studied the lay of the land ahead.

The spread of Port o' Porno showed in better proportion. It was one thin line of light-pricks off which angled fainter ones, extending only a short distance before dying widely off. There were perhaps two thousand men in the town— all the kinds of men from all the planets inhabited by crea-tures that might be called human—and of these at least three-quarters knew Hawk Carse as an enemy, because of his intolerance for their trade in isuan. His approach to the house Number 574 had to be swift, unseen, unheard.

He was able to make it so. Pointing the direction rod, he streaked forward until directly above a certain spot, then he dropped a thousand feet. A pause while he searched;

149

then another drop. He knew Kurgo's house well, but darkness and his height made its position obscure. The Street of the Merchants was always dark at night.

The Hawk made it out at last. The squat two-storied structure, similar to the strongholds of the other merchants, was unlit and seemed unwatched. He unfastened and swung back the hinged gloves of the suit so that his hands would be out, ready for action. In his left hand he took his ray-gun; then, moving the rod, he dropped straight, silent, swift, like the bird whose name he bore.

A single window-port, high up, broke the smooth rear of Kurgo's house. It faced a silent alleyway. The steel shutters were closed, but a pull swung them noiselessly outward. For a brief moment Carse's bulging figure hung black against the shadowed port. The room he peered into was solid black. He heard no sound. Clumsily he thrust out and stepped in.

Silence. Inky nothingness—but the air was weighted with a number of things, among them a smell which brought the short hairs on the Hawk's neck prickling erect. A smell! It was not to be mistaken—a faint, but altogether identifying smell—the body-smell of a Venusian!

For a moment Hawk Carse stopped breathing. Metal clanked once on metal as he moved from the window-port and became one with the darkness inside; then there was silence again, while his eyes trained forward and his hand held ready on the ray-gun. He waited.

Was it a trap? He had seen no guards watching the house; it had seemed deserted. But the steel shutters, unlocked, readily permitting entrance—and the smell! Even if not still there, a Venusian had recently been in the room —and a Venusian of Port o' Porno was an enemy. A Venusian. . . . There were only a few hundred on the whole satellite, and, of these, fifty were the men of Lar Tantril. Lar Tantril, powerful henchman of Ku Sui and director of the Eurasian's drug trade on Satellite Three. But that line of thought had to wait.

"I see you!" he whispered suddenly. "My gun's on you! Come forward!"

No answer. No sign or stir in the darkness. He breathed again.

Carse knew the arrangement of Kurgo's house. He was in the dead man's second-story sleeping-room. There was a door in the wall ahead, leading into the room Leithgow was accustomed to use on his visits, and there the papers should be. But first he would have to have light.

His ears pitched for any betraying sound, Carse moved heavily to his left until arrested by a wall. He felt along it, and located the desk he sought. His fingers found a flash he knew was there.

The darkness then was slit by a hard narrow cone of white light. It shot over the room picking out overturned chairs, a bowl that lay smashed on the floor amid a scattering of ripe akalot fruit, a sleeping couch, its sheets and pillows awry, and—something human.

A half-clothed body lay sprawled beside the couch, its hands thrust forward and its unseeing eyes still staring at the door whence had come the shots that had burnt out its life. Dead. Three days dead. Kurgo, the murdered master of the house, lying where Ku Sui's men had shot him down.

The Venusian-smell swept more strongly into his nostrils as the adventurer opened the door into Leithgow's room. No Venusian had ever been in those rooms before the abduction.

Carse's light danced over the room's confusion: a laboratory table overturned; apparatus spilled; several chairs flung wide, one splintered—mute signs of the resistance Eliot Leithgow had offered his kidnappers.

In a corner stood a metal chest. In the bottom drawer should be the all-significant papers. Carse crossed the room and slid the drawer open.

151

The papers were gone!

Methodically Carse hunted through every drawer and corner of the room, but he found no trace of them. Every article that would be of value to an ordinary thief was left; the one thing important to Dr. Ku Sui, the sheaf of papers, was missing.

The presence of the Venusian body-smell started an important train of thought in the Hawk's mind. It first suggested that the papers had been taken by a henchman of Lar Tantril, but this in turn came to prove that Ku Sui had survived the crashing of the dome and was alive and again aggressive. But was the Eurasian already on Satellite III? Was he already in personal possession of the papers?— and perhaps conducting a search for Leithgow's laboratory?

Or did it mean that Dr. Ku had merely radioed instructions for his Venusian henchmen to ransack the house, take whatever pertained to Leithgow, and wait for him?

Venusians. . . . There was only one logical man; and as Hawk Carse thought of him in that dark and silent house of tragedy, his right hand by old habit started to rise to stroke the bangs of flaxen hair lying low over his forehead.

His bangs were an unusual style for the period; they marked him, and attracted unwanted attention; but he would wear his hair in that fashion until the day he went down in death. He had worn them ever since one black day he had been trapped—trapped neatly by five men—and maltreated. One of the five was Judd the Kite, whose life already had paid for his part in the ugly business; there were three others whom the Hawk was not now concerned with; but the fifth was a Venusian.

That fifth, the Venusian, was Lar Tantril, now one of Ku Sui's most powerful henchmen, and director of his interplanetary drug traffic—Lar Tantril, who possessed an impregnable isuan ranch only twenty-five miles from Port o' Porno—*Lar Tantril, who probably had directed the steal-*

ing of the papers from this room! The papers, if not already in Ku Sui's hands, should be at Tantril's ranch.

Carse's deduction was followed by the inevitable decision. He had to raid Lar Tantril's ranch.

He knew the place fairly well. Once, even, he had attacked it, in a previous space-ship, seeking to wipe out his debt against Tantril; but he had been driven off by the ranch's mighty offensive rays.

It was impregnable, Tantril was fond of boasting. The ranch lay on the brink of the Great Briney, its other three sides flanked by thick, swampy jungle, in which grew the isuan that was gathered by Tantril's Venusian laborers. Ranch? More a fort than a ranch, with its electrified, steel-spiked fence; its three watch-towers, with lookouts always posted against the threat of hi-jackers and enemies; its powerful ray-batteries and miscellany of smaller weapons. A less vulnerable place for the keeping of Eliot Leithgow's papers could hardly have been found in all the frontiers of the System.

He, Carse, had raided it in a fighting space-ship, and failed. Now, with nothing but a spacesuit and a ray-gun, he had to raid it again—and succeed.

The adventurer did not leave immediately. He always made in advance what preparations he could. His important weapon was Ku Sui's revolutionary spacesuit; therefore, he took it off and studied its several intricate mechanisms as well as he could in the guarded light of his flash.

It was activated, he saw, by dual sets of gravity plates, in separate space-tight compartments. One set was located in the extremely thick soles of the heavy boots; the other rested on the top of the helmet. He saw why this was. The gravity plates for repulsion were those in the helmet; for attraction, those in the boot-soles. This kept the wearer of the suit always in a head-up position with reference to a planetary surface.

The logical plan of attack had grown in Carse's mind:

153

down and up! Down to the papers, then up and away before the men on the ranch knew what was happening. The success of his raid depended entirely on keeping the two gravity mechanisms intact. If they were destroyed, or failed to function, he would be locked to the ground in a confining prison; clamped down by the suit's dead weight. The suit was quite heavy, particularly the soles of the boots.

A chance to succeed—if the two vital points were kept intact! If they failed, he would have to slip out of the imprisoning suit and use only his wits and ray-gun in clearing a path to Ban Wilson's ranch.

It was characteristic of the Hawk that he never even considered calling on Wilson's resources of men and weapons. A Hawk he was: steel-tendoned and fierce-clawed, bold against all odds and danger, most capable and deadly when striking alone. . . .

After scanning the project, Carse attended to other needs. He ate some of the akalot fruit spilled over the floor of the adjoining room; opened a can of water and drank deeply; limbered his muscles; even rested for a few minutes. Then he was ready to leave.

Quickly he again was in the cold spacesuit, fastening on the helmet. He left the face-plate open. The left glove he hinged back, so as to be able to grip the ray-gun in his bare hand. Then, a denser shadow in the darkness, he shuffled to the rear window-port.

He steadied himself on the sill. There sounded in his ears the night-bedlam from the Street of the Sailors, punctuated by far-off bellows from the monsters of the swamps. Enemies, animal and human, ringed him in Kurgo's house; but up above lay a clean, cool highway, and open highway, stretching straight to the heart of the danger which was his destination. He set his controls for quick repulsion and leaped to the waiting heavens.

XXVI

Passage Through the Night

On the ground the satellite was a world of night; from a
mile above it was a tremendous circle of star-enclosed black,
one edge of which was faintly tinged with reflected light
from the rising of a smaller sister satellite.

Save for that far-off spectral reminder of another world,
Hawk Carse sped in darkness. Through the open face-plate
the night wind buffeted his stone-set face; his suit whistled
a song of speed as gusts of wind laced by. Dead ahead toward Lar Tantril's ranch his direction-rod pointed, and
with ever-gathering speed he followed its leading finger.
The lights of Porno dwindled to points, grew yet finer, then
were gone. Several times a sparse cluster of other lights,
lonely in the black tide of Three's surface, passed beneath
him, indicating the presence of a ranch. Then the last of
these melted into the ink behind, and there was a period
unrelieved by sign of man's presence below.

And then one bright solitary point of light appeared, far
ahead. It was a danger signal to the Hawk. He had to descend at once. From then on, speed had to be forsaken for
caution. Watchful eyes would be beneath that light; an intricate system of offense and defense lay around it. For it
was the central watch-beacon of Lar Tantril's ranch.

Carse swooped low.

He came into the night-world just above the surface of

the satellite. No faint-lit horizon showed now; there was only the darkness, and the darker shadows of the vegetation which filled it. At the height of a mile there had been few signs of the animal life of the satellite, but at an elevation scarcely above the treetops the flying man was brought all too close to its reality. Out of the black smother came clues to the life within it: sounds of large bodies moving through undergrowth and mud, occasional death-screams, howls and angry chatterings. . . .

This below; but there was more at his level. He was not the only living thing that sped through the night. Swift fleeting batlike shapes would appear from nowhere for one sharp second, would beset him one after another in an almost constant stream, perhaps thinking his bloated bulk easy prey, and would then be gone. At their first assault he had to shut his face-plate quickly. Sometimes there came different, more powerful wings, and he would weave in mechanical reaction, sensing the wings sweep past, often feeling the shock of contact as, with hammer pecks and thudding blows, the creatures sought to stun him. But the suit was stout; the repulsed ones could only follow a little, glaring with fire-green malevolent eyes, then leave to seek more vulnerable prey.

The watch-beacon began to wink stronger through the ranks of intervening trees as Carse neared the ranch. He now was gliding so low that the crowns of trees sometimes would rake him in his course. His low transit allowed one tree to loose great peril upon him.

The tree loomed a black giant in his path. Fifty feet away, swerving to avoid it, he saw its dark upper branches a-tremble. He had only this for warning, when what appeared to be the entire top of the tree severed itself completely from the rest and soared right out to intercept him.

It was a shape from a nightmare. He saw a multitude of small green-glowing eyes; heard, through the outside communicator, great leaf-wings rattling bonily as they spread to full thirty feet; heard the monster's life-thirsty scream as it enclosed him. Then the stars were blotted out.

But even in the sudden confusion of the attack, Carse knew the creature for what it was: a full-grown specimen of the giant carnivorous lemak, a seldom-seen, dying species, too clumsy, too big, too poorly adapted to survive. His ray-gun came up, but he was so violently knocked about in a leafy maelstrom that he could not use it. Without pause the claw-ended leaves of the lemak raked his suit. Unable to rend the tough material, it resorted to another method. With a strength so enormous that it could overcome both the force exerted by his gravity-plates and his forward momentum, the creature tossed him high in the air. As Carse rose he remembered that the purpose of the creature was to impale him on the long spike of an inner beak as he came down.

The lemak poised below, beak exposed. But it waited in vain, for Carse did not come down! A touch of his controls kept him at the new level. The lemak lifted to see what had become of the strange monster that did not descend—and received a searing pencil of heat through its beak. Screaming then with pain, it flapped into the distant darkness.

The Hawk dropped low again, hoping that the quick lance of his shot had not been observed. He had not wished to wound the lemak mortally, for no matter how accurate his shot, the monster would take a long time to die, and scream and thrash about as it did so. One shot through the beak was preferable to a prolonged hullabaloo; but even that might have betrayed him. . . .

With elaborate caution, he reconnoitered Lar Tantril's ranch.

From above, the ranch clearing was a pool of faint light contained in black leagues of jungle and the edge of the Great Briney. Slanting shadows and the dark bulks of unlit

157

buildings rendered details vague, but under prolonged scrutiny the larger elements of the setup became visible.

The clearing was a circle some two hundred yards in diameter. Just inside the jungle wall was the first line of protection, a steel-barbed, twenty-foot-high fence, its strong links interwoven with electrified wires. Centrally located within this fence stood five buildings, low, squat and one-storied, four of them forming a broken square around the central fifth. One building was pierced by rows of lighted windows, evidence that it was the barracks of the workers; others, used for processing and storing the isuan weed, were dark and silent. The central building was smaller, and had round window-ports that glowed like eyes in its smooth walls. It was the dwelling of the master, Lar Tantril.

Close to the central building rose a hundred-foot tower, topped by the watch-beacon. At three equi-distant points just within the encompassing fence were small, covered square platforms, held sixty feet aloft by mast-like triangular towers, traced by foot rungs. On each platform he could make out the figure of a Venusian guard.

Ceaselessly these guards turned and scanned the jungle, the heavens, the unbroken dark prairie of the lake, alert for anything suspicious. Lar Tantril had good reasons for maintaining a constant watch over his stronghold, and the eyes of his guards were sharpened by knowledge of the severe penalty laxness would bring. Close at hand were knobs which, when pressed, would ring a clanging alarm through all the buildings below; and each guard wore two ray-guns in holsters.

Despite the guards and the ugly spikes of the fence, however, the ranch from where he lurked appeared peaceful and harmless. No men were visible on its shadowed clearing. Even the surrounding jungle, beyond the shaded under-side of the watch-beacon, might have seemed nothing but a stage set, were it not for the sounds of the life that crept unseen through it—a long, far-distant howl, a quickly receding crashing in the undergrowth, a thumping from some small animal.

The guards were used to this pattern of nocturnal sounds. It was only when there came a sudden sharp shaking in the upper branches of a tree not thirty feet from one of the platforms, that the Venusian stationed there deigned to grip a ray-gun and peer suspiciously. All he saw was a large bird that flapped out and winged across the clearing, mewing angrily.

The guard relaxed his grip on the gun. A snake, probably, had disturbed the bird. Or some of those devilish little crimson bansees, half insect, half crab. . . .

Carse breathed again. He had been sure his position would be revealed when, drifting with almost imperceptible motion into the tree, the bird had pecked at him, then flapped away in alarm. A long, painfully cautious approach from tree to tree to the selected one had been necessary to the daring scheme of attack he had evolved.

He seemed to be safe. Through a fringe of leaves he saw the guard on the platform glancing elsewhere. Carse steadied himself, rose slightly, and again scanned the ranch.

Yes, it looked harmless, but he knew that nothing could be further from the reality. Spaced around the inside edge of that spiky fence were small metal nozzles protruding a few inches from the ground; on the turning of a control wheel, they would spit a fan of deadly orange thousands of feet into the sky. He had tasted their hot breath. There were also the long-range projectors whose muzzles studded the control building. And the ray-guns of the tower guards.

These were dangers that he knew of. What others the ranch held, he could not well surmise. But he saw one thing that was significant.

The ranch was expecting trouble. Over to one side of the clearing rested a great rounded object, on whose smooth

159

flank gleamed coldly the light from the beacon—Lar Tantril's own personal space-ship—and, alongside it, a smaller, somewhat similar shape, the ranch's air-car. The space-ship signified that the Venusian chief was present; the air-car, that all his men were gathered in the barracks— not dispersed in Port o' Porno for a night of revelry, as was their custom.

All waiting—all gathered here—all ready! All grouped for a strong defense! Did it mean what it seemed—that he, the Hawk, was expected?

He could not know. He could not know if a trap was lying prepared against his coming. He could only go ahead, and find out.

The only plan of attack he could think of had grown in his mind. Down and up: that was the essence of it: but some of the details were contingent. He had worked them out as far as he could with typical thoroughness. He had to reach the heart of the fort lying before him—had to reach the central house, Lar Tantril's own. The precious papers would be there, if anywhere.

The Hawk was ready. There was no sign in the face of the man that, in the next few all-deciding minutes, death would lick close to him.

He poised, his ray-gun in his bare left hand, his face-plate locked partly open. He raised his fingers to the direction-rod on the suit's breast, aimed it straight at the guard on the nearest watch-platform, and touched the switch.

XXVII

Trapped!

The Hawk struck so fast, so hard, so unexpectedly, that in only thirty seconds the quiet ranch was plunged into confusion.

He struck like a thunderbolt, using to its full power his chief weapon, the spacesuit. Sight of him alone might have been enough to strike terror. At maximum acceleration, from the dark arms of the tree he sped, and crashed with a clang into the platform he aimed at. Nothing there could withstand him. One second the guard was calmly gazing off into the sky; the next he was bowled over like a nine-pin, to spin heels over head to the ground sixty feet below. He lived for a little, he kept consciousness, but he was mortally injured; and he never saw the outlandish projectile that struck him, nor saw it streak to the second watch-platform, bowling down its guard in the same manner, then repeating it with the third and last.

A crash; a pause; a crash; a pause; then a third crash, and the outlandish object had completed the circuit, and all three watch-platforms were empty!

Then came confusion.

There had been screams, but now a crazed voice began crying out mechanically, over and over:

"Spacesuit! Spacesuit! Spacesuit! Spacesuit!"

It came from the second guard, who lay jerking on the

ground. His tongue, by some trick of nervous disorganization, beat out those words like a voice-disk when the needle keeps skipping its groove—and the effect was macabre.

The two lighted buildings disgorged a crowd of men. Short, wiry, thin-faced Venusians, each with skewer-blade strapped to his side and some with ray-guns in hand, scrambled out into the open, swearing and wondering. The second guard's insane reptitions brought most of them straight to his side, when they gathered around him in a crowd. They had no thought for what might be happening behind, within the buildings they had emptied. That was what Hawk Carse had planned.

A voice of authority roared over the crowd about the man.

"Rantol, what happened? What attacked you? Cut that crazy yelling, you fool! Rantol—answer me!—you, Rantol!"

"Spacesuit! Spacesuit! Space-suit! Space—"

"Lar Tantril!" shouted a man with slits of eyes. He caught the attention of the one who had spoken first. "Spacesuit, he says! A flying spacesuit! Ku Sui has spacesuits that fly! You know what that means! It's the Space Hawk!"

He paused, peering at his lord. The coarse yellowy skin of Tantril's brow wrinkled with this thought, then his tusk-like Venusian teeth showed as his lips drew apart in speech.

"Yes!" Lar Tantril said. "It's *Carse!*"

He ordered the now silent men around him:

"Circle my house, all of you, your guns ready. You, Esret"—to his second in command, the one who had given him the clue—"out gun and come with me."

Even as Lar Tantril spoke, a bloated shape was skimming through the kitchen of his house. Carse had entered from the rear, unseen. With gun in hand and eyes sharp he crossed the deserted kitchen, with its foul odors of Venusian cookery. Quickly he was through a connecting door and into the well-furnished dining room. All was brightly lit; he

162

could easily have been seen through the window-ports rimming one wall; but he counted on the confusion outside to keep the Venusians engaged for several minutes more.

He continued into the front room of the house, and saw at once the most likely place.

It was in one corner—a large flat desk, by the side of the broad screen of a telero (teleradio). Scattered over the desk were a number of papers. In seconds Carse was bending over them, scanning and discarding with eyes and hands.

Reports of various quantities of isuan . . . orders for stores . . . a list that seemed an inventory of weapons— and then the top page of a sheaf covered with familiar, neat, small writing. Yes!

Plans and calculations concerning a laboratory! And, down in the margin of the first page, the revealing, all-important figure—5,137!

He had them—and before Ku Sui! Now, only to get away: out the front door and up—up from this trap he was in—up to clean, empty space, thence to Leithgow and Friday at Ban Wilson's!

But, as the Hawk turned to go, his eye was caught by a little slip on the desk, a radio memo, with the name of Ku Sui at its top. Almost without volition he glanced over it, hoping to discover useful information about Ku Sui's asteroid—and with the passing of those few extra seconds passed his chance for escaping out of the door.

Carse's back was partly toward the front door when a voice, hard and deadly, spoke from it:

"Your hands up!"

The adventurer's nerves twanged; he wheeled; but even as he did so another voice bit out from the rear door:

"Get them up! One move and you're dead!"

Carse found himself caught between ray-guns held unswervingly on his body by men at each door. He was not fool enough to try to shoot, even though his own gun was in his hand: his best speed would be slow-motion in the hampering spacesuit. He was fairly caught. For a few precious seconds he had delayed his escape—and now it was too late.

At a shout from someone, Venusians pushed in through both doors, and thin faces appeared at the window-ports. Their ray-guns made an impregnable fence around the netted Hawk.

And then a well-remembered voice, harsh as the man from whom it came, cut through the room.

"Apparently you're caught, Captain Carse!"

The cold gray eyes narrowed, scanned the room, the blocked doors, the barricade of guns held by the grim men at doorways and window-ports.

"Yes," Hawk Carse murmured. "Apparently I am."

Lar Tantril, the Venusian chief, smiled. He was tall for one of his race, even taller than the prisoner he faced. He had the characteristic wiry body and thin arms and legs of his kind, and was clad in tight-fitting shirt and drawers, mud-colored, under a suit of iron-gray mesh. Spiky short-cropped hair grew like steel slivers from the narrow dome of his long hatchet head, and the taut-stretched skin of his face was burned a hard, patchy brown. He looked what he was: a bold and unscrupulous leader of his men.

"The gun in your belt," he said, "—drop it. Right on the floor. There—good. I like you not with a gun in your hand."

The Hawk regarded him frigidly.

"And now what?" he asked.

Lar Tantril continued smiling. His ray-gun was out, and did not move for an instant from the line it held on the chest of the bulky gray figure. He said at a tangent, cheerfully:

"Think fast, Captain Carse—think fast! Isn't that one of Dr. Ku's new suits? A little space-ship for a suit? Why not make a sudden sweep for the door?—crash through to the outside, then climb!—eh?"

164

"Why not?" said the Hawk.

"It might be possible," Tantril continued, "with your luck. *Unless something went wrong with your helmet gravity plates.*"

At this the Venusian raised his gun. Deliberately he brought it up, till it was pointed at the crown of the adventurer's helmet. He squeezed the trigger.

Spang! A pencil-thin streak of orange stabbed between Venusian and Earthman; sparks hissed out from where it struck the tip of the helmet; then, in an instant, life and strength seemed to leave the Hawk. He slumped obviously under sudden crushing weight. Weight! It bent him, and it was only with an effort that he was able to come erect again. For with the raying of the upper gravity plates, the suit's full weight came upon him, and the enormous boots bound him to the ground. A penciled hole in the compartment above the helmet still smoked.

Lar Tantril chortled, and though only one or two of his men understood what he had done, they echoed him.

"But even yet you've got a chance," the Venusian went on. "There's another set of plates in the boot-soles, for attraction. If you got a chance to stand on your head outside, you'd be gone! So—"

This time he lowered the gun, and carefully, accurately, he sent a spitting orange stream through the sole of each of the great boots.

The danger Carse had feared had come to pass. His one great weapon had been destroyed. He was more helpless than a clipped Hawk: he was in a prison, encumbered, all power of quick movement gone. Again he was planet-bound, tied to the surface, the way of the air hopelessly closed. Even the slightest step would cost much effort.

"You have protected yourself well, Lar Tantril," he said slowly.

Now Tantril laughed unrestrainedly. "Yes, and by Mother Venus," he cried, "it's good to see you this way, Carse,

165

unarmed and in my power!" He turned to his circle of men and said: "Poor little Hawk! Can't fly any more! I've put him in a cage! So thoughtful of him to bring his cage along with him so I could trap him inside it. His own cage!" He guffawed, shaking, and the others laughed with him.

Through it all Hawk Carse stood motionless, his face graven, his slender body a little bent under the burden of the dead suit. He still held in his right hand the sheaf of papers with their all-important figure—and the thumb and forefinger of his hand were moving, so slowly as to be hardly noticeable, in what seemed to be a lone sign of nervous tension.

"You know, Carse," Tantril observed after his laugh, "I've been half expecting you, though I don't see exactly how you knew I was the one who took those papers you're holding. Dr. Ku radioed me, you see. I think you were reading his message at the time I entered. Did you finish it?"

"No," said the Hawk.

"You'll find it interesting. Let me read it to you." And Tantril took up the memo.

" 'From Ku Sui to Lar Tantril: Search House No. 574 in Port o' Porno closely for anything pertinent to Master Scientist Eliot Leithgow or giving clue to his whereabouts. Keep what you obtain for me; I will come to your ranch in five days. Watch for Hawk Carse, Eliot Leithgow and a Negro, arriving from outer space at Satellite III in self-propulsive spacesuits.' " There followed some details concerning the suits' mechanism; then: " 'Carse caused me certain trouble and came near damaging my major inventions. I want him alive.' "

At this the gray eyes of the adventurer went frosty. All he and Leithgow had deduced, then, was true. Dr. Ku had survived the crashing of the asteroid's dome. The mechanisms also had survived—and certainly the Coordinated Brains—the Brains he, Hawk Carse, had promised to de-

166

stroy! Now, trapped, it seemed that that promise never would be fulfilled. . . .

Yet even through this depressing thought of a promise unkept, the Hawk's thumb and forefinger moved in their slight grinding motion on the first page of the sheaf he held. . . .

Lar Tantril put out his hand. "So, obeying Dr. Ku's orders, I had the house searched and got these papers. They must be valuable, Carse, since you wanted them so badly. Ku Sui will be pleased. Hand them over."

With but a bare flick of his gray eyes downward, Hawk Carse gave the sheaf to Tantril.

His brief glance at the topmost sheet told him all he wanted to know. Gradually, methodically, the motion of his thumb and forefinger had totally effaced the revealing figure 5,137, the one clue to the location of Leithgow's laboratory. Enough! What he had set out to do was finished. The chief task was achieved!

"And now, perhaps," Lar Tantril chuckled, "a little entertainment."

His men pricked up their ears. This language was understandable. Entertainment meant playing with the prisoner —torture. And alkite, probably, and isuan. A night of revelry!

But Hawk Carse smiled thinly at this.

"Entertainment, Tantril?" his cold voice said. He paused, and then added slowly: "What a fool you are!"

XXVIII

The Bluff of the Hawk

Lar Tantril was not used to being called a fool, but he was not annoyed with the words. He only laughed and slapped his thigh.

"Yes?" he mocked. "Truly, Captain Carse, you must be frightened, to try and anger me so I'll shoot! Do you fear a skewer-blade so much. We would leave most of you for Ku Sui!"

Carse shook his head. "No, Lar Tantril, I don't want you to shoot me. I'm telling you you're a fool—because you think I'm a fool."

With a wave of his hands the Venusian protested: "No, no, not at all. You're infernally clever, Carse. I'll always be the first to admit it."

"Then do you think I'd attack your ranch alone?"

"You'd like me to believe you have friends hidden somewhere?" Tantril asked, smiling tolerantly.

Carse's voice came back curtly. "Believe what you like, but learn this: It's your boast that your ranch is impregnable, guarded on every side and from every angle. I'm telling you it's not. It's vulnerable. It's wide open to one way of attack—and my friends and I know it well."

For a second the Venusian's assurance wavered.

"Vulnerable?" he said. "Open to attack? You're just stalling!"

168

"Wait and see. Wait till the ranch is stormed and wiped out. Wait twenty minutes! Only twenty!"

Hawk Carse was always listened to when he spoke in such manner. Lar Tantril stared at the hard gray eyes boring into his.

"Why do you tell me this?" he asked. Then, with a smile: "Why not wait until my ranch is wiped out, as you say?" His smile broadened. "Until these hidden friends attack?"

"Because I must insure my remaining alive. Nothing my friends could do could prevent your having plenty of time to torture me before you yourselves were destroyed. I think, under the circumstances—and in spite of Ku Sui's order—you would kill me. And I must go free. I have made a promise. I must be free to carry it out."

"Just what are you aiming at?"

"I'm offering," said the Hawk, "to show you where your fort is vulnerable—in time for you to protect it. I'll do this if you'll let me go free. *You need not release me till afterwards.*"

Lar Tantril's mouth fell half open at this surprising turn. He was unquestionably taken aback. But he snapped his lips shut and considered the offer. A trick? Carse was famed for them. A trap? But how? He scanned his men. Fifty to one; fifty ray-guns on an unarmed man helpless in a hampering prison. Even if there was a trap, Carse couldn't possibly escape death. But yet. . . .

Tantril walked over to his man Esret, and they conferred in whispers.

"Is he trying to trick us?" the chief asked.

"I don't see how. He can hardly move in that suit. It ties him down. We can keep our guns on him every second. He can't possibly get away. And at the slightest sign of something suspicious—"

"Yes—but you know the Space Hawk."

"What he says is sensible. Naturally he wants to live. He knows we'll shoot him if he tries to trick us, and he

169

knows we'll do it if we're attacked. We'll of course leave men at all defensive stations. If there *is* a weakness here, if the ranch *is* vulnerable, we should learn what it is. It won't cost us anything. We can't lose, and we might be saving everything. Of course we won't let him go afterwards."

Tantril considered a moment longer, then said:

"Yes. I think you are right."

He turned back to the waiting Carse.

"Agreed," he said. "Show this vulnerable point to us and you'll be released. But no false moves! One sign of treachery and you're dead!"

The Hawk's set face showed no change. It was only inwardly that he smiled.

Their very manner of accompanying him showed their respect for the slender adventurer.

He had no gun; he was stooped by the unrelieved weight of the massive helmet, the suit itself, and the large, heavy soles of the boots; his every step was that of a man overburdened and in chains—but he was Hawk Carse! And so, as he shuffled out through the front door of the house and moved with great effort across the clearing, he was surrounded by a glitter of ray-guns held by most of the men in the close-pressing circle. Tantril's own gun kept steady on his back, and he frequently reminded Carse of that fact.

Great floodlights now lit the entire area of the ranch. New guards already were on watch on each of the three watch-platforms, their eyes sweeping the clearing, the jungle and the dark stretch of the lake, then returning to the crowd which marked the progress of the shuffling spacesuited figure below. Each point of defense was manned. In the ranch's central control room, a steel-sheathed cubby in the basement of Tantril's house, men stood watchful, their hands ready at the wheels and levers which commanded the ranch's ray-batteries, their eyes on the miniscreen which

170

gave to this unseen heart of the place a view of all that was transpiring above. And all waited on what the bloated figure they so closely watched might reveal.

Watch—watch—watch. A hundred eyes below, above, around the Hawk, were centered and alert on each move of his clumsy progress. The barrels of two-score ray-guns transfixed him. Under such guard he arrived at the fence, where it paralleled the Great Briney.

"Open the gate," said the Hawk curtly. "It's down there."

He pointed to where the lake's pebbled beach shelved downward to the small murmurous waves—a ten-foot stretch of ghostly white between the guarding fence and the water.

"Down there?" repeated Tantril slowly. "Down to the water?"

"Yes!" Carse snapped irritably, and he waited. "Well, will you open the gate? I'm very tired: I can't bear this suit much longer."

Lar Tantril conferred uneasily with Esret, while his men cast doubtful glances over the dark, wind-rippled plain of the lake. But no enemy showed there. The beach was clear for a hundred yards on each side.

"By Iapetus!" the adventurer cried harshly, "are you children, to be afraid of the dark? Tantril, put your gun into me, and shoot if I try anything suspicious! Open the gate!"

After some further hesitation Lar Tantril ordered the gate opened. He stationed a man there, ready to close and lock it in case of need; and then Hawk Carse, still surrounded by the alert Venusians, shuffled down to the edge of the water.

Over the Great Briney was silence. No shape within range of the floodlights caused a catch in the nervous whispers of the crowd. The scrape and crunch of the lone Earthman's dragging boots made wide furrows in the pebbly sand as he shuffled down to the edge of the water.

171

The men now were a half circle around him as he stood at the water's brink. From them, lakeward, the watch-beacon regularly threw a great blot of shadow. All the ray-guns of the men were held ready as their narrow eyes darted from him to the water ahead, and back. Doubt and fear held them all.

The Hawk wasted no time, but stepped out knee-high in the water over the sharply shelving bottom. At this Tantril objected.

"Hold on, Carse!" he roared. "You play for time, I think! Where is this point of attack?"

The bloated figure did not answer him, but bent over as if searching for something under the small waves now slapping his thigh. He reached one hand down and probed around with it, apparently feeling. The eyes watching him were filled with fear.

"Here—or no," the Hawk muttered to himself, though a dozen could hear him. "A little farther, I think. . . . Here —but no, I forgot: the tide has come in. A little farther. . . . " He stopped suddenly and straightened, then turned to the Venusian chief. "Don't forget, Lar Tantril, you have promised I can go free."

Then he resumed his search of the bottom, the black surface of water now up to his waist. Again the fearful Venusian leader roared an objection:

"You're tricking us, Carse, you little devil—"

"Oh, don't be an ass!" Carse snapped back. "As if I could get away—all your ray-guns on me!"

Another part of a minute passed; a few more short steps were taken. A muttered oath came from one of the anxious men on the beach. Many of them were close to turning in a panicky dash for the safety of the buildings, guarded by ray-batteries—and yet fascination held them. What metallic horror under the surface was being exposed?

"Just a second, now," the Hawk was murmuring. "You'll

172

all see. . . . Somewhere . . . right about here . . . somewhere. . . ."

He held them taut, expectant. The water licked around the chest of his suit. One more step; one more yet.

"Here!" he cried triumphantly, and clicked his face-plate closed. And then the men who stared, hearts pounding, ray-guns at the ready, saw him no longer. The water had closed over his shiny metal helmet. Only a mocking ripple was left.

Hawk Carse was gone!

Gone!—and smiling!

The spacesuit, his heavy prison, would protect him from water as well as from space! It offered a golden opportunity—his only opportunity. It had been thrice pierced by Tantril's shots, back in the ranch house—but only the gravity-plate compartments, which were separate and sealed. It was still airtight after he closed the gloves—an effective little submarine in the dark waters of the Great Briney!

So Carse followed a black course over the lake-bottom, and he smiled. In his mind he could see what he had left behind: the men, shivering there in the edge of the water for an instant, completely befogged, and perhaps firing one or two shots at where he had disappeared; then turning and breaking in a grand rush for the fence and safety. He could see the ray-batteries, manned and centered on the lake; Tantril, in a very fury of rage, but fearful, preparing for a siege; preparing for anything that might loom suddenly from the water! And all of them wondering what lay beneath its inky surface; what he, Hawk Carse, had gone to join!

For days they would stare fearfully at the lake, while the tides rolled steadily in and out; for days the ray-batteries would be held ready, and none would venture outside the fence. It might take hours for the realization of his trick to sink in—but they still would not be sure of anything, and would have to keep vigilant against still-possible attack.

Not far up the coast was Ban Wilson's ranch, and Leithgow and Friday waiting there. He would rest for a while, and then the three of them would go to Leithgow's laboratory—its location now still secret. And then, after a few days, there was his promise to the Coordinated Brains to be kept.

But that was in the future. For the present, he went his dark, watery way smiling. . . .

Yes, first of Hawk Carse's traits was his resourcefulness!

XXIX

The Plan

At Ban Wilson's ranch on the edge of the Great Briney, Leithgow and Friday were waiting uneasily for the Hawk's return. More than half of a Three day had passed since he had set out alone, and they had heard nothing from him. They knew he had gone into great danger, so it was with growing fear that they watched the hours go by.

With Ban Wilson, they sat near dawn in the comfortable living room of the ranch house, fronting on the Lake. Largely rested now from the ordeal of the journey to Satellite III, the big Negro was restless, and even Leithgow, more controlled, showed the strain by continually rubbing his lined face with his thin, many-veined fingers. Wilson's men were on watch outside, but Friday from time to time had supplemented them—going out in the night to them, returning, stepping to the door, peering down along the beach, looking up into the sky, starting at unexpected sounds in the nearby jungle—staring, scowling and returning to sit and look gloomily at the floor.

But Ban Wilson was the most active. He was always active. He was a miniature dynamo of a man, throbbing with restless, inexhaustible energy. Ban was short and wiry, and he stared truculently at the universe through wonderfully clear blue eyes, surrounded by a bumper crop of freckles and topped by a mat of bristly red hair. His stub of a nose

175

had prodded into many a hostile place where it most emphatically was not wanted. All were sitting, at the moment, and Ban was speaking—no rare event with him.

"No, sir! I say the Hawk's safe and kicking! They can't kill *him*! By my grandmother's false teeth, I'd follow him to hell, knowing I'd come out alive and leaving the devil yowling with his tail tied into pretzels! He said he would meet you here. Well, then, he will."

Friday looked up mournfully.

"Yes, but Captain Carse was going into big trouble. And he was tired and worn out, and he only had a spacesuit and a ray-gun, and you know he wouldn't stop for anything till he'd done what he set out to. I kind of feel. . . . I don't know. . . ."

"Well, if he doesn't come—and come soon—I'll take that damned Porno apart till I find him!"

Eliot Leithgow put aside the late radio printcast from Earth he had been pretending to read. A brief silence fell over them, and through it the old scientist seemed to listen, seemed to sense something. He was not mistaken.

"Who's there?" cried someone outside.

It was a cry from one of the watchers. Friday leaped out of his uneasy seat and was through the door even before Ban. Leithgow, following more slowly, heard the Negro roar from ahead:

"It's Carse! He's come back!"—and they saw him go bounding down to the gray-lit beach to meet a slight, weary figure that came stumbling along its edge.

Hawk Carse had come as he said he would, but he was a sore figure of a man. Though he was not in the spacesuit now, for days he had worn it, and the marks of its grating metal and rubbing fabric lay all over him. Even from a distance the others could see that his once-neat trousers and soft blue shirt were torn in several places. On his haggard face was a nap of straw-colored beard, and in his bloodshot gray eyes utter exhaustion, both mental and physical.

176

He came stumbling along the beach, his feet dragging through the coarse sand, and it seemed as if he would drop at any moment. With a slight smile he greeted Friday, Ban, and then Leithgow as they came running to meet him.

"Hello, Friday," he murmured, "and Eliot—Ban—"

There he wavered, and leaned against the Negro's body. Friday wanted to carry him, but he would have none of it; by himself he walked up to the ranch house, where he slumped into a chair while Ban Wilson went shouting into the galley for a mug of hot alkite.

After draining it, Carse revived slightly. Again aware of the three men grouped around him, and seeing their eagerness for his news, he forced himself to speech.

"Sleepy—must sleep. But—some things I'll tell you." In brief phrases, his tired eyelids closed, he sketched his adventure at Lar Tantril's ranch. "But here's what's important —Ku Sui is alive. He is to have a meeting with Tantril at Tantril's ranch. In five days. And the Coordinated Brains —they're still alive. So, Eliot, these are orders: prepare plans for infra-red and ultra-violet devices—one of them ought to do it. We want to *see* the asteroid when it comes. Friday you go down and get my spacesuit; it's cached beneath a big watzari tree just this side of Lar Tantril's. Go in air-car, but be careful. And then—" His head slowly dropped, he appeared to have fallen asleep.

"Yes, Carse?" Eliot Leithgow asked softly. But the Hawk was only making an effort to gather the threads of his idea.

"Yes," he responded, "the plan. Ban stations a man to keep watch on Tantril's ranch. We go back to your laboratory, where you'll make the devices and repair the gravity-plates of my suit. Then, four nights from now, if the watcher's seen no one arrive, Ban, Friday and I return and lie in hiding around Tantril's ranch. When Ku Sui comes, he'll probably leave the asteroid somewhere near. While he's at Tantril's, we capture the asteroid—and my promise to the Brains will be kept.

177

"Then—but that's enough for now; I'm so tired. Ban, will you—some food—"

Wilson, who had been listening eagerly and, at the end, grinning in prospect of action with the Hawk, darted off like a spark. A few minutes later, after his third mouthful of food, Carse murmured:

"We'll use your air-car to go to Eliot's lab in, Ban, but maybe—have—carry me—aboard. So sleepy. Wake me when we get to—lab."

On the last word his exhausted body gave up, and sleep had its way.

While he slept, the others carried out his orders. Within two hours Friday, in the ranch's air-car, had retrieved the cached suit, Ban Wilson had delegated all the affairs of his ranch for an indefinite time, while he would be away, and Eliot Leithgow had jotted down a few preliminary plans for the instruments which Carse thought might serve to allow sight of the invisible asteroid of Dr. Ku Sui.

XXX

Three Figures in the Dawn

Much of the fourth night after the Hawk returned to his friends at Ban Wilson's was sunless and Jupiter-less, nor was there a breath of wind; and in the jungle which largely enclosed the isuan ranch of the Venusian Lar Tantril the sounds of night-prowling animals burst full and loud, making an irregular babel of varied and savage noise.

In the midst of this archaic night, Tantril's ranch was an island of stillness. Within the high guarding fence, the long low buildings lay quiet and unlit, brushed periodically by the light from the watch-beacon high overhead as it swept its shaft in turn over the jungle smother and the black, glassy surface of Great Briney Lake. Vigilantly, the eyes of three Venusian guards followed the ray.

They stood on the platforms of the three lookout towers. Below, in the buildings, seemingly asleep, wide-awake men were stationed at action posts, waiting for the clang of the alarm which would follow the pressing of a button in any one of the lookout towers. Lar Tantril's ranch was far from asleep. It was as alert and wary as the beasts tracking through the jungle outside its fence, and all its defensive and offensive weapons were at the ready.

No one within the ranch suspected it, but within two hundred yards sat the man Lar Tantril and his men feared most.

Regularly the watch-beacon swept around, lighting the

crown of the jungle with a white oval finger, the farthest edge of which reached perhaps two hundred yards. Over the western lake it passed—to make its inky ripples sparkle ominously. Over the jungle's confusion it turned—to make trees, vines and spiky creeper-growths leap into momentary visibility, then again be swallowed up in the tide of night. Here a cutlass-beaked bird, spotlighted in a tree for an instant, froze into surprised immobility, its nasty prey squirming in its mouth; there the coils of a seekan, lying in ambush on a branch, glittered in the sudden moment of illumination; or a nameless huge-eyed reptilian monster showed stark as it clawed at a nest of unfledged harees, while the frantic mother beat at it with wings and claws. . . .

But all this was usual, the ordinary routine of the jungle at night. Could the beacon have reached out another fifty yards, the guards on their towers might have seen something not usual at all—and would have summoned every weapon of the ranch below.

Or could the guards have heard, under the cries and crashings and yowls of the jungle folk, the man-intelligence carried on the tight radio beams which sped silently back and forth across the ranch—then, too, the alarm would have clanged.

The reaching beacon would have fallen upon a massive watzari tree, taller than most; and the guards, looking close, might have sighted in one notch of the tree's many limbs a glint of metal; might have detected, had the light held on that spot, a bloated gray thing that stood braced there, largely concealed behind a screen of leaves.

This gray thing, not native to the jungle, and odd, indeed, standing in a tree, was posted due north of the ranch. Another such thing waited to the south, in a similarly large tree; and another to the east.

Hawk Carse and his friends were abroad again, waiting to strike.

180

Ban Wilson, hot, itching and uncomfortable inside the spacesuit he wore, and restless as always, watched the ranch's beacon sweeping past him thirty or more yards away, and again sought relief from discomfort and tedium in conversation.

"Jupiter should be rising soon, Carse—right now's the darkest hour. Seems to me this is the most likely time for him to come. What do you think?"

Ban was the one posted south of Tantril's ranch. Carried on the tight beam of his helmet radio, which had been tuned by Eliot Leithgow so as to reach only two other radios, the words rang simultaneously in the receivers of Friday, who was east of the ranch, and Carse, who was north.

The Hawk responded curtly:

"I don't know when he'll come. It may not be till late in the sun-day.

Ban Wilson grunted at this discouraging possibility and for the hundredth time raised to his eyes the instrument that hung by a cord from the neckpiece of his suit. Through it, he slowly and methodically scanned the portion of black sky that had been assigned to him. The instrument would have resembled a bulky electro-binocular with its twin tubes and eyepieces, had not there been an additional element underneath the tubes, a small box containing components which by Leithgow-magic permitted observation of infra-red-lighted reality by one tube, and ultra-violet-lighted reality by the other.

"Nothing!" Ban muttered to himself, lowering the device. "And may Ku Sui sizzle for making these spacesuits so infernally uncomfortable! Why didn't he make 'em space-ships, with cot and kitchen, while he was at it! . . . Say, Carse," he began again, "maybe Dr. Ku's come already. I know my men said no one had arrived at the ranch in a propulsive suit like these—but hell, if his whole asteroid's invisible, why couldn't he make his spacesuits invisible, too?"

"It's not likely," the adventurer answered. He raised his tone incisively. "Now, both of you, quiet! Conceal yourselves carefully—Jupiter's rising!"

The western horizon, a moment before indistinguishable above the Great Briney, was now faintly flushed, a flush which steadily deepened and widened into a rosy arch which encompassed all that sector of the sky and sent long streamers out over the surface of the water, sparkling it with faint color. Soon, as the first feeble rays filtered into the matted gloom of tree and vine and bush, the night creatures began looking to their lairs, so that gradually their many-throated noises waned and then died altogether into the heavy, brooding hush that comes always with dawn over the jungles of Satellite III.

Jupiter thrust part of his bright arch upwards over the horizon, and climbed with his vast blood-blotched bulk into a sky now turned blue. Lake and jungle sharpened under the rapidly dissipating night vapors. The ranch beacon paled into unimportance. Jupiter-day had come.

And now the three figures crouched back behind the leaves of the trees that concealed them, and waited more tensely. Each one could see, through the intervening growth, the watch-towers of the ranch; but Friday, from his post in the tree to the east, could see the area best, and it was he to whom Carse's next words were addressed.

"Friday," he called, "do the guards in the towers seem to notice anything?"

The big Negro moved carefully for a better view.

"No, sir. I'm sure they don't suspect us at all. They're just pacing around on their towers, kind of nervous."

"Anyone else in sight?"

"No, sir. . . . Oh, now, there's something. Two of the guards are looking below, hands at their ears. Someone down there is telling them something. Now they're looking up to the sky—the northern sky. Yes, all three of them! They're expecting someone, sure enough!"

"Good. He must be coming. Use your glasses."

Then in all three trees the instruments that Eliot Leithgow had devised were raised, and the whole sweep of the horizon, and all the glowing, clear blue dome of the sky, was subjected to minute inspection. Ban Wilson, perhaps, looked most eagerly, for he had a violent interest in Ku Sui's asteroid, and still could hardly believe that one mile of craggy rock could be swung as its master willed in space.

But he saw nothing in the sky; nothing looming gigantically over any part of the horizon. He reported:

"Don't see anything, Carse."

"Don't see anything either, sir," the Negro's deep voice added. Both of them heard the Hawk murmur:

"Nor do I. But—ah! There! Careful! They're coming!"

"Where? Where is it?" yapped Ban excitedly, jerking the instrument to his eyes again.

"Speak low. Not the asteroid. Three men."

For a minute there was silence among them. Then, in a low crisp voice, the Hawk said:

"Three men in propulsive suits like ours, coming from the north straight for Tantril's. Visible to the unaided eye. Ban, you may not be able to see them till they get to the ranch, so keep hunting for the asteroid with your glasses. Friday, you see them?"

"Yes, now I do! Three! One ahead of the others!"

"Glue your eyes on them. No talking now from either of you unless it's important."

The incisive voice snapped off. Carefully, in his tree, Hawk Carse brushed aside a fringe of leaves and concentrated on the three figures brought by the dawn.

Hard and sharp they stood out in the flood of ruddy Jupiter-light, grotesque figures in spacesuits with transparent face-plates and large top-knobbed helmets and boots with thick soles like their own. They came gliding serenely, in vertical position, without sound or motion of limbs. They came rapidly, fifty feet above the crown of the jungle,

183

sparkling shapes in beautiful horizontal transit against the blue sky. One flew slightly in the lead—Ku Sui, the watching Hawk felt sure, the other two subordinates or attendants, probably men whose brains he had violated and were now dehumanized.

Straight in, without hesitation, the three figures glided, closer and closer to the watching man in the tree. More than ever did the Hawk feel that the leader was his old enemy. Into his eyes came a trace of the cold, deadly look that was talked of and feared throughout space, wherever outlaws walked or flew. Ku Sui—so close! There—in that even-gliding vertical figure, the author of the infamy done to Leithgow, of the crime to the Brains that lived though their bodies were dead. Capture the man now? The thought was in Carse's mind—but it was only a thought. Far too dangerous to try, with the powerful, watching ranch so close. He could not jeopardize the keeping of his promise to the Brains.

And so the three figures passed, observed by two pairs of eyes concealed in two high leafy trees. They lowered into the clearing just in front of the ranch house.

The meeting was at hand. But where was the asteroid?

Through his instrument, Carse scanned the sky for the massive body, but in vain. He called:

"Ban?"

"Yes, Carse?"

"See the asteroid anywhere?"

"Nowhere! I've looked till my eyes—"

The Hawk cut him short. "All right. Friday?"

"Yes, sir?"

"Can you see anything special?"

"No, sir—only that the three platform guards keep looking down towards the center of the ranch."

"Good. That means Ku Sui's being received," said Carse; "I'm positive that front one was Ku Sui." He considered for a minute, then said:

184

"Ban and Friday, you both wait where you are, keeping a sharp lookout. None of us can see the asteroid, but it must be somewhere near, for Ku Sui would not take a long, uncomfortable journey in a spacesuit. I think the asteroid must be close down, hidden by that distant ridge in the direction they came from. I'm going to go look for it. If and when I find it, I'll tell you to come to meet me. Inform me at once if Ku Sui leaves or if anything unusual happens. Understood?"

Assenting voices reached him simultaneously.

"Be careful!" he said.

Slowly, the adventurer moved backward for a few yards, then floated down through the watzari tree on the side facing away from the ranch. Near the ground he poised for a second, then, still slowly, floated off to the side, feeling a way through the shrouding leaves. Once well away from the neighborhood, he rose and risked more speed, making a way through the treetops.

Up there, threading the leafy lanes along the crown of the jungle, lowering, rising, turning, sometimes doubling back, but always tending north, Hawk Carse glided soundlessly for miles. By now he could maneuver with practised ease, and his speed increased as the need for remaining unobserved lessened.

He was familiar with the landmarks of the region, and it was toward the most pronounced of them that he flew. Soon it was looming well above him—a long, high mountain ridge, rearing a full two miles above the level of the Great Briney, nearly as dense with species of bushes and low trees as the vegetation of the jungle swamps.

He paused at the base of the ridge. There had been no warning from Ban or Friday, but, to make sure, he made radio contact.

"Friday?" he asked into the microphone. "Any activity on the ranch? Any sign they're aware of our presence?"

185

Clear and deep from miles behind, his satellite's voice answered:

"No, sir. Dead still. I guess they're inside the buildings —except the guards, and they're taking things easy. Where are you?"

"About ten miles from you, north and a little east, at the foot of the ridge. I think I'll know something soon now. Be careful."

He started up.

At the top he stopped. His eyes took in a long, wide valley, of which the ridge over which he poised was the southernmost barrier. He knew at once something was wrong. Through his opened face-plate he was aware of an unnatural hush that hovered over all the length and width of the region before him—a hush which seemed actually visible in the motionless leaves of the nearby trees. All the small, myriad sounds of life seemed to have frozen, save for the occasional faint, muffled cry of a single bird.

What had wrought the hush? Nothing showed to the eye.

From where he hung poised, Hawk Carse lifted Leithgow's glasses to his eyes. Then, the valley was suddenly changed, the hush explained. A miracle lay before him.

XXXI

The Raid

Dimly through the infra-red tube the valley lay revealed as a great natural cradle for a mammoth body of rock. This was the asteroid, moved far through the deeps of space, brought now to the surface of Satellite III.

Titanic, breathtaking in the majesty of its great bulk, the asteroid of Dr. Ku Sui now was made visible.

It hung suspended, low over the treetops of the valley, nearly filling it and rising halfway up its sides—this asteroid created in a time unthinkably ancient, exploded into separate entity by the cataclysm that gave birth to the planets, wrenched by the genius of Ku Sui from its age-old orbit in the belt between Mars and Jupiter and made into a private world of his own, to be swung through space as he willed, invisible to all who might try to prevent his System-wide goings and comings.

Carse scanned the asteroid closely.

It lay roughly head-on, its nearest end below him, some few hundred yards away. He was looking down on the end where the life of the asteroid lived, where were located all Ku Sui's works. On a space planed flat in the rock, rested the familiar dome, a titanic inverted transparent bowl laced with spidery supporting struts—a half bubble on the inside of which men lived and worked and guided their unique world through space. Already it had been repaired. Clearly

187

visible under it lay the group of buildings, in the middle the precious laboratory which held the Coordinated Brains to whom the promise had been made.

Carse lowered the glasses, and again the Jupiter-light lay normally around him, the asteroid gone, the valley hushed and seemingly empty. He called Friday and Ban, told what he had found, and ordered them to come. Twenty-five Earth minutes after that he saw their bulky figures come gliding through the top lanes of the jungle far below, and then, soon, they were together, concealed in the high brush of the crest.

Friday was speechless with wonder, in spite of knowing beforehand what he would see. Not so Ban Wilson. He, after a short, comprehensive stare, during which the amazement almost could be seen growing in him, sputtered:

"By Jumping Jupiter, Carse—I never would've believed it! That Ku Sui's certainly a genius! To have that whole asteroid there, and to take it with him wherever he wants to go! Look at it! And that dome—"

"No talk now!" the Hawk said curtly; "we've work to do. Now listen: Those are two port-locks in the near side of the dome. We're going to enter the smaller one. There'll no doubt be a guard there, so to him we're Ku Sui and the two men who accompanied him. We'll have to chance recognition; but at least there's no difference in the suits we're wearing. We'll use our glasses all the way, for surely Ku Sui has to use some similar device. Keep your gloves opened, keep your faces averted as much as you can when you get near, and keep your guns handy in your belts. If there's to be gunplay, leave the first shot to me. You both follow me just as the two followed Ku Sui."

Ban Wilson suggested, "Let's go down into the valley between the trees, then up the face of the rock. The guard won't see us then until we're right at the lock."

"No, he wouldn't see us, but he'd wonder why Ku Sui was being so cautious. We'll go straight down and across,

188

in full view. We'll get in easily, or—well, we won't. Now, get ready."

They opened their hinged gloves, eased the ray-guns in their external belts, swung wide their face-plates, and fastened their instruments before their eyes.

At a word from the Hawk they set their controls, then all three, as one, lifted from the brush and glided downward and out toward the port. It was not far away, so they approached it quickly. Behind the dome, larger and larger, grew the buildings—the low four-winged central structure and the supplementary buildings, probably workshops and coolie quarters and storehouses, all dim and unreal through the infra-red.

As they neared the Hawk said:

"I see no men, do you? It looks deserted."

"There!" cried Ban, after a second. "There! Beside the lock!"

Just then, beside the smaller port-lock, a figure had appeared, clad in the glistening gray smock of a servitor of Ku Sui. His smooth, round impassive Oriental face turned to scrutinize the approaching men; and Ban, though he had never seen one of Dr. Ku's robot-coolies, knew somehow that this guard was one of them. Being one, he would be only a mechanical man, who could obey no orders but his master's. Now he watched closely the three figures who glided down on him, his hand at a ray-gun in his belt. The same questions were in the minds of all three of the raiders. Would he be suspicious of their glasses? Would he find something too different in them? Would he summon others of his kind from the guard-box he had come out of?

But the guard showed no alarm. He could not of course discern the features of the raiders behind the instruments, and merely watched. Perhaps he was accustomed to Ku Sui's scientific innovations.

At the outer metal door of the small lock the Hawk came to a stop, and Ban and Friday, behind him, followed suit.

189

They hovered there like flies, and, like flies, they were powerless themselves to open the door to gain entrance. Only the guard inside could do that; and he, through the dome to one side, stood scrutinizing them closely.

Apparently he was satisfied, for after a moment there was a hiss of escaping air, and the door stirred and slid down out of sight, revealing an all-metal atmosphere chamber and the inner door at the far side. At once, Carse floated into the chamber, the two others following close behind. The outer door slid back up into position, leaving them enclosed.

They were in almost complete darkness.

"It could be a sweet trap," whispered Ban Wilson. If that fellow—"

"Quiet," the Hawk whispered. "I think we can take off the glasses now. Keep alert."

They took off their glasses, and dimly saw the walls of the chamber with their unaided eyes. Then for a full minute they waited.

At length the inner door too slid down, and immediately Carse glided through, no longer attempting to avert his face.

The coolie, standing just outside the chamber, drew the ray-gun from his belt.

Carse did not shoot. He struck the man with his suit. The move was quick, but not quite quick enough, for just before the coolie was smashed to the ground he got out a high-pitched warning yell; and then, as he lay sprawled out, a thin orange streak sizzled by Hawk Carse's helmet from a direction to one side.

This time Carse shot. His gun spoke twice from the hip before his companions could quite grasp what had happened. Seemingly without bothering to take aim, he had cut down two other coolies who had come running from the nearby guard-box.

As Carse looked down at their bodies, he was startled

190

by another shot. He turned, and saw it was Friday who held the ray-gun that had spoken.

The Negro said apologetically:

"Sorry, sir—I had to. The other coolie, the one you knocked down, was aiming at you. I guess they're all three dead now."

His captain said in a low voice: "In spite of what some men have said, I never like to kill; but for these coolies, more robots than men, with nothing human to live for, I think it may be release, rather than death.

"Well," he began, more briskly, "we're inside, and apparently no one else knows it yet. I expected more trouble. I wonder how many coolies Ku Sui has left? About fifteen that I know of were killed when we broke through the dome—and now these three—there can't be many more. Of course, there are the four white men, his surgical assistants."

Friday asked:

"What now, Cap'n Carse?"

"A search." At once the Hawk started giving orders. "Ban, you go through all the outbuildings. Keep your gun ready. Whoever you find, take prisoner. Keep in touch with me by radio."

"Friday," he went on, "I'm leaving you here. First get these bodies inside the guard-house. Then keep sharp watch. It's not likely Ku Sui will return within fifteen minutes, but we must take no chances. At the first sign of anyone coming in, warn me."

"Yes, sir. Are you going to the Brains?"

"First I'm reconnoitering the central building," said the Hawk. "After that, the Brains. I want no surprises this time."

"And what about Ku Sui?"

"Later," he said. "I'll take him alive. It should be easy. All right, Ban—get going."

The three parted.

191

XXXII

A Startling Request

Carse remembered well the central structure of the group of buildings, shaped like a great plus sign. Each of its four identical wings had a door at the outer end giving entrance to a corridor that ran straight through to the central laboratory.

Carse skimmed swiftly, two feet off the rocky plane—now bare of soil—towards the end of the nearest wing, where he gently landed. He tried the door. It was open. Cautiously he floated through into complete darkness.

He was prepared for that. With his right hand he drew a hand-flash from the belt of his suit, and standing motionless, ray-gun ready in his left hand, probed the darkness with a narrow white beam. Spaced evenly along the sides of the corridor were many identical doors, and at the end a larger, heavier door which gave entrance to the central laboratory. He found nothing that moved, so methodically he set about inspecting the side rooms.

The doors were all unlocked, and he moved down the line without causing alarm. Door by door he proceeded, giving each room a quick inspection; but he found no one, and nothing that promised danger. All the rooms of that wing were used only for stores and equipment. When he came at last to the end of the corridor, he knew that that wing was safe.

192

He paused a minute before the laboratory door. He had expected to find it locked, but it was not. Pushing softly against it, he entered.

The high-walled circular room was dimly lit by daylight tubes from above. The damage he, Carse, had wrought when besieged in it a week before, had been repaired—ceiling and door. The place was deserted—it seemed even desolate—but in Carse's memory it held many people. There had stood the tall, graceful shape in pastel green; there the operating table and the frail old man bound on it; there the four other men, mind-altered men gowned in the smocks of surgeons. . . .

They were gone from the room now, but there still remained in it one thing of life that had been there before. Five things. They lay in the case behind the wire screen which stood near the wall at one place.

To those five things he had made a promise—but this was not the moment to fulfill it. There were four doors leading into the laboratory, four avenues of possible danger, and he had inspected but one.

An open door to his right revealed a corridor similar to the one he had reconnoitered. He repeated his methodical search and found no one. Then he returned to the laboratory.

Surely there were men somewhere! It must be that they were in rooms along the two corridors remaining! Gun still in hand, Carse listened a moment at the nearest door.

Silence. He grasped the knob, turned it and quickly threw the door open. He saw no one. Wary and alert, he passed through, and discovered that this wing was the living quarters of Ku Sui.

There were five rooms: living room, bedroom, library, dining room and kitchen, and he skimmed through all five, his gray eyes taking in every detail of the comfortable furnishings. There was much of interest to him, but it would have to wait.

He skimmed back to the laboratory and went to the remaining door. Bending his head, again he listened. A sound —a faint whisper? He was sure he heard something.

Ready for whatever it was, Carse pulled the door wide. Before him lay the control room of the asteroid, and the particular men for whom he had been hunting.

They were the four white assistants, each once an eminent brain surgeon on Earth, each now altered like the mechanicalized coolies, so that Ku Sui could utilize unhampered their skill with medicine and scalpel.

They were clad in soft yellow robes, and were seated at ease at the far end of a long room crowded with a bewildering profusion of gauges, instruments, screens, and other controlling elements. They did not show surprise at the bulky figure that skimmed suddenly before them, for, like the coolies, their features did not change under emotion— if they still felt emotion. All they did was rise silently, looking at the adventurer out of blank eyes, saying nothing, and making no other move.

Carse tried simple measures in dealing with them. With quiet but firm voice, he said:

"You must not try to obstruct me. You have seen me before under unfortunate circumstances, yet I want you to know that I am your friend. I mean you no harm; but you must realize that I have a gun, and you must believe that I will not hesitate to use it if you resist me. I only want you to come with me. Will you?"

They were simple words, and what he asked was simple, but would the meaning reach these violated brains? Or would there instead be the desperate reaction of the coolies, who had tried to kill him? Carse waited with anxiety. It would be hard to shoot them, and he knew he should not shoot to kill.

A moment of indecision—and then with relief he saw all four, with apparent willingness, move forward towards him. He directed them through the laboratory and, without

194

any sign of resistance, herded them down the corridor he had first searched till all were outside.

In the Jupiter-light he at once made out the spacesuited figure of Friday, standing motionless by the small port-lock; and, an equal distance away, moving around a corner of one of the outbuildings, he saw another similar figure. He spoke by radio.

"Find any, Ban?"

Cheerful words came humming back.

"Only one coolie, Carse. I disarmed him and locked him inside a room in this building."

"Good," said Carse. "You can see I've got four men—white men. I believe they're unarmed and harmless, but I want you to search them and lock them in that room, too."

"Coming!"

The distant form rose a little and skimmed low over the open area between, until the opened face-plate showed Ban's freckled, grinning face. He grounded awkwardly, almost losing his balance, then surveyed wonderingly the four assistants of Ku Sui.

"By Jupiter!" he exclaimed. "Like robots!"

"You had no trouble?" asked the Hawk.

Ban grinned again. "Nothing to mention. This has been soft, hasn't it?"

"Don't be too optimistic! When you've put these men in the room, relieve Friday. Send him to me in the labora-tory and stand watch yourself. If Ku Sui appears—"

"I'll let you know!"

Hawk Carse turned back into the corridor from which he had just come. Now he would fulfill his promise. With no possibility of a surprise attack from anyone within the dome, and Ban Wilson posted against the return of Ku Sui, he could attend unhampered to the promise which had brought him there. He reentered the central laboratory.

Quickly he rolled back the screen lying across one part

of the curved wall and stood looking at the transparent case that lay behind it.

There they were—the most precious of Ku Sui's works, the consummation of his mighty genius, his treasure-house of wisdom as profound as man in that age possessed. They represented more—the consummation of all that was un-human in the Eurasian. There they lay, helpless, bound to his will—the brains of five of Earth's greatest scientists, kept unnaturally alive, all their knowledge and ingenuity subject to his call.

For a moment the adventurer stood lost in these thoughts, a mood rare with him, until he was brought out of it by the arrival of Friday, coming as he had been ordered. Carse greeted the Negro with a nod, and said:

"There's a panel in this room—over there somewhere— you remember—the place through which Ku Sui escaped when we were here before. It's an unknown quantity, so I want you to stand watch by it. Open your face-plate wide, and warn me at the slightest sound or sight of anything suspicious."

Friday skimmed over, and Carse turned again to the thing of life and metal to which he had made a promise.

He was not at all sure how to proceed. The case was full of a pinkish liquid in which were grouped, at the bottom, a number of complicated instruments interconnected by a maze of spidery silver wires. Bundles of other wires ran up from the lower devices to the case's main contents—the five grayish, convoluted, brutally naked mounds that lay in pans— Brains from bodies long since condemned to death —themselves long since condemned to life—to an exist-ence motionless, unlighted, unseeing, unhearing, unhoping. Alive—and with stray memories, which even Ku Sui could not banish, of Earth, of love, of the work and the respect that had once been theirs. Alive—and made to aid with their knowledge the very man who had brought them into slavery unspeakable. . . .

196

The Hawk's eyes were frigid gray pools. He moved to one side of the case and pulled a well-remembered switch. A low hum sounded; a ghost of rosy color diffused through the liquid, and increased until the case glowed jewellike in the dim-lit laboratory. Now, the narrow gray tubes leading into the under-sides of the Brains were plainly visible. Something within the tubes pulsed at the rate of heart-beats. The stuff of life.

When the color ceased to increase, Carse threw a second switch, and moved close to the grille inset in a small panel above the case.

Slowly and gently he said into the grille:

"Master Scientist Cram, Professors Estapp and Geinst, Doctors Swanson and Norman—I wish to talk to you. I am Captain Carse, friend of Master Scientist Eliot Leithgow. Some days ago you aided us in our escape from here, and in return I made you a promise. Do you remember?"

There was a pause, and then functioned the miracle of Ku Sui's devising. There came from the grille these words, in a thin, metallic voice:

"I remember you, Captain Carse, and your promise."

That voice from living brain cells, speaking through inorganic lungs and throat and tongue! That voice from five Brains, speaking, for some obscure reason which even Ku Sui could not explain, in the first person; that dead voice, vibrations of air, which expressed the living thoughts that sped back and forth among the mounds inside the case and were coordinated into unity by the Master Brain, the one which once had been in the body of Master Scientist Cram. To Hawk Carse, man of action, it was a macabre miracle. Even today, to you and me, it would be a macabre miracle.

Carse continued:

"I have returned here to the asteroid with friends. Primarily, I came to keep my promise to you, but I intend to do more. Dr. Ku Sui is not here now, but he will shortly

197

return, and when he does I am going to capture him. I am going to take him alive."

He was silent for a moment.

"Perhaps you do not know," he continued levelly, "but the people of Earth hold Master Scientist Eliot Leithgow responsible for your disappearance. He is a fugitive, presumed to be your murderer, and there is a price on his head. It is my purpose to restore Eliot Leithgow to his old place by returning Ku Sui to Earth to answer for the crimes he has done on you.

"I am now ready to fulfill my promise to you. I expect no interruption this time. I regret my failure to destroy you when I was here before, but I simply could not do it in the little time I had. I still do not know how best to go about it. I am asking you to tell me. I will wait while you think. There is no hurry. Your extraordinary position . . . your thoughts . . . I understand. . . ."

There followed a long silence. For once the Hawk was not impatient; there was in him the feeling that the pause was only decent and fitting. The situation of the Brains was without parallel in history. They, captive remnants of men, had asked him to murder them. Limbless themselves, his hand was to be the hand of their self-immolation. The present slow-passing minutes were to hold their last act of consciousness. . . .

Then spoke the voice:

"Captain Carse, I no longer want you to destroy me. I want you to give me new life. I want you to transplant me within the bodies of five living men."

The words, so unexpected, gave Carse perhaps the greatest surprise he had ever known. He could hardly credit his ears. It was some time before he could summon even the most halting reply.

"But—but could that be done?" He strove to collect himself. "Who could do it? I know of no one."

"Dr. Ku Sui could transplant me."

198

"Ku Sui? I suppose he could, but he wouldn't. He would rather destroy you."

Almost immediately the artificial voice responded:

"You have said, Captain Carse, that you will soon have Ku Sui captive. Will you not attempt to force him to do as I desire?"

Carse considered the suggestion, but it did not seem remotely possible. Ku Sui would have opportunities to destroy the Brains while enjoying the manual freedom necessary to perform the operations of reembodying them.

"I do not see how," he began—and then stopped abruptly.

Something had come into his mind, a memory of something Eliot Leithgow had told him once. Slowly the details came back in full—and as his right hand rose to the odd bangs of flaxen hair which concealed his forehead and began to smooth them, a faint smile appeared on his thin lips.

"Perhaps," he murmured. "I think perhaps. . . ."

He said decisively into the grille:

"Yes! I think it's quite possible that I can force Ku Sui to transplant you into living bodies! V-27! It's something of Leithgow's! I think—I think—I can't be sure—but I think it might be done. At least I will make a strong attempt."

The toneless, mechanical voice uttered:

"Captain Carse, you bring me hope. My thoughts are many, and they are grateful."

But the Hawk had made a promise, and wanted formally to be freed of it.

"You release me, then," he asked, "from my original promise to destroy you?"

"I release you, Captain Carse. And again I thank you."

The adventurer returned the switches motivating the case, and the faint smile returned to his lips at the thought that had come to him.

But the smile vanished at once at the quick, excited words that came crackling into his helmet receiver.

"Carse? Carse? Do you hear me?"

He threw over his microphone control.

"Yes, Ban? What is it?"

"Come as fast as you can. Just caught sight of three men flying straight here. It's Kui Sui, returning!"

XXXIII

"My Congratulations, Captain Carse!"

A moment later the trap was in readiness. It had been swiftly planned and executed, and it promised well. Both the inner and outer doors of the smaller port-lock now lay ajar. Hawk Carse was gone from view. The only figure visible was one which lay sprawled face-downward on the ground close to the inner door of the port-lock. The figure was clad in the trim gray smock of one of Ku Sui's guards. Its presence there seemed to be mute evidence that the asteroid had been attacked.

To one entering from the outside, the figure was that of a dead guard. The man that had worn those clothes *was* dead, but his clothes now covered the wiry length of freckle-faced Ban Wilson.

Ban played his part well. His cheek lay on the ground, face pointed away from the lock; he was the decoy of the trap. He could not see what was going to happen behind him; he knew that his life was going to depend on the action and skill and timing of Hawk Carse; but he did not worry. He had implicit faith in the Hawk, and trusted his life to his judgment without hesitation.

Still, it was hard for the naturally restless Ban to maintain the pose of a dead man for the long interval before there came any sound from behind. The Jupiter-light, flooding down on him out of the glittering blue sky above, was

201

warm and growing warmer, and of course he began to itch. Had he had the freedom of his limbs, he would not have itched, he knew; he never itched, except when he had to keep absolutely still. He cursed the phenomenon to himself. Minute after minute passed with no sound to tell him what was happening behind, or how close the three approaching figures had come. Obviously they were hesitating, reconnoitering, and taking their time at it. Ban waited . . . and itched.

Then suddenly he forgot his imagined itch. His ears had caught a sound.

It was quickly repeated—a faint grating noise from the direction of the port-lock. They had arrived!

Ku Sui would be there—alarmed, suspicious, glancing about for the enemies that had killed one of his men. He pictured him ray-gun in hand—and guns in the hands of the two others behind him—glancing warily everywhere. And then approaching!

Ban lay without moving an eyelash, a dead coolie, limp, crumpled. He heard the crunch of boots come right up to him and then pause; and the feeling that came to his stomach told him that a man was looking down on him. . . .

Now! he thought—now! while Ku Sui's attention was on him! If the Eurasian should turn him over and see that he was white!—

It was centuries later, it seemed, that he heard the voice of the Hawk:

"You are covered, Dr. Ku! And your men. I advise you not to move. Tell your men to drop their guns—*ah!*" . . . .

The sound of the voice from the guard-chamber was replaced by two spits of a ray-gun. Unable to restrain himself, Ban squirmed over and looked.

He saw, first, the figure of the Hawk. Carse had stepped out from the guard-chamber where he had been concealed, and was holding the gun that had just spoken. Standing upright, close to the inner door of the port-lock, were two

202

suit-clad guards. Ban saw that they had turned to fire at Carse, and that now they were dead. But they still stood there—dead on their feet, held erect by the stiff, heavy stuff of their suits!

Dr. Ku Sui was standing motionless above him, and through the open face-plate of the Eurasian's helmet Ban could see him looking at Hawk Carse with a strange, faint smile on his beautifully-chiselled ascetic face.

Ban got up, taking a ray-gun from his belt. The Hawk came towards them, ray-gun steady on his old foe; but while he was still yards away, and before he could do anything to prevent it, the Eurasian spoke a few unintelligible words into the microphone of his helmet-radio. Carse continued forward and stopped when a few feet away. Dr. Ku nodded, and in a courteous voice said:

"So I am trapped. My congratulations, Captain Carse! It was neatly done."

The two puffed-out figures faced each other for a moment without speaking, and Ban Wilson fancied he could *feel* the bitter thoughts that lay between the two, adventurer and scientist, there met again. . . .

Carse spoke.

"You take it lightly, Dr. Ku. Do not rely too much on those words you spoke in Chinese. I could not understand them—but such things as I do not already know about your asteroid I have guarded against; and I think we can forestall whatever you have set in action. . . . Get out of your spacesuit."

"Willingly, my friend!"

"Watch him, Ban," ordered the Hawk.

Ku Sui unbuckled the heavy clamps of his suit and in a moment stepped free. He stood at ease before them, tall, slim-waisted, clad in his customary green silk blouse, tailored to the lines of his body, with full trousers of the same material, all set off by pointed red slippers and red sash. The man was incredibly handsome, with his beautifully proportioned head, his saffron, delicately carved face, his fine black hair; but half-veiled by their long lashes, his exotic green eyes rested like a cat's on his old enemy.

The Hawk moved close to him, and deftly patted one hand over his body. From inside one of the sleeves of the blouse he drew a pencil-thin blade of steel from a hidden sheath strapped to the forearm. He found no other weapon. Stepping back, he also got out of his suit.

"And now, Captain?" the Eurasian murmured softly.

"Now, Dr. Ku," answered Carse, once again a slender figure in faded blue tunic and soft blue denim trousers, "we are going to have a little talk. In your living room.

"Ban," he said, "I don't believe there's anyone who can even see the asteroid, but we have to be careful. You stay on guard here by the lock. Close the doors, and yell or come to me if anything occurs."

He turned to the waiting Eurasian.

"You go first, Dr. Ku. Into the laboratory, and then to the living room of your quarters."

They found Friday still on guard in the laboratory where he had been stationed. The big Negro, on seeing the Eurasian, grinned from ear to ear, and could not refrain from saying:

"Well, well!—come right in, Dr. Ku Sui! Make yourself at home. We're glad to have you come visiting!" He laughed again.

But his words were wasted on the Eurasian. That man's eyes were on the Coordinated Brains. Carse said:

"No, I have not touched the Brains. Not yet. But that's what we're going to talk about." He motioned to one of the four doors of the laboratory. "Go into your living room— and no sudden moves. I have a certain skill with a ray-gun. Friday, keep doubly alert now. Better take off your suit. I will want you in a few minutes."

Ku Sui led the way to the first room of his quarters, the softly-lit living room. A thick velvet carpet lay on the floor;

204

ancient Chinese tapestries hid most of the pastelled metal of the walls; books were everywhere.

Dr. Ku sat down easily in an armchair, linked his fingers, and looked up inquiringly.

"We were going to talk about the Brains?" he asked.

Carse had closed the door behind him, and now remained standing. He met the hooded green eyes squarely.

"Yes." He was silent for a moment, then, quietly and coldly, he went to the point.

"When I was here before I talked with the Brains and gave them my promise to destroy them. Just now I have again talked with them, and been relieved of my promise. But I have committed myself to an attempt to restore them into living bodies."

"So?" murmured the Eurasian. "Very interesting."

"Very," the Hawk said calmly. "And some courtroom on Earth will find more than interesting the testimony of the Brains, given from the mouths of their new bodies."

Dr. Ku Sui smiled. "Oh, no doubt they would. But, my friend—this transplantation—you accept its possibility so casually! Won't it prove rather difficult, for you who have never even pretended to be a scientist?"

"For me, of course, it would be impossible."

"As for Master Scientist Eliot Leithgow—I have unbounded respect for his genius, but brain surgery is a specialty, and this task would be outside even his capabilities. I know he himself would admit it."

"That is so, Dr. Ku. There is only one person in the Solar System who could do it—you. You yourself will have to perform the operations."

"Well!" exclaimed the Eurasian. "Is this lunacy on your part, Captain? Or is it a joke at which in courtesy I should smile?"

The Hawk answered levelly: "I was never further from joking in my life."

205

With a slight shrug, Ku Sui averted his eyes. He glanced around the room as if bored. He unclasped his hands.

"I am a very fast shot, Dr. Ku," whispered Carse. "You must not make a single move without my permission."

At that the Eurasian laughed aloud.

"But I am so completely in your power, Captain Carse!" He held on to the last syllable, giving it a low, sustained hiss—and then he snapped it off.

"*S-S-Stah!*" His mood changed; the green eyes unmasked, to show in their depths the tiger.

"What insane talk! To say such things to me! Don't you know that to coordinate those Brains I worked for years with a devotion, a concentration, a genius you can never hope even to comprehend? Don't you realize they're the most precious possession of the greatest surgeon and the greatest mind in the System? Don't you understand that I've fashioned a miracle? Realize these things, then, and marvel at yourself—you who with your gun and your egotism think you can make me undo my achievement!"

The tiger departed, and Dr. Ku Sui relaxed, his eyes once more masked. Hawk Carse asked sharply:

"*Could* you transplant the Brains?"

"You insist on continuing this farce?" murmured the Eurasian. "Really, you try my patience!"

"*Could* you transplant the brains?"

Dr. Ku Sui looked at the grim face with its eyes of ice. With a trace of irritation, he said:

"Of course I could! What I have done, I can do again! But I *will* not reimplant those Brains—and my will no one, and no force, can alter. Perhaps it is clear now? You cannot touch my will! In some ways you are competent, Carse, and there are certain things about you that in a small way I respect. But here you are helpless."

"Not entirely," said the Hawk.

Ku Sui leaned forward a little. In that moment, perhaps,

206

he first felt a little concern, for Carse's voice was altogether confident and assured. He attempted to sound him out.

"A gun?" he asked. "Torture? Threats? These against my will? Absurd! Consider, my friend—even if I seemed to consent to the operations, could I not easily destroy the Brains while ostensibly working on them?"

"Your cooperation can be assured."

The Eurasian's eyes flashed brilliant with intuition.

"Ah—I see," he murmured. "Compulsion with the help of Eliot Leithgow!"

"Yes."

The two gazed at each other, Carse with a faint smile, the other genuinely disturbed. For once, Ku Sui's armor had been penetrated. Carse observed a small change in his eyes, and he knew that the swift, rich mind behind those eyes was working fast. What would it evolve? Those words in Chinese, uttered by the port-lock—what would they result in, and when? That something would come of them, he never doubted.

But this concern did not show in his face. Abruptly, he said:

"Enough of this. We're going back to the laboratory. I have a question to ask you."

A mocking light danced for an instant in the Eurasian's eyes, then was gone. Gracefully, he got to his feet.

"The laboratory? Of course, my friend. As for the question, I'll answer anything—almost."

XXXIV

The Deadline

Carse conducted Ku Sui straight to Friday, who greeted them with another grin. Looking the Eurasian squarely in the eyes, Carse said:

"I have Friday posted here because of the secret panel in this wall. The one you escaped through before."

"I remember. Alas, if I had merely a fraction of your luck then, how different my present situation would be!"

"This panel is an unknown quantity," the Hawk went on, "and I don't like unknown quantities. I want you to show me exactly where it is and how it works. You can refuse, of course, but I warn you, that won't delay things long. I can apply heat to the wall, or apply a certain something else to you. I suspect you have guessed what I mean."

Dr. Ku appeared to reflect a moment, then he smiled.

"You terrify me, Captain, with your subtle threats of compulsion. I suppose I'd better give up the secret. Really, though, your concern is wasted, inasmuch as the panel conceals nothing more than a small passage leading out of the building. Nothing important at all."

Were his words a screen? Carse wondered. Something else seemed to lie beneath them. He watched the tall figure make a few indecisive steps, then turn back again, considering. The smile and the easy words might be a camouflage—but for what?

"Nothing important at all," the Eurasian repeated. "Come, I will show you. Friday—if I may so address you —over on that switchboard you will find a small switch. It is the one with a Chinese character above it. Will you be so kind as to throw it?"

The Negro glanced inquiringly at his captain. For a second Carse hesitated, then he nodded. At once he turned to a position facing the suspected section of the wall.

An enigmatic light glimmered in the Eurasian's green eyes. Both men watched the Negro go to the switchboard and place his fingers on the lever.

"Only a small passage," Ku Sui said deprecatingly as Friday paused and the Hawk crouched a little, gun on the suspected place.

Friday pulled the lever.

Immediately there was a small, sharp explosion. Acrid smoke billowed out from under the case of the Coordinated Brains!

Carse sprang to Ku Sui, gripped one arm and cried:

"What have you done?"

"Not I, Captain—your obedient servant, the black. Please, your fingers—" He removed Carse's hand from his arm; and then, smiling, he said:

"I am afraid that all your threats are now but so much wasted breath."

"You mean—"

"Surely, Captain," said Ku Sui, "you must have supposed I would provide for such an emergency as this. I chose not to risk your darkly-hinted method of compulsion, and so had Friday remove the need for it. The Chinese character above the switch stands for 'Death.' "

Frigidly the Hawk asked: "You've destroyed the Brains?"

"I have destroyed the Brains." The Eurasian's voice held a deep, unusual tone. He sighed, reflected for a moment, then seemed to rouse. "No matter, it was time. I am far

209

ahead of that work, great though it was. It had a fault. The Brains were immobile, subject to meddling. The fault was inherent in them, and now it has brought their death. . . . Well, next time will be different. . . ." He lapsed into meditation, apparently oblivious of the two men whose prisoner he was.

But the Hawk acted.

"We'll see," he said shortly. "Friday, watch Ku Sui closely; he may have other tricks." He strode to the case, pulled the first of its two controlling switches, and stood grimly waiting. As on the previous occasions, light appeared in the liquid, and steadily increased until the five gray, naked mounds showed clearly. When it came to maximum, Carse threw the second switch. He said into the grille:

"I am Captain Carse. Do you hear me? I wish to know if you are aware of what has just happened. Did you feel anything?"

Silence. Friday, close to the Eurasian and watchful, hung breathless, praying that words might come from the grille in answer. But the man he watched was there only in body; Dr. Ku's mind was in a far space of his own.

Cold, metallic words spoke out.

"Yes, Captain Carse, I hear you. I did not feel anything, but I deduced what happened."

"Hah!" exclaimed Friday, immensely relieved. "All bluff! No damage to them at all!"

Carse asked quickly:

"You deduced the explosion, but do you know what it did?"

Again a pause, and again the metallic voice:

"A vital part of the processes by means of which I live has been destroyed. It cannot be replaced in time to save my life. I shall be dead in about three hours."

The Hawk turned to Ku Sui. "Is that true?" he snapped.

"Yes, Captain." The words were a whisper which came from afar. A man was turning back from memories of long years. "Three hours is all that is left to them. . . . There is a flaw inherent in such Brains; it is just as well. . . . No, it is *best* so. Ah, Carse, I am so far ahead of you. But I tell you, it is a painful thing to destroy so wonderful a work of my hands. . . ."

Silence filled the laboratory for a moment. It was again broken by the voice of the living—now dying—dead.

"I release you from your second promise, Captain Carse. No doubt what happened was beyond your control. . . . I think I grow weaker already. Dying is begun. . . ."

Quickly the Hawk directed a final question into the grille:

"Within what time will you retain enough vitality to undergo the initial steps of the transplanting operations? Do you know?"

Dr. Ku raised his head at this, though he seemed only mildly curious as to what the reply would be.

"Probably for two of the remaining three hours."

"All right!" said Hawk Carse, decisively. He threw back the switches. "Dr. Ku," he said, "you've only succeeded in accelerating things. Now for speed! Friday, we're taking this asteroid to Leithgow's laboratory. Go see that the portlock doors are closed tight, then you and Wilson hurry back here! Fast! Fast! Run!"

211

XXXV

To Leithgow's Laboratory

When Friday returned, breathless, with Ban Wilson, they found Carse in the control wing of the asteroid, studying the multifarious devices and instruments; and seeing him so concentrated, they did not disturb him, but went to where Dr. Ku Sui sat in a chair and assumed the job of guarding him.

The controls resembled those of any ordinary space-ship of the time, except that there was much extra apparatus of unknown function. Directly in front of Carse was the directional control in front of its complicated mechanism; above his eyes was the wide six-part miniscreen, which in space would record the whole "sphere" of the heavens; while to his right was the chief control board, a smooth black surface studded with squads of vari-colored buttons and lights. These were the essentials, familiar to any ship navigator; but in this place they took on awesome values, for they controlled not the fifty feet of an ordinary craft, but one mile of asteroidal rock.

"Yes . . . yes," said Carse to himself presently out of his study: then he turned and for the first time appeared to notice Friday and Ban. He gave orders.

"Friday, you see the radio over there? Get Master Leithgow on it for me—tight beam. Ban, you bind Ku Sui in that chair."

Wilson was surprised.

"Bind him? Isn't he going to run this thing?"

"No."

"*You're* going to, Carse?"

"Yes. I don't trust Ku Sui. The asteroid's controlled on the same principles as a space-ship; I'll manage. Hurry, Ban."

"Cap'n, here's the Master Scientist!" called Friday from the radio panel. The Hawk strode swiftly to it and clamped a pair of auxiliary receivers on his ears.

"M.S.?" he asked into the microphone. "You're there?"

"Yes, Carse? What's happened?"

"All's well, but I'm in a tremendous hurry; I've only got time to tell you we're on the asteroid with Ku Sui a prisoner, and that I'm undertaking to transplant the Coordinated Brains into living human bodies. . . . What? Yes, transplant them! They requested it. No, M.S.—not now; questions later. I'm calling primarily to learn whether you have any V-27 on hand?"

Eliot Leithgow, in his distant laboratory, suddenly understood. Excitement doubled in his voice.

"I think I see, Carse!" he said. "Good! Yes, I have a little—."

"We'll need a lot," the Hawk cut in tersely. "Will you instruct your assistants to begin preparing it at once? And your laboratory—clear it for the operations, and improvise five operating tables. Powerful lights, too, M.S., and all accessories. Have someone stand by your radio; I'll radio further details later."

"Right, Carse. All understood."

"I'm bringing the asteroid right to the laboratory. Is everything safe in your neighborhood?"

"There's a small band of isuanacs foraging around somewhere, but otherwise all's clear. They're harmless—"

"But possibly observant," interrupted Carse. "All right— I'll clear them away before descending. Until later, Eliot."

213

Carse switched off the mike and turned to catch a shocked expression on Friday's face.

"What's wrong?" he asked.

"Dr. Ku could hear all you said!" Friday whispered. "He'll know where the laboratory is!"

The Hawk smiled faintly. "No matter. He'll never use the information. His ride to the laboratory will be his last ride but one." He turned to Ban. "Watch him!" he ordered, and went over to the control-seat.

"Captain Carse," the Eurasian said, "may I ask you for a cigarro before we start on this journey?"

Carse's eyes were on the miniscreen, and he turned them to his old foe for a moment. "Perhaps later," he said levelly, "—if we survive these next few minutes."

Ban Wilson squirmed. He could not refrain from asking:

"Carse, are you going through the atmosphere all the way?"

"No. Haven't time for that. Up and down—up into space, then down to the lab—high acceleration and deceleration."

He grasped the control-stick, then in neutral, where it held the asteroid motionless in the valley. He glanced at the miniscreen again, then checked over the other controls.

"Ready, everyone," he said, and very slightly moved the control-lever up and forward.

The men in the control room had no sensation of power unleashed; only the screen and the bank of positionals told what had happened with that first delicate movement. It was an experiment, a feeler. The indicators of the positionals quivered a little and altered, and in the screen the trees of the valley, that a moment before had been quite close and large, began to diminish to green mounds below.

Then came the accelerating sensations. Carse began to get the "feel" of the asteroid-ship, and his control grew bolder. Under his fingers the mighty mass of the asteroid quickly lifted outward at an angle through the atmosphere of Satellite III toward the airless gulf beyond.

With dangerous acceleration the gigantic body rose, and from outside there came a moaning which rose quickly to a shriek—a sound made by the passage of thousands of jagged projections as they clove the atmosphere. A mile of rock was thrown upward by one slight hand; and that hand further increased the speed when in thinning air the shriek died away to the depthless silence of space.

In one special screen lay mirrored the craggy back-stretch of the asteroid, half of it clear-cut and hard in the Jupiter-light, the other half lost in the encompassing blackness of outer space. Over this shadowed portion hung a faint glow, the result of the terrific friction of the ascent. In miniature, in the under miniscreen, Satellite III lay dwindling.

The Hawk was visibly relieved. He turned to the silent Ku Sui.

"I must congratulate you, Dr. Ku," he said. "Your asteroid works as smoothly as any ship. Give him his cigarro, Ban. Do you have one?"

Wilson produced a plastic case from which he extracted a long black cylinder.

"You will have to put it in my lips," murmured Dr. Ku. "Thank you. And a light? Again thanks. Ah!" He drew in breath and exhaled a fine stream of smoke from his delicately carved nostrils. Then he looked up at the Hawk.

"And my congratulations to you, Captain. Not only on your expert handling of my asteroid, but on everything else: your resourcefulness, your decision, your caution. I have long admired these qualities in you, and the events of to-day, though for me perhaps unfortunate, only increase my admiration. My own weak resistance, my petty attempt to frustrate your plans in connection with the Brains—how miserable in comparison! It would seem, Captain, that you cannot fail, and that you will indeed succeed in giving the Brains new lives in other bodies, so swiftly do you move.

215

He drew at the cigarro, and the smoke wreathed a mocking smile. "But I have a question, Captain. Perhaps it is nothing, but still——"

"Yes?"

"The living bodies into which you propose to transplant the brains—where are they?"

Hawk Carse's face grew stern. Frigidly, he answered:

"They are on this asteroid."

"Here on the asteroid, Captain? I don't understand. What bodies are here?"

"The bodies of your four white assistants, and one of your guards. I don't like to use these five, but it can't be helped. There is no time to get others."

Dr. Ku's mocking smile remained. He did not seem at all surprised. He puffed quietly at the cigarro and nodded.

"Of course. You have five bodies right here on the asteroid. Yes."

"I do not regret having to use the body of the guard," Carse said. "He is no longer a human being, but only a kind of robot. You have already murdered him."

"Altered him. But I see what you mean."

"I suppose you find it unpleasant, to have to reassemble these parts into five whole, normal human beings?"

"On the contrary," said the Eurasian; "you inspire a very pleasant thought, Captain Carse—though I confess it is not the thought you mention."

The Hawk looked at his prisoner closely. The words had a hidden meaning, but what? What was Ku Sui's thought? The man's manner was superbly assured. In the back of Carse's mind an indefinite anxiety appeared.

That indefinite anxiety was still there when, forty-seven Earth minutes later, the asteroid had returned from its inverted U-flight, slowed in its terrific drop from space, and lay hovering over the secret laboratory of Master Scientist Eliot Leithgow.

216

XXXVI

White's Brain—Yellow's Head

To Friday it was a bad mistake to reveal the location of the laboratory to Ku Sui. From him above all men had that location, up to now, been kept. Just a few days before, Hawk Carse had risked his life to preserve the secret. And yet now, deliberately, he was showing it to the Eurasian!

Nervously, Friday watched Ku Sui, observing that his eyes were alive with interest as they scanned the miniscreen. It was too much for the Negro.

"Captain Carse," he whispered, coming close to the adventurer, "look, he's seeing it all! Shouldn't I blindfold him?"

Carse shook his head, but turned to Ku Sui, where he sat bound in the chair, eyes on the screen.

"Yes, there it is," he said, "—the laboratory you have searched for so long."

"There, Captain?" murmured the Eurasian. "I see nothing!"

And true, the screen showed nothing but a hill, a lake, a swamp, and the distant, surrounding jungle.

That spot on Satellite III had been most carefully chosen by the Master Scientist and Carse as best suited to their needs. It lay at least a thousand miles—a thousand miles of primeval jungle—from the nearest unfriendly isuan ranch, and it was diametrically opposite Port o' Porno. Thus it allowed Leithgow and Carse to come and go with but little chance of being observed, and the steady watch kept through the laboratory's instruments lessened even that. And even if their movements had been observed, a spy could have discovered little, so ingeniously was the camouflage of the laboratory contrived to use to best advantage the natural features of the landscape.

At this spot on Satellite III there was a small lake, long rather than wide. At its shallow end the lake lost itself in marshy, thick-grown swamps; at its deep end it washed against the slopes of a low, rounded hill. Topping the hill was a rude ranch house, which to the casual eye would appear the habitation of some poor jungle-squatter, with beds of various vegetables and fruits growing around it, and with what looked like a makeshift fence to guard against the animals in the surrounding jungle. The ground inside the fence had been cleared, save for a few thick, dead ozi stumps, gnarled and weather-beaten, which did much to make the outlay look even more crude and desolate.

So desolate, so poor, so humble, as not to deserve a second glance from the lowest scavenger, the pettiest pirate ship. So misleading!

Carse had brought the invisible asteroid to a halt about half a mile above the hill. The minutes were slipping by, bringing the two-hour deadline ever closer, but he did not skimp his customary caution in approaching the laboratory. From the control room, he swept the beam of the miniscope over the surrounding terrain, and soon sighted the band of isuanacs Eliot Leithgow had mentioned.

Magnified on the screen they seemed but yards away, though they were wandering knee-deep in marshes at the far end of the lake. All their repulsive details stood out clearly.

More beasts than men, were such isuanacs (pronounced ee-swan-acs), so called from the drug that had betrayed them step by step to a bestial life in which they had no

218

strength, no intelligence, no light, no hope—nothing but their mind-shattering craving. They were outcasts, driven out of Porno into the jungle, where they lived and moved always in swamp and mire, searching and preparing and eating the isuan weed until some animal ended their enslavement, or the drug itself brought terminating convulsions. They were the legion of the damned.

This band of half a dozen was typical. They went grubbing through the slime of the swamp, sometimes snarling at each other, now and again fighting over a leaf, squatting down in the mud where they were, to prepare and eat what they found, their torture of mind and body momentarily forgotten. Rags, mud-caked and foul, partly covered their emaciated bodies; their hair was matted, their eyes bloodshot. . . .

Carse noted their position and looked up at Friday.

"Get the Master Scientist for me," he ordered.

The radio connection took only seconds. Carse said into the mike:

"Eliot? We're directly above you. All well?"

"Yes, Carse. The laboratory's ready. But those isuanacs —they're still outside."

"I've seen them, and I'm going to chase them away. Then I'll be down to you. Have the upper entrance ready."

The Hawk turned back to the controls. Taking the control-stick out of neutral, he moved it very slightly down and to one side. Ban and Friday, not understanding his intention, watched the screen.

The asteroid gently changed position. In the screen the band of isuanacs came nearer and nearer. Completely oblivious of the great bulk hovering invisible near them, they continued their grubbing through the swamp. Carse stopped the asteroid when he reached them, then lowered.

Its under-side brushed the crown of the jungle. The trees bent, crackled and broke, as if swept by a windless hurricane. There was only a moment of contact; but in that moment a square mile of interwoven trees and vines was crushed into the soil, and to the isuanacs the effect was terrifying.

They stared at the phenomenon. There had been no sound, no wind, nothing—yet all those trees had bent and splintered to the ground! For a moment they crouched motionless, their slavering lips open, the isuan weed forgotten; then as one man, howling and shrieking, they broke and went splashing off panic-stricken through the marsh.

In a few minutes the band had disappeared into the jungle and the neighborhood was cleared; and by that time Hawk Carse was again in his spacesuit, out of the control room and busy at the mechanism of the large ship-lock in the dome, having left both Ban and Friday to guard Dr. Ku.

Using the formula given him by the Brains, Carse opened the port-lock quickly, and swung inner and outer doors open. He glided through and away, and came to a stop far out. For a moment he hung there, a soft breeze washing his face as he examined the hill below. As he did not use the infra-red instrument hanging from his neck, the asteroid might not have been there at all.

A moment later, after a straight, swift descent, Carse landed on the hill, beside a particular, gnarled ozi stump. The nearby ranch house looked deserted, the whole place seemed desolate. The Hawk pressed a certain crooked twig sticking out from the stump, and a section of the seeming-bark slid down, revealing the hollow, metal-sided interior of a cleverly camouflaged shaft.

There were rungs inside, but Carse did not use them. He squeezed himself in, closed the entrance panel, and, carefully manipulating his gravity controls, floated down. A descent of twenty-five feet found him on the floor of a short, level corridor with gray walls and ceiling.

Carse skimmed to the door at the other end of the corridor, opened it, and stepped into the secret underground laboratory of Master Scientist Eliot Leithgow.

"Welcome back, Carse!" was his warm reception.

"Hello, Eliot," the Hawk nodded, rapidly climbing out of the suit but retaining his infra-red device. "You've lost no time, I see."

The elderly scientist, his frail form clad in a buff-colored smock, turned and surveyed the laboratory. In the center of the square room five improvised operating tables were drawn up, each one flooded individually with light from focussed flood-tubes in the ceiling. Flanking them were tables for instruments and sterilizers, and, more prominent, two small sleek cylindrical drums, from one of which sprouted a tube ending in a breathing cone.

"The best I could do on such short notice," Leithgow commented.

"Where are your assistants?"

"In another room, working on the V-27. All I had on hand is in those cylinders."

"Much?"

"Enough for twelve hours for one man, but the manufacturing process is accelerating; fortunately I had plenty of ingredients. Of course I've divined your intention, Carse. Ku Sui to perform the operations under the V-27. And it's possible, possible! It's stupendous—and possible!"

"Yes," said the Hawk, "but more on that later. I'm going up now to get Dr. Ku. I'll use the air-car. It's ready?"

"Yes," Leithgow answered. "But, Carse—one question I must ask—"

The Hawk, already halfway to a door in the opposite wall of the laboratory, paused and looked back inquiringly.

"What bodies are to be used?"

"The only ones available, Eliot," the adventurer replied. "Ku Sui destroyed part of the apparatus which sustained the Brains, leaving only two hours—now one hour—to complete the first steps of the transfer. I'm using those four

221

white assistants of his—you remember them—men whose minds he altered—"

"Yes? And the fifth?"

"A robot-coolie."

"Merciful heavens!"

"I know, Eliot! It won't be pleasant for one of the Brains to find itself in a yellow body. But it's that or nothing."

"Come, Eliot, we need speed! Speed! We've but an hour, remember, to complete the first steps! I'll have Ku Sui and the five men down immediately."

The Hawk opened the door and ran down the long corridor. Behind him, in the laboratory, the old scientist resumed his work.

"A coolie!" he kept murmuring. "A scientist's brain in a yellow coolie head! What a cruel shock, when consciousness returns!"

XXXVII

Ku Sui Becomes Cooperative

Hawk Carse had run to Leithgow's hangar—part of the hollowed-out hill. It was seventy feet high and nearly a hundred feet long. Its wall, like all the others of the hideout, were of metal, sound-proofed. Leithgow's personal spaceship, the *Sandra*, rested there on its mooring cradle, and by its side was his air-car, an identical shape in miniature, designed for atmospheric transit.

Swiftly the adventurer ran to the air-car and climbed into its control seat. He tested the controls, found them responsive, then pressed a button set apart from the others. At once the door of a huge port-lock, set in the farther wall of the hangar, slid smoothly open, revealing a metal chamber similar to that of the port-lock on Ku Sui's asteroid. But there was this difference: the chamber of the asteroid's port-lock was for vacuum-atmosphere; this was for water-atmosphere.

The clamps of the mooring cradle were released, and the air-car moved gently into the lock chamber. Behind, the door swung shut. On the pressing of another button there sounded a gurgling and splashing of water, and quickly the chamber was filled. The air-car was now a submarine. All these operations were effected by radio control from within it.

When the water had filled the inside of the chamber, the

223

second door opened automatically, and the car started forward through a long, steel-lined, water-filled tube. It continued so on even keel until Carse, watching through the bow window, saw a red light flash on one side; at that he tilted the car and rose.

A second later, the shiny water-dripping shape of the car broke through the surface of the lake that edged on the hill, and forsook the water for the air.

To an outside observer, the appearance of the air-car and its subsequent movements would have been incomprehensible. There lay the hill, desolate, barren, apparently lifeless; there, washing against its slopes, the lake; nothing more. Then suddenly a curve of gleaming steel thrust up through the muddy water, rose swiftly almost straight into the cloudless blue of the sky, hung there, then suddenly disappeared, and remained gone from sight, as if space had opened and swallowed it.

Using his infra-red device, Carse brought the car in neatly through the ship-lock of the dome, sped it to the central building, and landed lightly beside one of the wings. Debarking, he ran down the wing's passage and in a few seconds was back in the asteroid's control room.

Friday was sitting in a chair close by the bound Eurasian; Ban Wilson, more restless, was pacing up and down. The Hawk nodded in response to their looks of welcome and issued curt orders.

"All ready. Ban, the air-car's just outside; go over and get those four men and the guard and put them in it. Have your ray-gun ready, but don't use it if humanly possible. We're going down to the laboratory. I want speed. Hurry!"

"Right, Carse!"

"Friday," the Hawk continued, "help me untie Dr. Ku."

In a moment the bonds were off, all save those on the wrists. Stretching himself, the Eurasian asked:

"You are taking the Brains down now, Captain Carse?"

"No—just you, your assistants and that one guard, this trip. Master Leithgow and I wish to have a talk with you."

"I am always agreeable, my friend."

"Yes," said the Hawk, "you'll be surprisingly agreeable. And truthful and helpful, too. Now—outside, and don't attempt to delay me in any way. I'm in a great hurry, and won't be patient at any tricks." He turned to the Negro. "Friday, I'm leaving you here on guard. Stay alert, gun handy, and keep in radio contact. I'll be back soon."

"Yes, sir!"

Walking behind his captive, the Hawk left, passing down the wing to the air-car outside. There, Ban Wilson was bringing up the four white assistants of Dr. Ku and the one robot-coolie, all unarmed, stolid, apparently without feelings. Carse placed them all in the rear seats of the car's compartment, and set Ban facing them with drawn ray-gun. Then with a hum from its generators the car raised, wheeled, skimmed forward through the large port-lock, and lowered to the lake.

Dr. Ku Sui watched everything with an interest he did not attempt to disguise. There was being revealed to him the secret entrance to Eliot Leithgow's laboratory, and long had he sought for that laboratory, long pondered its probable location. No doubt, at various times, passing over, he had seen the barren hill and its flanking lake, but had never given them a second glance. Yet here, right *in* the lake, was the doorway to Leithgow's refuge!

The air-car lowered to the lake's surface, paused, and dipped under. The water pressed around, dark and muddy. Slowly downward the car sank, apparently without direction, until ahead, out of the blackness, winked a spot of red.

At once the air-car made towards it and slid into the tube leading through the hill. Quickly it was in the chamber of the lock; the outer door closed automatically behind, and the water of the lock was forced out; and then the inner door opened and the car, dripping, emerged into the bril-

225

liantly-lit hangar and floated to rest in its mooring cradle beside Leithgow's *Sandra.*

A minute later its passengers were in the laboratory of the Master Scientist.

Dr. Ku Sui with a swift glance took in the arrangements made in the laboratory; then his eyes went to a door that opened in the opposite wall, and to the slight figure in a buff smock that came through it. He smiled.

"Ah, Master Leithgow! A return visit, you see. At Captain Carse's invitation. It is very interesting to me, this home of yours, so cleverly concealed!"

Leithgow vouchsafed his arch-enemy no more than a look, but turned to the Hawk.

"You are ready, Carse?"

"Some preliminaries first, Eliot. These men, the four whites and the yellow, must be put in some place of safety. You take care of them, Ban. One of the store-rooms—lock them in. Your remember the way? Then, better get out of your suit."

Ban nodded, and led the five robot-humans out. Leithgow, Hawk Carse and Ku Sui were left alone in the laboratory, and for a moment there was silence.

How much had passed between these three! How many plots, counter-plots; how much blood; how many lives affected! The feud of Hawk Carse and Ku Sui—and Eliot Leithgow, who was the chief cause of it—here again had come to a head. Here again were all the varied forces of brains and guile, science and skill, marshalled in an immense effort on whose outcome depended the return of Eliot Leithgow to Earth, the restoration in bodies of the Coordinated Brains, and, indeed, though more distantly, the fate of all the tribes of men on all the planets. For if Ku Sui even now won free, he would proceed irresistibly to his goal, the domination of the Solar System. . . .

Three men stood alone in an underground room—and the course of the species Man was being affected by their every move. Large words, these, but the histories of the period bear them out. Though, doubtless, only Ku Sui realized how great were the stakes in the game taking place there.

Hawk Carse still was uneasy. The odds seemed all on his side—yet there was Ku Sui's almost imperceptible smile, his mockery, his mysterious words up on the asteroid, his smooth, unruffled assurance! What did these things mean? He intended now to find out. He said tersely:

"Eliot, I have informed Dr. Ku that he is to be the means of the transplantation of the Coordinated Brains to living human bodies, since he is the only person capable of performing the operations. He does not believe that we can force him to do our will, yet all the same he took no chances: he started the death of the Brains. We shall have to work very fast. But I think Dr. Ku has another card to play against us, and I don't know what it is. You and I are going to find out what's in his mind—right now."

"I somehow feel that you mistrust me," interposed the Eurasian with mock sadness. "Ah, if you *could* only read my mind. . . . Or can you? Is that what you are coming to?"

The Hawk glanced at Leithgow. Leithgow nodded, and placed a metal chair close to one of the cylindrical drums —the one fitted with a tube and breathing cone.

"Sit there, Dr. Ku," Carse ordered.

The green eyes scanned the drum.

"A gas, Master Leithgow?"

"That is all. Not harmful, not painful."

"I see. Well, I expected it," the Eurasian murmured. Suddenly he smiled at the two men facing him, and said to Carse almost pleasantly:

"Things repeat! Not long ago I asked you to sit in a chair and submit to a treatment of mine, and you did as I asked. After so gallant a precedent, how could I refuse? All right, Master Leithgow, your gas!"

227

With skillful fingers Eliot Leithgow fitted the cone on the Eurasian's face and fastened it there. He placed the fingers of one hand on a vein in Dr. Ku's wrist; with the other hand he pulled a control set to the side of the drum. A ticking and slight hissing became audible, and two indicators on the drum quivered and crept to the side.

A minute of this—the ticking and soft hissing, the indicator's slow fall, the green-clad figure in the chair, watched closely by Carse on one side and Eliot Leithgow on the other—and a change was apparent. A ripple flowed over the Eurasian's soft garments; his body appeared to loosen up, to become free of muscular tension. The gas hissed on.

"The first step," murmured Leithgow abstractedly, out of his concentration on dials and patient. "The muscles—notice—relaxed. The will—the ego—the nexus of emotions and volitions which oppose external direction—all being worked upon, submerged, neutralized— but not his knowledge, not his skill. No—all that he will retain! You'll notice nothing more until you see his eyes. A few minutes. What says the red hand? Thirteen. At nineteen it should be completed."

Carse watched intently. It was wonderful to know that when the correct amount of this substance, which he knew only as V-27, had been administered, and Ku Sui awoke, there would be no enmity in him, no opposition to their demands, no fencing with wits; that this same Ku Sui, his great mentality unimpaired, would be subservient to their will and entirely dependable.

"Seventeen," murmured the old scientist. "Eighteen. . . . Now!" With a flick of his fingers he shut off the stream of V-27 and unloosened the cone from Dr. Ku's face.

The ascetic features were in repose, the eyelids closed, their long black lashes lying quietly against the delicate saffron of the skin. Dr. Ku Sui seemed resting in dreamless sleep. But for only a moment. Soon the eyelids quivered

228

and slowly opened. At once a great change was apparent in the man's green eyes.

Many observers have recorded that under the hooded, enigmatic eyes of Dr. Ku Sui there lurked a glimmer of evil fire. No doubt the observers who met these eyes always imagined the evil, being conscious of the devil and the tiger in the man. But Carse and Leithgow now saw that the fire was gone.

No veil lay over the green eyes now, no spark of evil showed in them. They were clear and serene; they hid nothing; almost, they were the eyes of an innocent child. This Dr. Ku Sui of a hundred schemes, a score of plots—this monstrous egotist of magnificent capacity and untiring brain, bearing ever toward his despotic goal—it was as if he had been dipped into a magic pool whose waters had given him innocence and eyes of peace. . . .

The Eurasian breathed deeply, then smiled at the two men standing by him.

"Now," whispered Eliot Leithgow. "Ask him anything. He will answer truthfully."

The Hawk lost no time. He asked:

"Dr. Ku, you will perform the brain operation for us?"

"Yes, my friend."

The man's tone was different. Gone was the suaveness, the customary polite mockery; it was frank, open, pleasant.

"Is it true, Dr. Ku, that your Coordinated Brains will die, if left in their case?"

"Yes, they will die, if left there."

"Within what time, to save them, must the operations to transplant them into human bodies be started?"

"Within about thirty minutes."

"Can all five Brains be given the initial steps for transplantation into the heads of your four white assistants and the guard within thirty minutes—the remaining part of the two hours the Brains said they would retain the necessary vitality?"

229

Dr. Ku smiled and released a thunderbolt. There was no malice in it. He simply told what he knew to be the truth.

"By fast work the steps could be taken and the Brains saved, though the subsequent operations would take weeks. But the Brains can't be transplanted into the heads of my four white assistants."

"What?" Both the Hawk and Leithgow cried out together. "They can't?"

Dr. Ku looked at them as though astonished.

"Why, no, my friends! I wish I were able to, but I cannot perform the operations by myself, unaided. That would be impossible! . . . You seem startled. Surely you must have supposed that those assistants might be vital to the work! I have taught them, you see; trained them; they were specialists in brain surgery to begin with, and I do not believe there are any other surgeons this side of Mars who could take their place in operations of this type. Without them, I could never transplant the Brains."

This, then, had been the trick up his sleeve! This was why, in the control room of the asteroid, he had shown relief when the Hawk told him what bodies were to be used for the transplantation! For he had known that, whatever Eliot Leithgow's method of forcing him to perform the operations might be, the Coordinated Brains simply could not be put in the heads of his four assistants—because the assistants were themselves needed for the operations!

"Then—it's hopeless!" said the Master Scientist bitterly. "All this for nothing!" He sat there, overwhelmed. "You might find other bodies in Port o' Porno, Carse—condemned men, criminals—but Porno's an hour away, two hours' round trip, and in thirty minutes the Brains will be too weak to save. . . ."

"I am sorry," Ku Sui continued. "I should have told you before, perhaps. If there were any way out, I would tell you; but there does not seem to be any way."

"Yes," broke in Hawk Carse suddenly. He added coldly:

"Yes, there is a way."

Leithgow and Ku Sui looked at him inquiringly.

"We need four bodies," he went on. "We have one—the guard; he is not needed to assist in the operations. Four bodies—here, ready, in twenty-five minutes. Not the bodies of normal men, of those with life ahead of them. That would be murder. Four bodies of condemned men—men with no hope left, nothing left to live for. I can get them!"

He brushed aside Ku Sui's and Leithgow's questions. He was all steel now, frigid, intent, hard. "Ban!" he called.

Ban came running. "Yes, Carse?"

"Get into your propulsive space-suit. Hurry! Then come here."

"Right!"

Carse ran over to where he had left his suit and rapidly got inside. As he did so, he said:

"Eliot, there's fast work to be done while I'm gone with Ban. You must take your assistants and Ku Sui up to the asteroid in the air-car and transfer down here all the equipment Dr. Ku says he'll need. Be extremely careful with the Coordinated Brains. If you possibly can, have everything in readiness by the time Ban and I return with the four bodies."

Ban Wilson skimmed into the laboratory. The Hawk gestured him to the door which led to the tree-shaft connecting with the surface and started to follow.

"But, Carse, *what* bodies? Where can you get four more living human bodies?" Leithgow cried.

"Later, Eliot!" the Hawk snapped, passing through the door. "Just do as I say—and hurry! I'll get them!"

And he was gone.

XXXVIII

The Four Bodies

Although puzzled by the Hawk's promise, Leithgow could only put his trust in it and go ahead with the preparations as he had been directed. He lost no time. He took two of his three laboratory assistants off their hurried manufacture of V-27 and with Ku Sui went out to the air-car. Passing by way of tube and lake and air, they were quickly inside the dome on the asteroid, and then in Ku Sui's laboratory, where Friday waited on guard.

Completely docile, the Eurasian indicated the various instruments and devices he would need for the operations, and they quickly were transported to the air-car. Then came the case containing the Coordinated Brains. Dr. Ku detached its connections with expert fingers, and he and Friday took opposite ends and rolled it with infinite care to the air-car outside.

"Do I stay here, sir?" Friday asked the Master Scientist in a whisper. Though informed of the change in Dr. Ku effected by the V-27, he was still very suspicious of him. "Seems to me he's a bit too meek and mild. I think I ought to go down and watch him."

Eliot Leithgow did not quite know what answer to give. The Eurasian forced the decision.

"I will need all the assistance you can possibly give me," he observed, in his new, frank voice. "I am faced by a tremendous task, and the use of every man will be necessary. I would suggest that Friday be brought down."

And so Friday came, and the asteroid was left unguarded. A mistake, this turned out to be, but under the circumstances Eliot Leithgow could hardly be blamed for it. There was so much on their minds, so much work of vital importance, so desperate a need for speed, that quite naturally other considerations were subordinated. The asteroid, to the naked eye, was invisible; it could attract no attention; every man found in it had been disposed of. Certainly it seemed safe to leave it unguarded for a while.

However, Eliot Leithgow took one precaution. Down in his own laboratory again, in the midst of the work of transferring Dr. Ku's operating equipment from the air-car, he called aside one of his assistants and instructed him to go and survey the asteroid through the infra-red device every ten minutes; and with this order the old scientist dismissed the matter from his mind, and turned all his energies to preparing the laboratory for the operations.

Under Ku Sui's directions his cases of equipment were brought in and arrayed, and the various drills and saws, and such other instruments operated by electricity, were connected in readiness. Everything was sterilized. Soon the plain, square room assumed the appearance of an operating arena, the five tables in a row in the center, spotlessly white and clean under the direct beams of the tubes hanging over them, at the head of each table a stand on which were containers of antiseptics, bottles of etheloid, a breathing cone, rolls of gauze and other materials, and along the edge of the stand identical, complete sets of gleaming steel instruments.

The case containing the Coordinated Brains was brought into the laboratory last. The inner liquid was now dark and apparently lifeless; to the uninformed eye, it would not have seemed possible that life was beating in the five grayish

233

mounds immersed in it. And, indeed, Leithgow looked at them doubtfully.

"Are you sure they're still alive? Do you think there's still time?" he asked Dr. Ku.

The Eurasian picked up a long, slender, tubelike instrument topped with a dial; then, going to the case, he touched a cleverly concealed catch, and a square pane set in the top swung back. He dipped the instrument he held into the liquid, and for a moment stood silent, watching the dial. Then he took it out, reclosed the pane and turned to Leithgow.

"A test," he explained. "The indicator, interpreted, means we have something like forty-eight minutes in which to complete the first phase of the transplantation of the Brains into human heads. It might be done if we start in eight minutes. But the heads—? He paused.

"Eight minutes!" said Leithgow worriedly. "Eight minutes for Carse to come! He promised the bodies, but . . . well, we can only go ahead with the preparations and trust to him. Is everything ready?"

"All but my assistants. I had better see them now."

The Master Scientist issued an order to one of his men, and the four white assistants were led into the laboratory. For these men, no V-27 was needed; their brains already were subservient to Ku Sui, and they would obey his orders unquestioningly, no matter what the work. There was no danger from them.

They stood motionless, their eyes fastened on their master, as he spoke to them.

"Brain operations," he said. "These"—he indicated the case—"are to be transplanted again into human heads. You have done work similar to it before; you know the routine. But now it must be quick. Synchronize your speed with mine; I shall be working very rapidly, and it is vital that you be in phase with me every instant. When the bodies come, you will prepare the heads; and then you will attend me through every step." He turned to the old scientist. "Operating gowns, gloves, masks, Master Leithgow?"

"I have your own. Over there. Your green smock is among them."

But Leithgow's answer was abstracted. Four minutes for Carse to come! Or everything lost! He busied himself helping the four surgeons and two of his own assistants into the white, sterilized gowns, then the masks that left only the eyes free, and then the skin-tight rubber gloves; but his mind was not with his actions. The old man looked very frail now; his age showed in the deep lines now on his face. Three minutes. Swiftly, two. . . .

"At least," observed Ku Sui, "we have one body, the guard, I had better start immediately on him."

"Bring him out," Leithgow instructed one of his men. "One Brain will be saved. But—*there*! Thank God! Hear that? They're coming down the shaft! It's Carse, returning!"

It was Carse. He and Ban Wilson were banging against the sides of the shaft in their crowded drop from the tree at the top. Leithgow hurried to the door, and looked out.

"You've got them?" he called.

"Yes, Eliot. Here—we need help."

The Hawk's voice sounded weary. Friday and the scientist ran along the passageway until they reached Carse, near the shaft. He was holding a limp body. He laid it carefully down on the floor.

"Ban's coming down with another," he said, "and there are two more above. Go up and get them, Friday."

The Negro started to obey. But Eliot Leithgow was staring as if he had seen a ghost. His eyes were on the body Carse had laid down. At that moment the parchmentlike skin of his face seemed whiter than usual. When Ban Wilson floated down the shaft with another unconscious body, the old man winced, and slowly brushed his eyes with his hands. He whispered:

"They're all—like that?"

235

"Yes," answered Carse. "There were two others, but we let them go. They were worse." The cold gray eyes looked steadily at Eliot Leithgow. "I know," the Hawk said. "It's bad—but it can't be helped. It was these or none. There was no choice."

Hawk Carse had fulfilled his promise. He had brought back four isuanacs.

XXXIX

Ordeal

Five bodies lay on the operating tables in Eliot Leithgow's laboratory. The air, hushed and heavy, was pervaded by various odors, particularly those of antiseptics and etheloid. A breathing cone had been applied to each of the bodies, and they were now locked fast in controlled unconsciousness.

On the first table lay the body of the robot-coolie, a man of medium size with the round yellow face and stub nose of his race. His short-cropped, bristly black hair had been shaved off, leaving him bald. That head was destined to hold the mighty brain of Master Scientist Raymond Cram.

On the second table lay a twisted, distorted body, an apelike thing with which fate had played grotesque pranks. It was hairy, of middle height, and its dark skin all over was wizened and coarse, almost like the bark of a tree. The legs were short and bowed, the hands stubby claws; the face, puckered even in unconsciousness, was that of a gargoyle in pain. His long matted hair had been shaved off, and the large pate washed with antiseptics. Soon, if the operation was successful, that head would hold the brain of Professor Edgar Estapp, world-famous chemist and bio-chemist.

On the third table lay a shape like a skeleton, so emaciated was it, so closely did the bones press into the dry, fever-yellowed skin. Of one leg, only the stump was left;

237

this creature had been forced to hop or crawl his way through the isuan swamps. The head was no more than a skull, with great sunken dark-rimmed eyes, discolored fangs and loose, leathery lips. There had been no hair on this death's head; it had long been bald; and now, washed, clean for the first time in years, it was to hold the brain of Dr. Ralph Swanson, Earth's one-time leader in the science of psychology.

On the fourth table lay a giant's body; but a hollow giant, a giant made thin and pitiful by the ravages of his destroyer, isuan. A roistering, free-booting space-ship sailor, this man may once have been, but isuan had twisted and shrivelled the mighty arms and strong legs. One ear had been torn from the skull, probably in a recent brawl, for the root remaining was one big festering sore. Behind that drug-coarsened face would be the new home of the brain of Sir Charles Esme Norman, wizard of mathematics and once a polished, charming Englishman.

On the fifth table lay a dwarf. Its ridiculous body was not over four and a half feet long, though the head was larger than that of a normal man. In the old dark ages on Earth this body would have served for the jester of a lord, or a butt for the wit of a king; or perhaps, in more recent times, as an exhibit in a circus side-show. The huge head, with its ugly, heavy face, the runt's body below—this was for the brain of Professor Erich Geinst, the solitary German who had stood preeminent on Earth in astronomy.

These creatures were the result of Hawk Carse's desperate search. They had composed more than half of the band of isuanacs that had been rooting in the swamp when the asteroid arrived. The Hawk had remembered them, and had quickly seen that they were the only answer to his need. So, with Ban Wilson, he had gone out for them, his mind steeled against the thought of the great scientists' brains in such bodies. In spacesuits they had swept down on them. There had been no time for considerate measures; all four had

238

been abruptly knocked out by the impact of the heavy suits as they fled in terror.

Eliot Leithgow had been concerned at the thought of a scientist's brain in the head of the robot-coolie; what was his horror when confronted by the need of using these appalling remnants of men! But he could not protest. What else was there? Ku Sui, under the V-27, had spoken the truth; the operations would be impossible without the aid of his four assistants. The Brains even now were dying. The choice was: bodies of isuanacs or death for the Brains. The adventurer had chosen, and the scientist approved.

Circumstances had combined to require their use. The request of the Brains; Ku Sui's attempt to kill them, thus setting a time limit to their life; the presence of the band of isuanacs near the laboratory: each circumstance had a long train of other, minor ones behind it. Chance or Fate, whatever it is, whether predetermined or accidental—men may wonder at its workings, but they must accept, however reluctant, its patterns and compulsions. Seldom, certainly, can there have been a pattern more strange than the one now being worked out in the laboratory of Master Scientist Eliot Leithgow.

The bodies lay there, washed, shaved and swathed in the customary loose operating garments; globules of etheloid dropped steadily down into the breathing cones of robot-coolie, gargoyle, living skeleton, twisted giant and dwarf. One by one the isuanacs fell back deep into unconsciousness—and *this* was their farewell to the brains that always had been part of *them*.

Movement began. White-clothed figures, masked and capped, used gleaming instruments held in skin-gloved hands; and all the figures in that laboratory were mute—mute from the alterations in their brains—mute from their concentration on the delicate work in progress—or mute from horror that would not die. . . .

So began the ordeal.

239

Of its details, Hawk Carse knew little. Probably he cared little. They were not of his world. Only for the first half-hour could he follow intelligently what was being done. He too had put on a white robe, as had Ban Wilson and Friday; and for a while he stood at one end of the room, a silent, watching figure beside the other two men of action, Ban and the Negro, while all the rest moved in a kind of rhythm. The center and focus was Ku Sui in his smock of delicate green—Ku Sui, moving from one table to the next, his slim gloved hands flying, pausing, moving again, steadying, concentrating on a detail, once more continuing the round. No more than single words came from him; he and his assistants worked as one, in perfect sympathy and coordination; and a constant stream of instruments flowed to him and then away, their task of the moment done.

The first table, and then to the second, with one white figure staying behind at the first, finishing off details of the work left by the master. The third table; the fourth; the fifth; then back to the first, while two white figures detached themselves from the main group and went to the nearby case holding the Coordinated Brains. An object held in a specially formed pan was lifted out and carried to the first table; and Carse sensed a crisis in the attitudes of the working men. This, he knew, was the first great step. A brain was to be re-born. The fingers of men, and of one man in particular, were fashioning a miracle.

How could he hope to understand? He could only hang on the movements of that group of figures, and feel relief as he saw them settle into smoothness again. Evidently the first crisis was past. A few minutes more were spent at the first table; then once more Dr. Ku Sui went to the next table, and another object was lifted from the liquid of the case.

And in a deep, open pan standing on short legs beside the case, something gray and shapeless and warm was placed.

The first phase came to an end when there were five

similar warm things in the open pan, and nothing, except the liquid and a multitude of spidery wires, in the case that but shortly before had harbored the brains of five scientists. . . .

A pause. Relaxation. Tests. The figure in tinted green spoke to one in light tan in a low tone of relief.

"Successful so far, Master Leithgow! We may congratulate ourselves on the consummation of the first step. It has been done well within the time limit, I believe."

"Yes, Dr. Ku. And how long will be needed to finish?"

"That is up to you. Normally, I would require a month. In that time all could be done safely, with small chance—"

"That's too long!" said Leithgow, with an abruptness unexpected in him.

Carse intervened.

"Why too long, Eliot?"

The old scientist went close to him and, in a lowered voice, explained:

"Ku Sui would develop immunity to the V-27 in a month. Two weeks of it would give him partial immunity. Even ten days might. He has to be re-gassed four times a day."

"But, letting him come out of it every night and resting normally?" the Hawk objected.

"I have allowed for that. The gas would still be in his system. No—nine or ten days is the limit." He raised his voice again to reach the Eurasian. "Can you complete the work within nine days, Dr. Ku?"

Ku Sui considered it. At last he said:

"That is a lot to ask, Master Leithgow. But— it might be possible. It would mean prodigies of concentrated application. We'd have to work in shifts, naturally."

So it was arranged. All the assistants, both Ku Sui's and Leithgow's, were portioned off into shifts of four hours' sleep and eight hours' work; Carse, Ban Wilson and Friday, too, for now every one of them was needed.

Nine days for the work of a month—and work as delicate as work can possibly be! Small wonder that in the minds of all of them—the Hawk and the old scientist, Bán and the Negro—that period, when remembered later, seemed no more than a confused, chaotic dream; or, rather, a nightmare time, connected imperishably with the odors of an operating room, antiseptics, etheloid, V-27, and the glint of innumerable small, sharp instruments.

It was a titanic task, an ordeal that stretched to the limit the powers of the men working in that confined space. Normal life for them ceased; the operating room became a new universe. They lost all consciousness of time, even with the routine of the changing shifts and the food which was brought in at regular hours. Antiseptics, etheloid, the never-ceasing flow of the instruments, the five bodies lying death-like on the tables, the hard white glare of the lights—all this —sealed underground from the life of a forgotten world above—on and on and on. . . .

It is impossible even to conjecture how the mind of Ku Sui regarded the titanic task that he was performing to aid his most bitter enemies. Even at other times, when his mind was not drugged, there were only moments when, through some recorded speech or action of his, we can see past the man's personality into his brain; how great a mystery must his thoughts remain to us, then, when held in abnormal bonds by Leithgow's V-27! Envision it; this arch-foe of Hawk Carse and Leithgow helping their designs, lending all his mighty intellect, all his great skill, to their purposes, aiding them in everything! Certainly, afterwards, the memory of what he had been forced to do must have occasioned him many bitter moments.

Regularly, every four waking Earth hours, Dr. Ku Sui was led to the metal chair and gassed afresh with the V-27; and his expression remained pleasant, his eyes always friendly. But the artifical state in which he was kept showed soon on his face. It lost its saffron clearness and became a jaundiced yellow, and it also grew peaked and drawn.

But the other faces around him were peaked and drawn, too. The terrific strain showed on all, no matter what stimulants they took to keep going. Many a man would have been driven to insanity by such sustained concentration, and the knowledge that five lives hung on every action, however minute. . . .

On and on and on it went, science made into a marathon. Four hours of exhausted, deathlike sleep; eight hours more of the smells, the glaring light, the stream of instruments. Days of this, sealing the Brains permanently into their second homes, into their hideous second bodies. . . .

But the climax came, finally, and the last spurt of exhausted effort. For the concluding twelve hours there was no rest for anyone. At the end of that session Dr. Ku Sui, a shell of his former self, reviewed the results of the nine days' ordeal. His verdict was:

"Four have come through safe, I think. The fifth—I do not know. His body was near death when he was brought here. But it is finished."

Then the men slept. Some slipped to the floor and slept where they were. In nine days, the work of a month had been done, and a miracle wrought. The Brains had been born again.

XL

Flight

It was to Hawk Carse that the news of imminent danger came first.

He had staggered from the laboratory into a sleeping room and, clad as he was, fallen over into a berth. He probably would have awakened in a few hours, from his custom of years to four-hour watches on ships, but he was permitted less than an hour of sleep. A hand pulled at him; a voice kept calling his name.

"Captain Carse! Captain Carse! Wake up, sir!"

It was one of Leithgow's assistants, a man named Thorpe. His tone was excited and his manner distraught.

"Yes?" the Hawk muttered. "What is it?"

"It's the asteroid, sir! I was instructed to watch it at intervals, but I—I guess I fell asleep, and just now—"

Carse sat up. "Yes? What?"

"—when I looked through the glasses—it was gone!"

"Gone? You're sure? Let me see."

Thorpe at his heels, Carse half ran from the room to a cubby just off the laboratory, the watch-post, where observational miniscopes with their screens provided a panorama of the surrounding territory.

One 'scope had been equipped with an infra-red device and trained on the asteroid. A glance at its screen showed that where the asteroid had been poised, there now was nothing. Only the light of midafternoon and a cloudless sky.

244

Carse changed the adjustment. Nothing came to sight. The heavens were bare. The asteroid was gone.

Quickly, the Hawk found a reason for the disappearance, saw the consequences and made the inevitable decision. Vanished now was the long weariness of the laboratory. During the operations he had been able merely to obey orders and do manual work. This was a crisis; this was *his* work. He assumed command.

"Your lapse has imperilled us all," he said curtly to Thorpe. "From now on we're in great danger. Stay here and keep on watch, and sound the alarm immediately if the asteroid reappears."

"Yes, sir. I—I'm sorry—"

The Hawk cut him off with a frigid nod and ran to the laboratory, where both Ban Wilson and Friday lay fast asleep. Roughly Carse shook them awake, and in staccato sentences explained the news.

"The asteroid's gone. That means danger to everyone here. We'll have to evacuate. Ban, you wake all the men, including Ku Sui and his assistants, then come to me for further orders. Friday, see that Leithgow's ship is ready for instant departure. Quick!"

Alarmed, without questions, the two parted on their separate errands. Carse went to the room where Eliot Leithgow was asleep, awoke him and told him, too, the alarming news.

The old scientist took the news with spirit.

"What does it mean, Carse? What must we do?"

"Leave, Eliot—at once. We have no choice. Our danger while here is immense. In the hands of enemies, the asteroid could crush us like a fly, simply by coming down on the top of the hill."

"But who could have taken it? There was no one on it, was there?"

The Hawk said wryly: "I thought not, but—well, you remember the secret panel in Dr. Ku's laboratory?"

245

"Through which he escaped before? Yes."

"I suspected that he might have someone hidden behind it, and I intended to question him when he was under the V-27, but in the terrific rush of things it slipped my mind. Sheer carelessness, Eliot; I'm sorry. I should have suspected trouble, for when we captured Ku Sui he spoke some words in Chinese through his helmet-radio. Now I am sure they must have gone to some man of his hidden on the asteroid; and that man, obeying instructions, simply lay low, and then, when it suited him, took the asteroid away in search of allies. He knows Ku Sui is a prisoner here, and unquestionably he will be back to release him. We must be far away by the time he arrives."

"Yes." Leithgow nodded slowly. "As you say, there is no choice."

"But your work here is finished, Eliot," Carse went on. "If only we can get to Earth safely, with Ku Sui, and with the Brains in their new bodies, we will have done everything we set out to do. We have proof of the crime done to you, and we have Ku Sui. You will be restored to your old position and the blame put where it belongs. But we must leave for Earth at once! Who knows how near the asteroid is, or who's on it!"

"All right, Carse." The scientist got up. "What are your instructions?"

At that moment Ban Wilson appeared in the door, reporting that all the men had been accounted for and awakened. Carse started more wheels moving.

"Everything of value here must be transported aboard the ship. Eliot, you know better than I what to take, so you'll assume charge of the loading. Ban, you and all the men except two of Eliot's assistants will help. I'll need them to move the bodies. Send them to me in the laboratory. But first, be sure Ku Sui and his four men are safely confined. All right—let's go."

246

Within an hour the general evacuation was finished and the ship loaded.

The *Sandra*, Leithgow's ship, bearing his daughter's name, was a sturdy vessel designed more for comfort and utility than speed, and so her appointments, including offensive and defensive weapons, were limited. Her commodious cargo-holds were easily capable of accommodating all of the Master Scientist's laboratory instruments and devices, the volumes of his extensive library, and his great mass of personal papers and more intimate effects; could hold, too, much of the more important stores of the place, too, and its furnishings. The laboratory and its surrounding rooms were pretty well stripped.

The largest of the *Sandra's* cabins was transformed under the direction of Leithgow into a hospital bay, and the five cots bearing the unconscious bodies of the patients were put there. Though hastily improvised, this hospital was complete, nearly as fully equipped and as efficient as if it were on Earth and not in the belly of a space-ship. The chances of the patients for complete recovery were not diminished in any way by the sudden necessity for flight.

In a second, much smaller cabin, Ku Sui was confined by himself. Its walls, of course, were of metal, and there was no means of exit from it save the door, which bore double locks. The Eurasian, silent and drugged and dull, immediately stretched out on the single berth and was again sound asleep. A third cabin was made over to his four assistants.

With everything completed, the underground refuge largely bare of articles of value and the *Sandra* made ready for her long trip, the ship was floated slowly out of her cradle and into the water chamber. Her flight to Earth had begun.

Eliot Leithgow stood near the Hawk in the control cabin, and his lined face was sad with many memories. For years, this place that he was now leaving had been his only home, his one sure haven. How carefully he and Carse had planned and built it! How many times had they met there, often when danger was close and enemies near, and cemented still more firmly the bonds between them! To Leithgow, the hill symbolized safety and friendship and his beloved work. Those were dangerous, weary years he had spent in the hill, but they were priceless nevertheless, warmed as they were by his achievements and the friendship of Hawk Carse.

Now he was leaving it and going back to Earth. The years of exile, it seemed, were ended; Ku Sui was a prisoner, and the proof of his singular crimes was aboard. Earth—green Earth! Separate, distinct, peerless in the System; home of men of his kind! He had loved and worked and known honor and respect on Earth; it held the grave of his wife, and the fresh, warm young love of his wife reincarnate, his daughter Sandra. He was at last going home to Earth from his exile on this desolate, raw frontier post.

There was a choking in Eliot Leithgow's throat, and he turned away from the eyes of his friend. . . .

The *Sandra* lifted through the lake and launched herself, dripping, into the warm air of afternoon. Her generators hummed, and soon she was arrowing into the blue. With a few words as to the visual course, Carse turned over the controls to Friday, and devoted himself to the matter of the watches.

Satellite III became a concavity, then, as the *Sandra* passed through the thin outer layers of the stratosphere, appeared a true globe again. The Negro reported:

"Through the atmosphere, sir. Orders?"

"Full acceleration. Continue visually for the present. I'll start working out the true course in a few minutes."

"Yes, sir!"

The hum of the generators seemed to deepen. In a matter of ten minutes, shipboard routine was arranged—Carse, Friday, and Ban splitting the watches. The Hawk, as was his custom, took the first watch. Friday was relieved of control and immediately went back for more sleep, as did Wilson. Eliot Leithgow did not retire right away, however.

He watched Carse switch on the automatic control and go to a miniscope which had been equipped with an infrared device. He adjusted it for view toward Satellite III, back along the course the *Sandra* had taken, and watched the screen. He repeated this for views to the side and ahead, and above and below. Then turned to the scientist.

"Nothing," he said. "No sign of the asteroid. We'll have to keep careful watch. The usual screen is useless against the invisibility of the asteroid; and the high magnification of this 'scope, with its resulting small field of view, will require continuous, methodical search at all angles, in the attempt to pick up the asteroid, should it appear. A tedious job, with chances of sighting it not very great. At any rate, we may have some sort of a head start," he finished.

Leithgow had waited for this opportunity to have a few words with his friend.

"Carse," he said slowly, "I've been wondering where the man who is running the asteroid has taken it."

"I've wondered about that, too," replied the Hawk. "We may be pretty sure that he went for allies; Ku Sui has several on Satellite III. Of them all, I think he would go for Lar Tantril.

"Lar Tantril, the Venusian. A fellow of much self-confidence and one of Ku Sui's chief agents. At present"—he smiled faintly—"he nurses a special grievance against me. You remember how I tricked him on his ranch. He'd be very eager to pursue us in the asteroid if only for the opportunity of repaying me for that trick." The adventurer's left hand rose to the bangs of flaxen hair covering his forehead, and he murmured, musingly: "I rather hope it *is* Lar Tantril. . . ."

"You hope so?" Leithgow repeated, surprised. "When he hates you so? Why?"

"Lar Tantril is not notable for intellect. He's blustering,

249

domineering—pretty much a braggart and bully. Certainly he's no model of caution; and he's not acquainted with Ku Sui's asteroid, for he didn't even know it existed. He will be able to run it, of course, with the help of the man left on it, but I doubt if he will have the perception to discern the weaknesses in it. Yes, I hope he's the one."

Leithgow went on to the main thing on his mind.

"I'm a little worried, Carse," he admitted. "I've been imagining this as the end of my years of exile, and the resumption of my old life on Earth. But this ship is slow, and I see now that if the asteroid does pursue us and capture us. . . . What do you think of our chances?"

The Hawk pursed his lips slightly, and for a while he looked away and did not answer. When his voice came, it was tinged with regret.

"Eliot," he said, "I've been trying to find an excuse for my lapse, but there isn't any. It was the blunder of a novice, my not remembering to question Ku Sui about that secret panel. That was the cardinal point, yet it slipped my mind, in my preoccupation with the emergencies and fatigues connected with the restoration of the Brains.

"Our chances are not more than fair, Eliot. That's how it appears to me. I think we'll be pursued. The asteroid's far more powerful than we, and there's no telling what new offensive resources Ku Sui may have given it; I had no time to study the strange apparatus I saw in its control room. No nearby merchant ship would help us if we were attacked, for to them the asteroid would be invisible, and they'd think us crazy."

He paused. But seeing the somber expression on the other's face, he smiled and cuffed him on the back.

"But maybe we won't even be pursued, Eliot! Maybe we'll be too far ahead for them to catch us! No doubt I've made it look too serious, so cheer up! We're alive, we've got everything we wanted, and we're making full acceleration

250

for Earth! You know the luck of that man they call the Space Hawk!"

Leithgow smiled gently, then left the cabin for the sleep he needed so badly. Hawk Carse was left alone on watch in the fleeing *Sandra*.

A lonely, intent figure, he stood over the chart-table, working out their best course to Earth. Presently, however, he went back to the infra-red 'scope and adjusted it for view of the leagues behind. He could not detect any sign of the asteroid, but he remained looking for a while at Satellite III. There it lay, a diminishing globe, three-quarters of it gleaming in the light from nearby Jupiter. The great dark patches which mottled it—they would be the jungles. That scintillant sheet would be the Great Briney, with Port o' Porno not far from the margin at one place. On the other side of the little world, now, lay the hill containing Leithgow's laboratory. All going . . . going . . . falling swiftly behind. Satellite III, scene of so many clashes, where so many times he and Eliot Leithgow had fought off the reaching hand of Ku Sui—soon it would be millions of miles away. What adventures would he have before he saw it again? . . .

A little sound came from the Hawk, a half-sigh. Abruptly he called one of the men of his watch and stationed him at the 'scope; then he returned to the chart-table and the work of calculating their course to Earth.

XLI

In Earth's Shadow

Hour after hour and day after day, for a week the *Sandra* tracked on through the boundless leagues, the waxing sunlight beating steadily on her starboard bow, and her silent gravity-plates and singing generators bringing Earth ever nearer. Friday, who possessed an extensive knowledge of all the practical sciences, did extra service in the role of cook, and his regularly served meals disguised the undifferentiated hours of space into Earth-mornings, noons and nights. Watch in and watch out, nothing occurred to disturb the even routine.

As for the ever-feared pursuit, there was no sign of it. Systematically and carefully the men stationed at the 'scope searched the surrounding space, especially the region behind, but with no result. The disappearance of the asteroid, and the kindred mystery of who had been on it, remained unsolved.

Peace came to Eliot Leithgow's face, and the tiredness left his eyes. The long, hunted years were beginning to be washed from him, and daily, to Carse, he appeared younger. Often in the control cabin or over a meal he talked of what lay ahead, and the happiness Earth held waiting for him. There was his daughter, Sandra, whom he had seen last as a girl of fourteen, but who even then was interested in his work. She would be mature now, and perhaps eager

252

to help him in new work already planned. There was so much of it! Discoveries, theories evolved during his fugitive years—now he could complete them and give them to his old circle of brother scientists. All this was in his conversations; but secret and unworded in his thoughts were anticipations of the dear old beauty of Earth, the beauty for which his aging heart had pined so long. . . .

And Earth was drawing nearer.

Another week passed.

Twice a day the door of Dr. Ku Sui's cabin was unlocked and he was brought out under guard for several turns through the ship. Though they continued to dose him with the V-27, it was apparent that the gas had less and less effect on him. Eight, then twelve times a day they regassed him—that was as often as they dared, considering its ultimate effect on the mind—but more and more of the recent frankness and serenity of his green eyes melted away. Gradually the old, enigmatic veil came to hide their depths, and sometimes there again was in his face the hint of something tigerish and cruel lying waiting. They no longer trusted him to attend to the five patients. He seldom spoke. Once each Earth day, a reserved figure in an exotic costume of green, attended either by Ban Wilson or Friday, he strolled through the ship for a few minutes and was returned to his lonely cabin. Of all the marks his experiences must have left upon him, the only one apparent was his silence.

One day he forsook that silence and directly accosted Carse. He had a request. His saffron face impassive, the long lashes lying low over his eyes, he said softly:

"I wonder, Captain Carse, if I might be permitted a glimpse of the five subjects?"

Leithgow and Wilson were with Carse in the control cabin at the time, and they observed their friend closely, curious as to what the reply would be. They saw his gray eyes meet

253

the other's eyes squarely—Hawk Carse, the complete victor at last, and Ku Sui, the vanquished.

The Hawk answered:

"Your request is only natural. Certainly you may see them, and perhaps you will offer an opinion on their progress, which has so far been in the hands of your assistants. But I shall have to accompany you."

"You are kind."

"Take the controls, Ban," Carse directed, and together they left the cabin.

There was little visible change in the five bodies. They lay on cots placed in a line, sheets drawn up to their necks. It might have seemed as if they were asleep and would presently wake up; though in reality consciousness would not return for weeks, and normal consciousness not even then, if the healing processes were not successful. Bandages swathed the upper half of their ugly heads. An assistant of Leithgow's, at present on watch there, moved occasionally to attend them.

"I must ask you to stand back here, Dr. Ku," said the Hawk, indicating a spot some five feet from the nearest cot. His left hand hung easily near the butt of his holstered raygun; the position was not accidental.

Ku Sui nodded and perhaps noted the gun, but his eyes were on the bodies. He stood regarding his handiwork in silence, his face inscrutable, and Carse did not disturb him. At last, in a low tone he asked the assistant:

"The food injections were successful?"

The attendant nodded.

"I remember," the beautifully modulated voice went on, "I was not sure of one subject. Swanson's brain, was it not? Is his condition any better?"

"It is still precarious."

"Ah, yes . . . yes. . . ." He appeared to muse. Finally he looked away and said:

"It was a great feat. Thank you, Captain Carse. I am

254

pleased by this glimpse of the miracle my hands were made to perform. I am ready to return."

But at the door of his cabin he paused, and his eyes turned to the cold, firm face close to him. He said:

"I suppose, Captain Carse, you intend to bring me before Earth's World Court of Justice?"

"Yes. Along with all our proofs."

The Eurasian smiled. "I see. The proofs being the five monsters. Since there is no questioning those proofs, it would appear that Earthmen will soon levy punishment on Dr. Ku Sui. . . . So. . . . You know, Captain Carse, I find your caution a great handicap. You keep gassing me; I am locked in; and since I have observed no excitement aboard the ship, apparently there are no friends anywhere near me. You have stripped me of everything." His eyes lowered for a moment. "Everything save this ring."

On the forefinger of his right hand, set simply in a platinum band, was a large stone which in some aspects looked black.

"A black opal," said Dr. Ku. "I have worn it for years and I prize it highly. Perhaps at the last I will give it to you as a memento of these past years, Captain Carse." And he went into the cabin, where they gassed him again.

Another week passed.

Crossing the orbit of Mars, the *Sandra* arrowed on into the last leg of her long voyage. The sun was a small, flame-ringed disk on her starboard side, and ahead lay Earth, growing each day. Cheerfulness pervaded the ship, nerves were relaxing, faces lightening. Carse could not remember when Eliot Leithgow had worn a smile so constantly. It was natural, for to the old scientist and his assistants Earth was home, the symbol and reality of normal life amid the race of men.

But to Hawk Carse the Green Planet was not home. He was the adventurer and wanderer, the seeker of new places with the alluring lustre of peril. Earth was to him little more

255

than a port of call, and it brought him sadness to see how eagerly Leithgow stared at her growing face. Their parting was not far away now.

The *Sandra* logged off miles by the thousands. Then came the day when only ten thousand were left, and, soon after, five thousand. Deceleration had long since been begun. Slightly but unvaryingly the ship's momentum had slackened, until she arrived at the two-thousand mile mark, where the great mass of the planet filled all of the space ahead, and the well-remembered continents and seas lay outlined as clearly as on a classroom globe.

Carse leaned musing in a corner of the control cabin, oblivious to the well-meaning but toneless voice with which Ban Wilson, at the 'scope, was butchering a song. A gentle tap on the shoulder summoned him out of his study.

He turned and found that Leithgow had come to him. Carse smiled at the old scientist, and said:

"Well, Eliot, we'll be in soon now. Apparently we've made it safely, and there's nothing to stand between you and the day you've waited for so long."

"Yes. But Carse—what of you? How long will you stay? I only wish I could persuade you—"

"To retire, Eliot? Settle down? Became a bored, landlocked Earthman?" The Hawk smiled, and shook his head. "No, no, old friend. Oh, I'll stay on Earth for a few weeks; I suppose I'll have to, to testify before the Court; but after that's settled, I'll be going back. You know me, Eliot; I'll never change. There are a number of things I must attend to at once. My ship, the *Star Devil,* is still on Iapetus; I must find her and get her tuned up again. She's the fastest craft in space, thanks to you. Then I must make the round of my ranches and see how things are running. I've a lot of work on the Iapetus ranch, particularly. Then, there's that Pool of Uranium—not that I need the wealth, if it's there; but the search has killed so many that I'd like to take a crack at it myself. Oh, I've plenty to do!"

Leithgow looked at him, and there was deep affection in his eyes, and friendship as close as it can be between men.

"No, Carse," said Leithgow softly. "I suppose Earth will never get her gravity on you for keeps. But I hope you will come down occasionally to see me, and perhaps once a year, say, spend a month with Sandra and me in our—"

"*Carse!*"

Ban shouted the name. His face, turned from the 'scope, was live with excitement.

"Here! Look!"

"What is it?"

"The asteroid! It's close!"

In two strides, Carse was at the screen. One look served to verify Ban's report. The asteroid of Dr. Ku Sui had at last appeared.

It was not more than fifty miles from the *Sandra,* a craggy fragment of a world, peanut-shaped, and tipped by its gleaming dome. Its speed seemed the same as theirs, but its course was different; and to Carse, that fact immediately explained its sudden appearance. He turned from the eye-piece, with a face grown hard and cold.

"Well, it's happened," he said. "Instead of a-stern, they've been on our flank. Now they're cutting in, no doubt ready for business. All right, Ban, sound the alarm."

The harsh alarm bell rang throughout the ship, an emergency call to stations. Like a gladiator about to step sword in hand into the arena, the *Sandra* girded her loins and made herself ready for what at best could be but an unequal struggle. She was not designed for space duels. She was outclassed in weapons, weight and speed—in all save pilots. Carse, at the controls, snapped out another order.

"Defensive web on, Ban, and build up power for the ray-batteries."

As the echoes of the bell died, a piercing whine grew amidships, and shreds of blue light flickered along the

257

Sandra's outside hull. They were quickly gone, but they left behind an almost invisible envelope of blue which enwrapped the ship completely. The defensive web against attacking rays was on.

Friday ran into the control cabin, on his heels two of Leithgow's assistants. Carse briefly explained. "Friday," he ordered, "you take the stern ray. Ban—"

But Ban Wilson was watching the screen and had more news. Interrupting, he cried out:

"They must be attacking! A light just flashed from the dome!"

They all saw the light. The miniscreen, though it did not reveal the asteroid, showed the first weapon with which it struck—a ray of pastel purple which in a blink had leaped out and enfolded the *Sandra*. A shower of sparks crackled out from the ship's defensive web, but the purple ray held on.

"I think I know that ray, Eliot," Carse said. "What's on our speed indicator?"

The scientist gasped as he read the dial. "It's dropping! Much faster than our deceleration accounts for! It's a magnetic ray! Carse, the asteroid's stopping us!"

258

XLII

Scratch of a Tiger

Alone among them, the Hawk and Friday showed no surprise. They had felt a magnetic ray only a few weeks before.

"Williams," Carse said to one of Leithgow's assistants, "get Thorpe and go and dose Ku Sui with V-27. Give him plenty. Then both of you station yourselves, guns in hand, outside his cabin. We'll take no chances with him, gassed or not. If he tries to escape, prevent him. If you can't prevent him, kill him. Our speed, Eliot?"

"Relative to Earth, seven hundred, and dropping steadily.

Carse gave the controls to Ban, then went to the 'scope screen.

Squarely behind the *Sandra,* and within twenty-five miles, the peanut-shaped body had come. It was an ominous approach. While the *Sandra* remained pinned by the purple ray, the Hawk studied her aggressor. As he watched the asteroid, the others watched him; Ban Wilson fidgety, Friday clenching and unclenching his yellow-palmed hands, Eliot Leithgow anxious, with shoulders that sagged a little.

The forward speed of the *Sandra* decreased to four hundred miles an hour, and still the Hawk watched the massive body.

A sputter sounded in the radio speaker. Not taking his eyes from the screen, Carse listened to a heavy Venusian voice that suddenly spoke to him from it.

"Carse, I've got you! You've seen our ray, but have you

looked at your speed indicator? You're caught—and this time you're going to stay caught. You can't possibly resist the ray I have on you, and in a few minutes you'll be drawn right to our side. I advise you to surrender peacefully. No tricks—though there's no trick that could do you any good! I've got you this time!"

A frosty smile appeared on the Hawk's lips.

"I was right, Eliot," he murmured. "The asteroid was taken to Lar Tantril. He is our opponent."

Those were his words, but he did nothing. He only stood coldly watching the screen. The *Sandra's* speed sank to three hundred, to two hundred and then to a hundred, and the asteroid, which also, of course, was decelerating, remorselessly came nearer. Ban Wilson had every confidence in the Hawk, but finally the inaction grew too much for him to bear.

"Jumping Jupiter, Carse!" he sputtered, "—aren't you going to do anything? Use our rays! Try maneuvering to the side! Damn it, we're just letting them take us!"

The adventurer might not have heard, for all the sign he gave. The second hand of the Earth-clock kept turning; seconds built into minutes, and the minutes passed. The asteroid was only ten miles astern.

"Eliot," said Carse quietly, "get me one of your infra-red glasses."

He took over the controls again. Carefully he varied the forward repulsion and sent current of different magnitudes to the side gravity-plates, and the *Sandra* answered by slowly rotating, longitudinally reversing her position. Though still under Earthward velocity her bow turned from that planet and came to face the invisible asteroid. When the turn was complete, the men in her control cabin were looking straight ahead into the brilliant center of the pale cone of the purple ray.

Lar Tantril's voice again boomed from speaker, this time harsh with anger.

260

"Try no tricks, Carse! I see what you intend. You plan to suddenly *answer* my ray, instead of continuing to resist it, and so drive right past me and escape. But I warn you I have terrific power, and if you move towards me of your own volition, I can burn you to a cinder in three seconds, and I'll do it. You can't escape! If I have to destroy Ku Sui, all right—but I'll get you!"

The Hawk strapped over his eyes the infra-red glasses Leithgow now gave him.

Swapping ends had neither increased nor decreased the rate at which the purple stream was bringing the *Sandra* towards its focus—which was all of the asteroid their unassisted eyes could see. The space-ship's momentum continued to drop normally until the moment came when she had no Earthward velocity at all; then she started to move toward the restraining focus.

With his infra-red glasses, through the bow windows, Carse could see the massive body in considerable detail. There was the dome, a gleaming bubble now showing wisps of blue, from the defensive web around it; inside were the several buildings, and minute black dots which probably were the figures of men. There were many of them. The largest group was clustered near the ship-lock. The outer door of the lock was open, and it was there that the purple ray originated. Obviously the intention of the enemy was to draw the *Sandra* right in. Five miles now separated asteroid and ship.

Again the Venusian chief spoke.

"I warn you once more, Sparrow Hawk, try no tricks. You may see the men I have here, but you can't see my projectors. One of them is centered right on you, and my right hand is on the control that fires it. We have terrific power, Carse. Better not attempt anything!"

The Hawk switched on the extension microphone at his side. Levelly, he said into it:

261

"Lar Tantril, I'll make a bargain with you: a favor for a favor."

"What?" shot from the loudspeaker.

"I will agree to surrender peaceably when you've drawn my ship inside if, for your part, you promise to free Eliot Leithgow, who is aboard with me, and the five patients on whom Ku Sui operated. If you don't grant me that, I will oppose you to the last second."

"But, Carse—" the Master Scientist began, horrified; but his objection faded when the slender man at the radio turned his head and half-closed one eye in a wink.

"You will agree to that—and no tricks?" Tantril's voice repeated.

"I will agree to it. And as for tricks, what could I possibly try? Your rays could burn through my web in seconds, as you say: I know it as well as you."

"All right!" the Venusian replied decisively. "I agree. I'll release Leithgow and the five patients. Keep away from the controls and I'll draw you in."

Carse switched off the microphone.

"A hell of a lot Tantril's word is worth!" muttered Ban Wilson. Once more, surprisingly, the Hawk winked. This was unusual behavior. Friday began grinning. For once in his life he had guessed his master's intention before the others.

A mile and a half to the front lay the near end of the asteroid, on which sat the dome. Perhaps nine hundred miles behind lay the tremendous disk of Earth, her dangerous atmosphere all too close. In the very face of Earth, all three on a line, the ship lay linked by a stream of purple to the rough-hewn, errant asteroid. Half the bulk of asteroid and Earth lay sharply outlined against the black of space by the intense white light of the distant sun.

The asteroid neared to a mile, then a half-mile. Hawk Carse said curtly:

"Ban, when I give the word, put all the power we've got

262

into our defensive web. Load the generators; overload them; tax them to the limit. The web must be as tough as possible for five seconds."

"Got you, Carse."

"You've—a trick?" ventured Leithgow timidly.

"I think I have, Eliot. Lar Tantril might have caught on when I turned the ship, but unfortunately for him his brain is incapable of proceeding past a certain point. . . . Now, Ban!"

"Feel it!"

In answer to Ban's hands, the deck of the control cabin began to vibrate under the mounting speed of the generators in the power-room. The generators could not stand that terrific overload long: they would burn out. But Carse needed only a few seconds of it.

The asteroid was a quarter of an Earth mile away, seen through the infra-red. The dome loomed large.

"All right!" whispered Hawk Carse. "Hold on!"

With the words he unleashed full acceleration.

It was a risk and a big one, but the Hawk had it calculated to a fraction of a second, so, without hesitation, he took the chance. A little less than four seconds to reach his objective, he reckoned; a little more than one second for Tantril to release the asteroid's rays as he had threatened; therefore a little less than three seconds for the *Sandra* to be exposed to those rays. The chance that her defensive web could resist them for that long would decide it.

From almost a standing start the *Sandra* swept ahead, generators humming, her web a blue mist around her, acceleration at maximum. Straight through the axis of the narrowing purple ray she sped, a hurtling metallic projectile, thousands of tons in mass, her stub bow levelled dead at the dome.

After a second the asteroid bared its fangs.

A cone of brilliant orange washed around the *Sandra's* bow, and a storm of soundless sparks engulfed her. She was caught in a maw of fire, and held there for all the remaining seconds of her wild dash. But the seconds passed; the hands of Hawk Carse were delicate on her control; and the *Sandra,* now a little off the axis of the ray, struck the dome, crashed, wrenched terribly in every joint; and then the jolt and the wrench and the sparks were left behind, and there was around her only the deep silence of lifeless space.

At three hundred miles an hour the *Sandra* had nicked the upper plates of the dome and streaked on, unharmed!

It was not necessary now to use infra-red glasses to see the asteroid. It lay there on the miniscreen for naked eyes; but for seconds not one of the men in the ship's control cabin thought to look. The awful acceleration and shock had dazed them. They had not known what was coming, except Friday and the Hawk, and only the latter was able to retain reasonable alertness. Almost immediately after the impact, he had cut down the load on the generators and brought the *Sandra* out of her drive forward, then began rotating the ship until she was facing back towards the asteroid and Earth. Only then did they look through the bow windows, and discover what had happened.

"It's visible!" cried Friday. "See—the invisibility's gone!"

A score of miles away the asteroid lay, fully revealed, its starboard half gleaming hard and sharp in the sunlight. Cautiously the *Sandra* drew closer. Carse gave the controls to Ban and examined the dome carefully on the miniscreen.

He saw that the keel of the *Sandra* had made a great rent in it, so that through this the air had rushed out. Airless space had taken possession. The ray which had been burning at the *Sandra* had snapped off with the cracking of the dome; in that one wild second of impact, all of the asteroid's functioning mechanisms must have gone dead. It appeared that Lar Tantril had not thought far enough: he had not sealed the buildings against possible crashing of the dome, and for that reason alone he and his men had gone down in full defeat under the drive of the Hawk.

264

Shreds of flotsam, rotating, moving in space outward from the dome, were visible—bits of wreckage and a number of white, bloated things which once had been living men. The outrushing tide of air had taken them along.

"Merciful heaven!" whispered Eliot Leithgow, staring at the desolation. "In one second, snuffed out!"

The Hawk brought the *Sandra* to a position a quarter of a mile above the asteroid.

"They're all dead in there, I'm sure," he explained. "For the asteroid is now visible, which means that the doors of the power building were open. If those doors were not sealed, none of the others would be. It's a dead world. But it had to be done. It was the asteroid or the *Sandra*. Tantril might have been a good straw boss—but space is dangerous for men who can't think."

"Look!" cried Friday, "—it's turning!"

All watched. Very slightly, but definitely, it was beginning a long slow turn that would reverse its ends. Its angular velocity seemed to increase before their eyes.

"A last kick of the side plates," murmured the Hawk.

The dome started sliding under, out of their sight, the other end of the asteroid slowly coming up in a great arc to take its place. The asteroid was falling, too. Nine hundred miles away was Earth—less than that, by now, for the body now was free to accept the tremendous gravital pull of the planet so near. Soon it would plunge to destruction there. . . .

A thought came to Carse, and he said:

"Perhaps Ku Sui would like to see what has become—"
On the last word he stopped and whirled around, startled.

"I heard a hiss!" cried Friday.

"You too? Then it was a port-lock!" Carse turned to the miniscreen. "Look there!" he exclaimed.

Sharply visible in the brilliant sunlight moved a dwindling figure in a propulsive spacesuit. Slowly on the screen—rapidly outside, against the colossal background of Earth

265

—the figure moved; and as they watched they saw it begin to turn longitudinally in flight, until it was upside down with reference to the space-ship, *but right-side up with reference to the dome of the asteroid, toward which it was headed.*

"He's going to enter the dome!" Carse exclaimed. "Ban, take the controls—and watch him!" He ran aft.

Leithgow and Friday, following at his heels, found him inside Ku Sui's cabin, examining two figures sprawled at his feet. They were Thorpe and Williams, who had been sent to gas and guard the Eurasian. Carse said:

"Both dead. Poison. Look at Thorpe's wrist."

On the right wrist of the dead Thorpe was a red scratch, and the flesh beneath was swollen and discolored. One cheek of Williams bore a similar patch. Both had been armed with ray-guns, but now they were gone.

"Poison," Carse repeated for Leithgow, who just then entered. "It might have been in Ku Sui's ring. Everyone else was in the control cabin. The men entered the door; Ku Sui was waiting and struck. Scratched! Well, I'm going after him."

Not quite understanding, the two younger men gaped at the Hawk.

"But, Carse!" Leithgow objected, "—you can't! How can you possibly—"

"Ku Sui's going back to the dome," the Hawk cut in. "We saw him heading there. Where else can he go? He can't make it to Earth, for we'd pick him up. No; he's got some reason for returning to the dome. He thinks he's escaped! Well, he's mistaken!"

Carse was in a frigid rage. Friday shuddered when his glance, in passing fell on him. His eyes were deadly.

"Let me by, Eliot," the Hawk said, almost in a whisper. "This time he goes or I go, but by the gods of space it will be one of us!"

266

XLIII

The Passing of Ku Sui

Carse ran to the stores cabin, just as the Eurasian must have run there a few minutes before. Quickly he lifted a propulsive spacesuit from the rack and got into it, transferring his ray-gun to its belt. Not speaking a word, he skimmed to the rear port-lock, Leithgow and Friday close behind, attempting to dissuade him. They wasted their words. Carse only turned and gave them orders.

"Keep the ship as close as you can without danger. Be careful of Earth's gravity! I'm going—and I'm going by myself." Eliot Leithgow reached him at that moment. "Eliot, if I don't come out, you've everything needed to prove your case—the re-embodied Brains, Ku Sui's four white assistants—"

Leithgow wouldn't listen. "You're going to your death, Carse! You'll be caught inside! Earth's pulling strong on the asteroid, and in a few minutes it will be plunging through the atmosphere with terrific speed! The friction will make it a meteor! You'll burn! You'll die in flames!"

The Hawk was closing the outer door of the lock.

"Have to risk that, Eliot," said the immovable man. He opened the inner door of the lock and stepped into the chamber. "Remember, keep as close to the asteroid as you can, and keep a sharp watch for Ku Sui and me." He looked levelly at them, white men and black, then turned away. "Good-by," he said.

The door swung shut in their faces.

In the chamber the Hawk closed the face-plate of his helmet and rapidly spun the controls in one wall. There was a hiss, and the outer door opened. He jumped into space.

The view below was breath-taking; Earth seemed almost to hit him in the face. He had not realized it was so close. The mighty sphere filled his whole view, stretching far to the left and right, far up and far down; and clearly on it, in sharp outline, he saw the continent of Europe, the Atlantic Ocean and, bordering it, the edge of North America.

To his left was the flaming orb of the sun; almost underneath, rotating end over end against the glittering background of the North Atlantic, was the asteroid. He himself was rotating with respect to the asteroid. Quickly he moved his controls, and slowly his rotation was corrected. He started for the asteroid, and at maximum acceleration began to overhaul it.

The asteroid was falling free, and the speed of its fall was mounting fast; but under power he soon came close to it. As the dome swung over and the sunlight flooded its buildings he looked hard for a moving shape, but saw none. Was Ku Sui inside? He would have to go and see.

Any attempt to get into the dome would be hazardous! The asteroid now was describing a complete rotation in about thirty Earth seconds—which would give the dome a peripheral velocity of about 360 miles an hour! At the least misjudgment of space or time either his suit would be ripped or he would be dashed to instant death. He had to slip cleanly down through the jagged tear in the dome, planning his motion accurately to the fraction of a second.

Never cooler, the Hawk made it. Building a parallel speed equal to that of the rotating dome, he followed it over in its dizzy whirl; and as the rent came below he shot curving down and in with a precision that was sufficient.

For alternating fifteen-second periods the sunlight flooded the dome and its buildings; and at the end of the first of these, just as the returning darkness blotted all vision, the Hawk arrived at the door of one wing of the central building. He had not seen Ku Sui, and he had no time for exploration, but he did have a hunch as to where the Eurasian had gone, and he followed that hunch. He passed through the blackness of the corridor—not along the floor, but along the right wall, pulled there by Earth's gravity. He felt he was making a terrific noise. Did Ku Sui know he was being followed? Was he waiting in ambush? Carse could not be sure, but he felt that at any moment a lance of orange light might come to meet him.

Down plunged the asteroid, Earth's atmosphere, with all the danger of friction, coming ever closer, and the great face of the planet lying waiting to receive all that was not vaporized in the passage. It was just too bad; but somewhere near was Ku Sui, his blood enemy; and while one muscle was capable of motion, he was going to move forward for a final accounting.

Before Carse realized it, he was in the laboratory. He groped his way to the place of the secret panel. As he bumped against the wall, feeling for an opening, the wall gave way, and he found himself in the very place he sought. At his feet was an open shaft, and in the side of the shaft a ladder. Clumsy in his suit, he tried to place one of his great boots on a rung; he slipped; and he slid along the side of the shaft to the bottom, landing with a gentle thud.

He felt about him, and decided that he was at one end of a passageway. As rapidly as he could, arms stretched wide, he pressed along it.

By now he was ignoring the controls of his suit; they were of no use to him in the darkness and confusion in which he moved. Continuously he was bumped and pulled against the four sides of the passage. Where did it lead? How far did it extend? Was Ku Sui at the end of it? There was not much more time. The asteroid might be in the outer layers of Earth's atmosphere—already might have begun to glow

269

with the heat of friction of its passage. Once that started, incandescence would follow quickly—and there he would be, down in the heart of the asteroid, blind, in inky blackness without clue to what was happening, still hoping foolishly to find his man. There would be no heat-warning through his insulated suit. Even now, perhaps, there was no time to get out; already he may have passed the point of no return; he could not know. But he went on.

How far had he gone? A hundred yards? Two hundred? More, it seemed. There was still no variation in the blackness around. The passageway seemed straight. Did it lead straight to the center?

Then, ahead, for just a second, Carse saw a faint wisp of light!

Automatically, his hand reached for the ray-gun, but, almost before it had moved, the light was gone and the blackness was as deep as before. But he was coming to something! He went on, perhaps a little faster. He was sure he was going to come to something. If only Ku Sui were there!

Again the light winked somewhere ahead. This time it seemed stronger, and he thought it lasted longer. An interval of blackness while he bumped ahead. There it was again! As he fought forward he suddenly realized that it came at regular intervals. Perhaps it came from an apparatus, worked by the hands of the Eurasian! On—on. The seconds flew by, building to the small total which would bring friction to the asteroid, then incandescence and scalding death for the man groping within it!

Again, suddenly, the light. This time it revealed the end of the passage! Quickly Carse traversed the remaining distance and felt around with his hands. He found an opening, a doorway, to his right. Surely the room beyond the door held the final secret of the asteroid. If Ku Sui were anywhere, he would be in there.

Carse restrained an impulse to rush in. He waited for the recurring light. Everything in him told him that this was

270

the climax of his chase—that the room to the right held the man he was bound to kill.

It seemed ages that he stood there waiting—picturing in his mind the great rock turning end for end, dropping with awful speed toward Earth—and himself standing far below in silence and darkness, determined to finish the feud! (Was there no weakness in this man? Did it not frighten him to realize he might not escape from that rock in time?—that it might already be too late to try?)

The darkness suddenly melted. For a second a ghostly light filtered through. He stared, and in its brief maximum saw before him a high, bare rectangular room, burnt out of the rock—and at its far side, shimmeringly, a man in a spacesuit. Ku Sui, brought to bay!

Or did he? Carse, for one of the few times in his life, doubted his eyes. Were his eyes playing him a trick? For it was not a hard, clear figure that he saw; it was an indefinite one, vague and elusive, like a thing seen without focus. A prank of the strange light, perhaps? But surely Ku Sui! Ku Sui trapped!

After that one second's hesitation the Hawk leaped forward, gun in hand, but even as he moved the ghostly light departed, and in the blackness his eager searching arms closed on—nothing!

Surely Ku Sui had been there! Surely he had not just imagined he saw him!

Baffled, and coldly raging, the Hawk turned and groped frantically. Earth's gravity pinned him to a wall; he pushed off and continued his groping. He found no one. Nothing.

Again came the light. This time, positively, he saw that no one was in the room.

In some incredible way, Ku Sui had eluded him. The instant the previous light had failed, he must have slipped by and escaped down the passageway behind. It seemed impossible, but there appeared no other explanation. Recovering somewhat, Carse pushed his way to the door, ready to follow back through the long, unlit passage. Perhaps he could still overtake the other. If there was still time.

But *was* there still time?

Many seconds had passed. Inexorably, they had brought him closer to the attracting Earth. Now he stared around the room in dismay.

For its blackness was softened by a faint glow. It was not that of the recurring light; it was constant, and came from somewhere above. Friction! Carse saw that within numbered seconds the surface of the asteroid would reach incandescence!

One thought raced like lightning through his head. He could not get free through the corridor and dome behind: that would take minutes, and only seconds were left. Ku Sui, if he were back there, was trapped and finished. A flaming meteor would be his coffin. But Carse's, too!

Hideous death! Trapped within fiery walls of melting rock!

At that moment came the regularly recurring flash of light—and Carse, in his great need, understood. It was sunlight! It occurred with the rotation of the asteroid! It came each time one side faced the sun!

But sunlight could reach the room only by way of some channel overhead!

Swiftly, helped by the waxing glow, Carse found the channel. It was a vertical bore several feet wide, in one corner of the ceiling. Its rock sides glowed redly, but at their far end was a black patch that made him thrill with hope. Outer space!—and a short, straight escape to it! In a flash he saw how Ku Sui may have eluded him!

The Eurasian's exit might also be his!

He didn't lose a fraction of a second. Setting his controls to maximum acceleration, he rose with a rush into the bore. Despite his aim, Earth's gravity and the rotating asteroid threw him heavily into one red-hot wall. If the fabric of his suit burnt through! But no time for such worries—must make the frigid air outside—fast—fast—never mind bumps —quick out—and must stay conscious—*must* stay conscious to exert repulsion against Earth!

Like a projectile Hawk Carse shot out of that fiery tunnel at an angle to the asteroid and in a direction away from Earth, and in an instant the glowing body was far below him, streaking faster and ever faster to the grave that lay now so near.

He fought to come out of his dizziness, shaking his head to clear it. He searched the sky for sight of a minute, suit-clad figure. If Ku Sui had preceded him through the emergency exit, he should be visible somewhere, a point of light against the black depths.

There was no sign of him.

Carse's eyes dropped to the asteroid. Already it was a hundred miles below, a breath-taking celestial object, a second sun, increasing in brilliance as it diminished in size. Was the Eurasian in it, trapped in the long corridor to the dome, not yet dead on this his last flight in his extraordinary vehicle of space?

The end came at once. For just an instant the second sun seemed to hang reluctant over the watery plain waiting to receive it; then its last tremendous flight through space was over, and it was received in the blue waters of the Atlantic.

A cataclysmic burial. A titanic meteorite—a screaming, incandescent streak—a tremendous wreath of billowing steam—a high wall of water racing through the oceans of half the Earth—this, the burial of Ku Sui's asteroid, brought so far from its accustomed orbit beyond the planet Mars. If Ku Sui was in it, he died as he had lived, spectacularly, with brilliance—and with a parting tidal wave to disturb the lives of men.

For some reason sadness fell over the heart of the Hawk. . . .

273

Far back in the sky he saw a space-ship, moving in his direction—the *Sandra,* coming to pick him up. In it would be his good friends, who stood by him: gentle, old Leithgow, the faithful Friday, cheerful, fidgety Ban Wilson. But in it, too, those repulsive ones, heir to Earth's greatest intellects. . . .

What would the Brains think when they found themselves in such bodies? How would their wives receive them? He, Carse, had done the best he could, but. . . .

Should he cut in his mike and tell them he was safe? No. It was not his way. He would feel uncomfortable. Sentiment was not for Hawk Carse, who wore bangs and let no man see his forehead.

They would want to know about Ku Sui. What could he tell them? Was he dead? But he didn't know. He really didn't know. . . .

Carse sighed. He did not cut in his mike. He waited. The ship very slowly grew larger. In due time it arrived and picked him up.

www.ingramcontent.com/pod-product-compliance
Lightning Source LLC
Chambersburg PA
CBHW031004260626
47169CB00002B/686